Desire

Also by Amy Wallace

THE PRODIGY

Desire

Amy Wallace

Houghton Mifflin Company

BOSTON · 1990

For information about permission to reproduce selections
from this book, write to Permissions, Houghton Mifflin
Company, 2 Park Street, Boston, Massachusetts 02108.

Library of Congress Cataloging-in-Publication Data
Wallace, Amy.
Desire / Amy Wallace.
p.   cm.
ISBN 0-395-51951-9
I. Title.
PS3573.A425627D47   1990   90-35205
813'.54—dc20   CIP

Printed in the United States of America

BP 10 9 8 7 6 5 4 3 2 1

The author is grateful for permission to quote from the following:
page vii: "The pearl in the poor one's clothes," from *Understanding
Reality: A Troist Alchemical Classic*, by Chang Po-tuan, translated by
Thomas Cleary. University of Hawaii Press, 1987.
page 112: "How we squander our hours of pain," from *The Selected
Poetry of Rainer Maria Rilke*, edited by Stephen Mitchell.
Translation copyright © 1982 by Stephen Mitchell. Reprinted by
permission of Random House, Inc.
page 116: "Vigils," by Arthur Rimbaud. From *Rimbaud*, by
Wallace Fowlie. Copyright © 1966 by Wallace Fowlie. Used by
permission of the University of Chicago Press.
page 174: "My worst habit is I get so tired of winter . . . ," by
Jelaluddin Rumi, in *These Branching Moments: Forty Odes*, translated
by John Moyne and Coleman Barks. Copyright © 1988 by
Coleman Barks. Used by permission of Copper Beech Press.

11-90 BA 1500

For my parents

"*Keep away from people who try to belittle your ambitions. Small people always do that, but the really great make you feel that you, too, can become great.*"

— MARK TWAIN

*The pearl in the poor one's clothes is originally
    round and bright;
If one does not know how to find it oneself, one
    will count others' treasures instead.
Counting others' treasures is after all of no benefit
    — it just makes you expend your labor in vain:
How can it compare to recognizing your own jewel,
    which is worth more than billions in gold?
The shine of this precious pearl is most great, as it
    lights up all worlds in the universe.*

—CHANG PO-TUAN

PART I
The Great Horror

The need to go astray, to be destroyed, is an extremely private, distant, passionate, turbulent truth.

— GEORGES BATAILLE

What we call fate does not come to us from the outside: it goes forth from within us.

— RAINER MARIA RILKE

"This is the book," said Great-uncle Mordecai. "This is a great horror."

He pushed it across the desk. Gingerly, Lily touched the dusty binding, causing crisp, yellow pages to crackle and break. The book was bound in thick leather encrusted with tiny jewels, most of which had fallen out over the course of centuries, leaving small sockets where sapphires and seed pearls had been. She ran the flat of her hand over its surface. A pain like a bite shot into her palm. A little diamond had scraped her, and she pressed her hand to her lips.

"Are you quite all right, my dear? Do be careful."

"Fine. I'm just clumsy. I didn't realize they were so sharp."

"As if you didn't know jewels."

Lily laughed. "I should know to be careful, shouldn't I? I guess I'm not always that cautious."

"Impulsiveness is charming in a young girl."

"You always say that. I'm not so young."

The old man shrugged. "You're barely thirty, far too young to be reading the book. I myself did not read it until I was much advanced in years. But when you told me you were engaged . . . and now that she's died . . ." He paused, running his fingers over the edge of his desk. "I thought for a very long time before showing it to you. God help me if I've made a mistake."

Lily laughed nervously, high in her throat. "Well, let's just see what's in this famous book." She reached awkwardly to open it, and a flurry of dust rose from the pages. Raising her hand to swipe the air, she jostled the forbidden book with her elbow, causing a page to slip out and waft to the floor. She recognized her great-uncle's handwriting, the letter written at a time when his grip had still been strong. She felt him start across the desk, but she could not raise her eyes. They both stared silently, stupidly, at the piece of paper. It read:

O my dearest dear, my own true heart,
Where were you last night? I waited and waited, but you didn't come. I've been sick with worry that you won't come back. I couldn't sleep. I wrote letter after letter to you and I threw them all away. I don't know how you came to love me, I'm loathsome, and I'm ill. Haven't I suffered enough punishment for what I've done? But the worst is when I wait, when you don't come. When I don't hold your white breasts in my hands. Come back, just one more time. Even if you've stopped. Please, or I don't know what will become of me. Dearest, I don't need you to be cruel to me, for I do the job well enough myself. I

Here the fragment was broken. The two of them stared at it. Lily was unable to avert her eyes not to read, like one who touches frozen metal and finds her skin seared to it by the cold. Mordecai broke the silence.

"It is part of the history. But I want you to read it at the right time."

He bent his aged, long limbs, and took up the paper with dignity, replacing it carefully inside the book. Then Mordecai leaned forward to address his great-niece.

"Did she say anything about me? At the end?"

"She said the same things she's always said. She rambled . . . The same old thing."

"Tell me again."

"That you were like a father to her, and she loved you. But

she was too ashamed to see you. I thought maybe she'd tell me why, this time, but she wouldn't. It was the same to the very end. Besides, she was on so much medication . . . You know, Uncle, I don't know why losing her should make me feel like such an orphan. She was just a distant relative. Besides, she's been crazy for as long as I can remember."

"You've had too many losses. Losing your parents. Nothing can recompense a child who loses both her parents, and grows up with aunts and uncles instead."

Lily shrugged. "I hardly remember my parents, so what's the difference? We've been over all this. Besides, I have you. I've always had you . . ."

"What are you reading?" Mordecai spoke to her gently now, beginning their familiar ritual.

Lily sighed. "I've been reading the *Tao-te Ching*, actually."

"Good. I've always said—"

Lily fidgeted in her seat, then blurted, "Look. I'm sorry I saw that piece of paper. I didn't know. I don't know anything about it. If there are secrets in this family, just tell me, I'll be careful . . ." She drifted off, avoiding her great-uncle's eyes.

The old man lifted his patrician gaze from his hands.

"I'm a little weak today, child . . . I'll arrange for the funeral. Take these pages. I don't want the book to leave my house."

From the book's innards he fished out a sheaf of documents so old Lily feared they would crumble in his hands.

"These are the originals. Too fragile for you to read. I've copied them, and I've translated them from the French. I did it a very long time ago. Even these copies are delicate." He handed her a second stack of papers.

"There is a legacy, you see. These letters were written by your ancestor, and they concern . . . matters that travel inside us."

"Oh no. The pox. Don't tell me I come from a long line of syphilitics. Well, I guess that would explain a few things. I thought my hair was falling out."

Mordecai shook his head, and gave her a wan smile. "Ah,

my dear. I don't want to alarm you. But you must listen. I'm prescient when it comes to the heart. And I have my fears."

Lily tugged nervously at a handful of long brown hair, and pulled it behind her ear. She was not a superstitious person.

"What is horror, Lily?" The old man leaned forward. "What do most people think it is? Death? Dismemberment? Spilt blood? I say horror is something else. Something that creeps inside us, that crawls in us, that rambles in our veins — something like our worst kind of regret, regret that never leaves us . . . I want to prevent you doing something wrong, Lily, something that will cause you this regret. One can't erase mistakes. To say 'What's done is done' is to spout tripe. To say 'It was meant to be' — that's another stupid salve that only feeds the pain, when you discover that it changes nothing." He sat back in his seat. "I won't let you be haunted. Now we mustn't discuss it further. Chen Li will show you out."

"But, Uncle . . ." she whispered.

"Yes?"

"What are you reading?"

"Oh yes. Baudelaire. And Swinburne. He's been out of fashion for decades. But I've always been fond of him. Do read Swinburne."

He looked away, over her shoulder. "Chen Li will show you out," he said absently.

For 28 years the Chinese man had been showing her out, longer than she could remember. He was grave, graceful, and ironic. The old mansion in Pacific Heights ached with mysteries, but sometimes she imagined he was at the very heart of them. He had watched her grow up here, first on Sundays when her aunts took her on the obligatory visits to see her peculiar great-uncle, and later, when she was old enough to take the bus by herself, at any time of the week, day or night, that she felt like visiting. Sometimes she came rarely — whole weeks went by and she never gave it a thought — and sometimes she went day after day, to do nothing but putter through her great-uncle's library, drink tea and, later, brandy, and discuss literature with him by the hour. The aunts and uncles had long stopped visiting. As far as she knew, she was the only guest. She was grateful for the changelessness of it. Great-uncle Mordecai aged so slowly and steadily that she never noticed it. He was old beyond counting, and she was grateful for that, too. It was another of the house's mysteries.

It was always a little hard, when she visited him on her lunch break, to go back to work. Dusty shades kept out the light, and it always seemed like night in the house on Pacific Street. Whenever she crossed the house's threshold onto the street the daytime cut at her, and her heart gave an angry crack at being returned to the world.

Within twenty minutes, she was at Van Velsen's Jewelers. The establishment, which had stood for 60 years on the corner of Maiden Lane and Grant Avenue in the heart of downtown San Francisco, exuded a quiet, expensive severity. Mordecai van Velsen had founded the business in 1931. No one knew how old he was when he began it. Van Velsen's had established an international reputation beyond that of ordinary prestige or elegance; although the company dealt in all manner of stones, the Van Velsen name had become synonymous with the finest pearls in the world. No house in London or Paris could boast an artist like the elder van Velsen, who shaped and worked and sold pearls worth hundreds of thousands of dollars. His great-niece, Lily, had learned the art at his knee, and had been carrying on the tradition since the old man's retirement over a decade before. Lily was one of a dozen people living who knew the secrets of pearls, but even she, with all her skill, could not match her great-uncle's mastery. The market for natural pearls was now so small, however, that there was little call for Lily's art, and she worked instead at cutting and setting rubies, diamonds, and emeralds.

It was at the Gemological Institute of San Francisco that Lily met Alan Purdue. She grudgingly attended the Institute's classes; Mordecai insisted that she acquire a degree. She moped her way through dull afternoons, speaking to no one, waiting to return to the pleasure of her work at Van Velsen's.

The first time she saw Alan, he was peering into a microscope, his broad shoulders leaning into the small instrument, the sleeves of his white shirt rolled up. She noticed his forearms first, brown from the sun and lined with strong veins. His eyeglasses lay abandoned beside him while he peered, half absorbed and half irritated, into the microscope, running his fingers through a thick head of russet hair. He was humming and muttering, and tapping a pencil against the table.

Lily stood in the doorway watching him, fascinated. She thought he would burst out of his chair. After a few moments he pushed himself away from the desk and plucked a gem, a small sapphire, from the grading tray. He tossed it up as if it were a coin, catching it in the air, then slapping it against the back of his hand. He blinked at it, grinned broadly, and announced, "Heads, I win." He turned to her. "I'm taking you to lunch."

She stared, as if she had been caught reading someone's diary. Alan made a deep, mock bow.

"Young lady," he began, "have you been watching me?"

"Oh, I'm sorry, I—"

"Never mind. I've been watching you, too. Out of the corner of my eye. Lunch?"

Lily saw his eyes, behind the glasses—they were a russet color, like his hair, and bright. They're safe eyes, she thought, bright and without secrets. Before she had time to reply, he had her by the elbow and was leading her to the door.

"You see," he explained to her later, "I have no real aptitude for gem cutting." He inclined his head to one side, and laughed. "I wish I had, but I don't have the eye. My father made a fortune in zircons. Have you heard of him? Lucas Purdue, the Zircon King. I was supposed to manage the family business, but I prefer real diamonds. I thought I'd give it a try here . . ."

He suddenly seemed almost shy, and this emotion was so incongruous that Lily found herself staring, unable to think of anything to say.

Finally she said, "Perhaps you have other talents."

He smiled gently. "Ah, and I do." He tapped his brow with his forefinger. "Business acumen. I possess this. It's easy for me, too easy. But cutting diamonds, ah . . . now that, that is *difficult.*" He leaned forward on the last word, and took Lily's hand in both of his. "I like difficult things." He squeezed her hand, inspecting her face. "Your eyes are a strange color, Lily. I don't believe I've ever seen that shade of green before. A little yellow in them, and feline . . ." He sat back in his chair. "I imagine you can see a lot with those eyes."

Alan's talents were so extreme it hardly mattered that he was a poor cutter. He could calculate the angle of a refraction in seconds, assess weight and grade, compare the output of Zanzibar emerald mines to those of Tanzania with barely a moment's thought. He courted Lily with the same precision he applied to his work, a precision leavened with charm and whimsy, until she relaxed her habitual guard, until his presence became soporific and necessary. He gave her little gifts; he petted her; he bossed her and amused her. Watching his eyes for danger, she saw instead an easy sparkle, a sane and simple spirit. Bright, she told her great-uncle, and without secrets. She spoke to Mordecai about him carefully at first and later, resenting her caution, she spoke of him often. She waited for some kind of blessing, but none came. After the two men finally met, Mordecai told her, "Ah, Lily, if only people could save us! And don't you think I would have saved you, if it were possible?"

"From what? What on earth are you talking about?"

"Nothing. I like your young man. He has very little malice."

Lily felt the resentment rise inside her, then she shook it off like so much rain.

"You're being cryptic, Uncle. It's irritating. It's a disease with you." She mock-glared at the old man, then continued. "I want Alan to manage the business at Van Velsen's. It will leave me free to work with the jewels. I'm tired of the paperwork, and the books. He has a talent for that sort of thing, and he gets along with people. Unlike present company," she added dryly.

She expected some rebuke, some rejection, but there was none. Mordecai smiled. "Fine, my dear," he said. "I think it's just the right thing."

The customers liked Alan immediately; he made the establishment seem less severe. His presence charmed away old ghosts, and brought a modern touch into its rooms. Lily and Alan worked together easily, and she felt as if the store itself were calmer, less forbidding. They rarely spoke about the old man, but she told herself it was better that way. Sometimes things are best kept separate.

There was a thrill in the shop when Lily arrived. Alan rushed up to her, coloring with excitement.

"Lily! We've got the most incredible commission! Mrs. Franstein bought the Nakamura pearls—the Nakamura pearls! I've never seen anything like them. Never. I can't believe it. Two of the stones are damaged. She wants them replaced. The center stone and an adjacent one. It's going to be very difficult to match that center pearl."

"But how could she buy the Nakamura pearls? They belonged to that Dutch family . . . I don't understand it. You know they can't be needing the money, not even that kind of money."

"Well, it's the most incredible thing. There was some kind of scandal in the family, and it involves the pearls. Someone damaged them, I don't know how. All very mysterious. And Mrs. Franstein said something about the pearls being bad luck, and the Ebels wanting them out of the house. Here, I'll show you."

The pearls were full and heavy, like pieces of fat. They had an ancient glow, having ripened in foreign seas and rested against royal necks. The center pearl, for all its magnificence, was irreparably damaged by an ugly dent. Even without its centerpiece, the necklace was worth upwards of $800,000. If it were replaced with the proper pearl, it would be worth twice that. Mrs. Franstein had taken her find to the only shop in the world that could restore it.

Lily let the strand fall from one hand to the other, weighing it, bouncing it, like a knife in a gangfighter's hands. Then she let the necklace dangle from her index finger. The heavy, sick pearl swayed over the ground. It was decadent. It was almost unseemly. She imagined the maw of the oyster that had grown it.

Alan interrupted her reverie. "The most important thing that's ever happened in this store. The publicity . . . I've got some leads already. Beaker, out on Van Ness, might have something. He was in with that Japanese firm. I'm not worried about matching the color, it's the *size*. They're really enormous. Well, I want to get over there, so would you see about that *Bijou* layout? What, didn't I tell you? I'm forgetting everything on account of these pearls. Some sculptor—Penthe. Johnny Penthe. Never heard of the guy, but he's supposed to be really good. I saw a few pictures of his stuff. A little morbid, but people think it's high ideals. Anyway, *Bijou* magazine called. They're doing a layout on Penthe, and somebody there got a *concept*: a layout with his statues wearing our pieces. He just does people, you know. And they're good-sized. *Bijou* is huge. I'll bet the circulation is eighty thousand. So we'll round up the best stuff, and maybe pull out the Paxton ruby, see if we can't beat that deadline—Are you listening, Lily?"

"I just got distracted. Sorry." She was still holding the pearls.

"So let's have dinner tonight. We can talk more about this."

"I . . . I can't. I have something I have to read."

"Oh?"

"From my great-uncle."

"Some eighteenth-century French perversion, I suppose."

"Well, no, actually, this time—"

"Okay, sixteenth-century Scottish perversion. I just don't see how those damn novels can be more important than a dinner with your beloved. And I am not being ironic. Do not forget," he said with mock solemnity, "we are newly engaged."

"Oh, you know how it is, it means so much to him."

Alan sighed and shook off his jocular tone. "I guess marrying you is marrying into this lending library thing. Well, what is it?"

"What? Oh. It's . . . it's Thomas Hardy. *Tess of the D'Urbervilles.*"

"God, I read that in high school." He looked at her for a long moment. "If you insist, then. I guess you do look a little peaked. Curl up with a toddy and a sad book. I've got to do some catching up here anyway. Say, why aren't we living together?"

Lily laughed.

"She'll sleep with me, she'll marry me, but she won't live with me. You go figure it. Just you wait—it's only a matter of time. I'll *thrill* you with domesticity—you'll ache for it—you'll dream of laundry soap and toothbrushes, you'll—Come here." He gave her a long kiss and let her go. "Hey, Lily—Don't walk out with those!"

He plucked the pearls from her hand. They were warm and moist from her palm.

Lily sat down to work, but having held the Nakamura pearls disturbed her concentration. She had three pearls to shape for a brooch that belonged to a movie star, and an emerald to set for an Iranian prince. She examined the memos on her desk, and discovered that a Texas oilman had commissioned a cattle brand to be made out of platinum for his prize herd. She set an employee to work on this last order, and took up the emerald. The prince had designed a tiara for his mother, and the Austrian stone was its centerpiece. It had a bright, young glow, and sat in a bed of diamonds. The task required her attention for a full hour, and when she had finished she lit a cigarette and looked at her three pearls. They were a little misshapen, but it would be possible to alter them, to make them into near-perfect spheres. It was pleasant, easy work, predictable and simple, but Lily looked at the little orbs without interest. Her assistant knocked, and she and Lily passed the next hour on the design for the cattle brand. There was a shortage of platinum, and a number of hasty phone calls had to be made. In the end, she set aside the little pearls.

Lily thought she should take some air. The feel of the Nakamura pearls had gone to her head. It was dusk, and she felt warm, much warmer than the night allowed. She opened the windows of her apartment and stared out at the bay. The *Tao-te Ching* lay open by the bed, and a tattered copy of an Eric Ambler novel. She meant to read them, but there was a clutch in her stomach, a pull toward her briefcase.

As she opened it, the odor of the documents inside filled the room, conquering the scent of fresh freesias and the thick coffee smell that hovered in the kitchen. It was the smell of age and dust. "Eau de old," she muttered to her cat, and laughed nervously. Curse flicked an ear back at the sound of her voice. He was stretched languidly in a still-hot patch of dust and fading sun. She walked over to him and ruffled the fur of his belly. He cast her a dark, sloe-eyed look, and set his ears a little farther back. The tip of his tail flicked.

Sighing, Lily took off her clothes, pulled on a T-shirt and crawled into bed. She cast one last lamenting glance at the indifferent Curse, and began to read.

| | Madelaine Hubert | | Nicole Charcot |
| | Laon, Aisne | to | Montreil-les-Dames, Aisne, 5 February 1566 |

My dearest friend,
    To think that I will never see you again outside the convent walls. That we will never again laugh and play as we have so long been accustomed to. Oh Nicole, I know there is only one

matter you wish to know about. I will not make you wait and guess. He is gone. He has been sent away to his uncle's home in Paris. No one in his family will speak to me, as you know. What little I know I heard from the LaFaver boys. They say he may be sent to Germany, or perhaps even farther, until his parents are satisfied that all is forgotten and they can make a proper marriage for him. As for my own parents, they will not speak of the matter at all, and they guard me closely for fear that I have been tainted by your influence. I am ostracized for knowing you. Nicole! To think of the days of our loving friendship, who could have imagined such sorrow and affliction coming upon us? And what is my own next to yours?

There is little else to tell you. Mother is with child again —and at her great age! Jean has taken several prizes at school. Pray, write me quickly and tell me all you can.

Your loving friend,
Madelaine

27 February
My dearest Madelaine,

I scarcely know how to begin. Your letter has brought me joy and pain alike, and the two conditions commingle within me here, so that I do not know what I truly feel. In memories I find a sweet sorrow, which relieves me of my burden. I now believe, Madelaine, that I have had my portion of joy, I used it all and must spend what life is left to me suffering the portion of my pain.

As for my life here, it is cold and strange. How I miss you! You cannot know. Each morning we rise long before dawn, and wearing our coarse habits we begin a round of devotions and prayers, and tedious tasks such as I never imagined possible. There is a vow of silence among us, and speech is permitted only for one hour before our evening prayers. But there is little to say. I believe I am shunned here too, Madelaine, though I suppose I shall never know—perhaps I just feel it so. We see no one from the world outside, and the faces of my sisters are so hard. Ah, there is the bell for supper: I have no more time. Madelaine, I beg you, give me news of him, all you can. The little you have told me is a beginning, at least.

Yours in God,
Nicole

19 March

My dear Nicole,

I must always be on the watch for my mother, who suspects me of writing to you. I am closely watched by my tutor as well. I have stolen a moment here, dear friend, by feigning a migraine while my family is at church. I will not waste time in coming to the point. I visited your mother yesterday afternoon, on the pretext of reclaiming a few books and sewing things. I hoped, by using my guile, to acquire some news of him you hold so dear. But I found your mother at the hearth, burning his letters to you! She was startled, but stern, when she saw me, and would not speak of the matter. She held a great many papers in her hand, but these she carried with her into the next room. While she gathered my things, I snatched what I could out of the fire. I enclose the fragment that remained; it is only half a letter, but it will be dear to your heart, I know.

I must go now, and cover my head with a cloth and pretend to be ill! If my pretense is too good, I fear I will be leeched for my trouble, so I will be well again tomorrow. I do not know when I can write again.

Your,
Madelaine

what joy you have brought me! The midwife Loyse sent a boy to me straightaway with the fine news. Shall we name her Colette, after my grandmother? How I wish to be with you. And how soon we will be freed from the constraints of our situation. We will go to Italy as soon as possible. It is God's will, I assure you, that two who love as we do should marry, even if it is only in God's eyes, for He cares little about rank and caste. I pray this letter finds you and our

daughter as well and as contented as you are in my dreams.
Goodbye, my Nicole, until our happy rendezvous on Saturday!

Charles

21 March
Dear Madame Charcot,

As I have promised, I shall make you a monthly report on the condition of your daughter Nicole. Since she has taken vows to our Lord Jesus Christ, a strange constraint has come over her. She speaks little, and her eyes are often cast downward. In her devotions she is constant, and properly respectful, but I fear she is not earnest. As yet, I have not spoken to her of this strange listlessness. It has only been a fortnight since her arrival at the convent, and a month since she was delivered of child, a matter of which she does not speak. Two letters have arrived from Paris, from Charles Desnos. I deemed them best destroyed. Two letters from Madelaine Hubert were given to her, although in future I think it will be wisest if we examine them first.

In Our Lord Jesus Christ,
Soeur Henriette La Rochelle

3 April
My esteemed Holy Mother,

The darkness of my daughter's unholy love will be washed clean by her marriage to our Lord Jesus Christ. The child has been given to a wet nurse who will give it a Christian upbringing. I write to thank you for your report. Our lives are empty here, without the light of our daughter Nicole. The villagers mock us, even in the house of the Lord! We bear this cross, Holy Mother, as an atonement for our daughter's great sins, and pray that her heart and spirit will be cleansed alike, and that the doors of heaven will not be closed to her.

Yours in the sight of Our Lord,
Mme Eveline Charcot

12 May

Dearest Charles,

Are you as far away as they tell me? I imagine we are speaking to one another, all the time. I am supposed to pray to God, but I do not. I pray to you. As I kneel on the stone floor of the priory, I imagine that it is you I address. God will forgive me! Perhaps He even blesses me for it. I know when you are thinking of me. I can feel it. Even though we rarely speak, here, I am not often truly alone. At night I am so tired after all the day's hard chores. But even so, I do not sleep for hours. I do not really know if I sleep at all. You are there—I just start to think of you, I just imagine you, your face, and then I speak to you, and you answer.

I will try to get these letters to you by sending them to Madelaine, perhaps she will be able to find you. But for now, it is not safe. I will keep them all here.

Nicole

17 May

Dear Madame,

The duties of the nunnery allow me little time for correspondence. I sympathize with the maternal concern you have expressed in your letter, but there is little I can do to allay it. I do not know why you have not heard from your daughter. I often see her with pen in hand, scribbling furiously. The other sisters tell me the same. As we are forbidden to keep diaries, I have assumed she was writing letters to you, her faithful and devoted mother.

Her condition does grow stranger, week by week. In the day, at prayers, she is peaked. Occasionally, her head droops and we are obliged to prompt her to continue her devotions. On other occasions, she is possessed of a religious fervor that is most unseemly in a young girl. She forgets her prayers, and begins to mumble I know not what as she fondles the beads of her rosary. Last Tuesday she fell into a faint at such a moment. One of the sisters went to her aid, and found that Nicole was damp with her exertions. Her ecstasies are certain to have a bad influence on the other nuns. I hold nothing back from you, Madame. I place my faith in Our Lord, and I pray for your daughter, as I know you also do.

In God's name,
Soeur Henriette La Rochelle

3 July
Dearest Madelaine,

These pains are worse than those of childbirth! I die for my Charles, and my only relief, other than these letters to you, was my diary. Sister Renée has taken it away. She came last night as I lay sleeping—I dreamt of Charles, I often do—they told me I made low moaning sounds in my sleep—Sister came and woke me, and rifled my bedding until she found the little book hidden beneath the pillow. Madelaine! If you get this letter at all, it will be by God's grace—I will sneak it out by giving it to the groundsman with a few francs. Perhaps I will not be able to write any more. If only I knew what I said in my sleep! It must have been something awful, for now I am shut in most hours of the day, and am rarely left to myself. The Mother Superior crosses herself when she sees me, and the nuns look away. What have I done to lead such a life of misery? I have not had a word from Charles, nor any news of my little Colette. Write to me as soon as you possibly can.

Your loving friend,
Nicole

10 September
Dear Holy Mother,

I try not to write to you often—I know the labors of your office keep you much employed. But this piece of news is most pressing. It concerns my daughter and her misfortune. Charles Desnos is dead. He attempted to steal the baby from its home, and was apprehended in the act. In the ensuing struggle, he was killed. Although it is harsh news, my daughter had best know of it. Perhaps it will help her to treat her vows with greater piety.

Your obedient servant,
Mme E. Charcot

29 September
Dearest Madelaine,

I heard the Mother Superior talking to Sister Renée. They thought I was asleep, but I was only pretending. Mother wrote to tell them that Charles was dead, and that they ought to decide whether or not to tell me!

I know he is not dead, Madelaine. Shall I tell you how I know? They are just trying to change me, they want me to be like them, to love my devotions. I know only one devotion! I know he is not dead because he comes to me, he sends me messages. He speaks to me when I sleep. It began a few weeks ago. He receives my letters although I dare not send them. I hide them in a hole in the floor. But when he comes to me he has read them.

They leave me alone often now. I am rarely with the others. So I have much more time to speak to him. When I am supposed to pray to our God, I know He will understand that I address Him through my prayers to another. Madelaine, this is a treacherous lie. My Charles is very well.

Your loving,
Nicole

19 October
Dear Madame Charcot,

It is the saddest of tasks to write you this letter, Madame. I hesitated long before taking up my pen. Since we gave your daughter the news you requested, she ceased to eat, and fell ever more deeply into the reveries of which I spoke previously. She slept often, and deeply, and each morning it took the efforts of the sisters to wake her. We thought she suffered the disease which afflicts our kind — the accidie of the cloister. But she did not suffer its ordinary symptoms. Her melancholia was most pronounced, it is true, but she had neither the irritation nor the boredom that characterizes it. This fatigue, as you know, is one of its first signs. We attempted the usual cures — work in the garden, the activities of the parish — but none produced an effect. We believe she has unclean thoughts, poisonous thoughts that she does not bring to confession. We began to feel her state was unsuitable for the sisters, and we began to fear the worst for Nicole.

We think it is another thing now—the influence of Satan, in the form of one of his unholy servants. He visits her at night, and performs the lewdest operations upon her. We know this because we discovered certain letters, which we have burnt. They were addressed to Charles Desnos, but since he is deceased, and she has been informed of this, it is surely an incubus which visits her. Madame, I have summoned an exorcist from Paris, he will arrive on the Sabbath. I will inform you of his success or failure. I trust you will pray, as we all do, for the salvation of Nicole's soul.

Yours in God,
Soeur Henriette La Rochelle

4 November
Dear Madame Charcot,

It is over. The exorcist attempted to drive the Devil from your daughter's flesh, but Satan's grip was firm, and her delusion remained to the end. She fell into a fever on the third day of the proceedings, and she remained in this state for seven days, during which she discoursed with her incubus. Her words were transcribed, and I enclose a page of these ramblings. The original will remain in the files of the church.

We are sorry for your loss, Madame, and pray for the salvation of your daughter's soul. She is in the hands of our Lord and master now, and He will dispose of her as He sees fit. When Satan takes hold with such vigor, his grip is unyielding.

We received your donation, and we thank you in the name of Our Father.

Soeur Henriette La Rochelle

Charles . . . are you there? I hear you. Yes. Yes, I hear you. But it is a thirst to quench, oh yes, yes it is. I have an ache, it is unbearable, the sisters—take it away! Away from here, away from me! It is better like that . . . what is that sweetness? I smell you. You must stop now, someone's coming. Ah . . . you have not done anything, Father. Stop, Father. No sin. Your hands. Charles. She is Colette, I see her . . . do not let it happen to her too — There are dreams about people like us . . . it is a long night of them. The Devil is in me surely, yes he is, right inside of me, like that, like that! Oh! It is the end coming. It is a thirst to burn like that, sisters . . . Have you found him yet? Bring him here, I want to touch him — ha ha! Stop that! It is a heathen soul with the devil in it . . . beside me . . . burning for the thirst, to the ground . . . oh no! That is where the Devil visits . . . he is very cold, but I itch, Charles . . . when is the night coming? I want to sleep . . . Mother? Where is sleep? Uh-uh, not so . . . I want to . . . yes, that is what I want, he was cold in the dream. I am burning.

Lily's nose felt stuffy from the dust of the pages. The whole room smelled like antiquated dust, the bilge of another century. She looked sourly at the letters. She pushed them into as neat a pile as possible and pulled the blankets more closely around herself. Curse was meowing, looking for something. She picked him up and placed him in bed with her.

She lay awake. It was impossible to sleep. Curse was restless and he felt hot. She got up and telephoned Alan.

"Lil? Are you okay?"

"Yeah. I couldn't sleep."

"It's all that coffee. It's curdling your nerves."

"Can I come over?"

"Of course. Right away."

When she arrived, Alan was reading a book and drinking a beer. He set his glass down, and pulled her into his lap.

"I've been thinking. We could do this every night. You wouldn't have to come skulking over here in the wee hours."

"I'm just not ready."

"Well, fine. Makes it romantic and all that. Couldn't sleep, huh? That *Tess*. Pretty hard-core."

"Tess?"

"And Angel and the D'Urbervilles. I haven't forgotten my high school education." He looked at her curiously. "Well, weren't you reading it?"

"Oh, I . . . no, I got restless."

"What did you do then?"

"You know. I talked on the phone and tried to sleep."

"Uh-huh. Well, let's go to bed. You're going to see Penthe tomorrow morning, right?"

"What's he like?"

"Huh? I don't know. Like an artist, I guess. What else?"

The studio occupied the upstairs of an old building in the Mission district. A tired taqueria downstairs catered to a decaying clientele of pimps and winos, and a few junkies drinking sodas. Finding the street door open, Lily padded quietly up the stairs — she hoped to get a quick glimpse of the work before she had to face the artist.

When she reached the studio threshold, she saw his back. He was reaching up — the figure he was working on was taller than he was. It was not a well-defined form, but she could see that it was a woman holding something like a bowl in her hands. With a chisel, he was making her face.

"Hello. Are you Mr. Penthe?"

He started so faintly that she could only see it in his shoulders, then he turned to her. A lock of black hair hung over green eyes. His cheekbones were high and strong, and his mouth was curious — the upper lip was thin and tense, and the lower was lush. It was appallingly sensual. She stared at it.

"Yes. And you must be —?"

"Lily. Lily van Velsen. From Van Velsen Jewelers. My secretary made an appointment —"

"Of course." His smile was sudden and bright. He regarded her carefully for a moment, then brushed at the plaster dusting his sleeve. "Would you do me a favor, Miss van Velsen?"

"Lily."

"Lily. I need a model for the hands. You have lovely hands."
He took her left hand and studied it. "What a magnificent ring."

"I . . . I just got engaged. I didn't want this ring. I wanted
a pearl, but . . . that's bad luck, you know."

"Do you mind if I take it off, just for a minute, while you
hold your hands up, like this? Here, hold this cup." He handed
her a rusty tin mug. "Pretend it's a chalice."

Before she could reply he slipped the ring off her finger and
set it down beside some broken heaps of plaster. She posed with
the mug. Such a cliché, she thought, taking off your engagement
ring. She stared at the upraised cup.

"What's in this grail, anyway?"

"Mmmmm . . . the milk of paradise. Honeydew."

Lily laughed. Her arms began to ache from holding it, and
a pain traveled like a fuse from her shoulder to her neck. Johnny
worked steadily at the hands, as if he were indifferent to her
discomfort.

When he was finished, he said, "Thank you, Lily." He
reached for her hand again, touching it gently. "Yes, just the
hands I wanted. Come on, I'll make coffee, and I'll show you
my work."

Most of the statues were ugly. Their execution was impec-
cable—the hideous made compelling. Men reduced to tears,
stone heads in stone hands, bearing an agonized weight of pain.
There was a couple wrapped in an embrace that might have
been lovemaking or violence, their faces consumed with a passionate hate.

But Johnny Penthe appeared to love women, and these figures
were beautiful. They were of all descriptions—fat and thin,
aged and nubile. Their breasts sagged like sacs, or pressed
against the air like sweet fruits. Their thighs were thick and
heavy, or taut with muscles like great cats. He saw into the
hearts of women. Four or five of the statues were women in lan-
guorous poses, an arm outstretched, a long, white neck arched.

"These four would be suitable for *Bijou*, don't you think?"
He took a piece of cord from the floor, and wrapped it around

the neck of a woman. "Can you imagine that it's an emerald necklace?"

Lily looked more closely at the statue. Around its wrists were small colored stones, set in a circle—a bracelet of crude gems. Against the whiteness of its arm, the rough ornament was stunning.

"Do you like that?" He smiled. "I try to adorn them. Come here."

A statue of a nude woman lay on her back in brazen repose, one leg propped up, one arm fallen like Marat's in the bath. She conveyed the appearance of a woman who had been making love. In the plaster around her neck was pressed an elaborate necklace, composed of moonstones.

"That must have cost you a fortune," said Lily. "It's exquisite."

"It did." He flashed his brilliant smile. "I wouldn't be a starving artist, would I, if it weren't for their jewelry. But I see them that way. It's mostly glass, of course."

The coffee was made, and he poured hers into the tin cup. His own cup was a little plaster mug, and it too had small gems and pieces of polished glass pressed into it. He laughed. "I see everything that way. Adorned."

"That isn't very realistic."

"No." His voice was dry. "I told you I was a starving artist, didn't I? I took some slides to a gallery in North Beach yesterday. No one there had heard of me. I was just dismissed." He shrugged and reached for a cigarette. "Sometimes I do believe the world doesn't want me. Sometimes I do believe the world would like me to rot in hell."

"But *Bijou* . . . the circulation—"

"Yes, *Bijou*." He was suddenly serious, and she felt the shock of his dark green eyes and their violent gaze. "Let's make it very good. I want it to be very good. It matters to me." They stared at each other, and Johnny broke the silence.

"Well, go on, ask me about my work. You haven't asked."

"I don't have to, do I? It's here." She waved her hand through the air.

"That's very unusual. You're supposed to ask me all kinds of things—where I've shown, where I went to school—"

"But that's not asking you about your work."

He eyed her sharply. "You can't be very successful at what you do."

Lily arched her brows. "Of course I am. Van Velsen's is one of the finest jewelers in the world. It's very small, but I make all of the aesthetic decisions. My great-uncle began the business and trained me. He always wanted me to continue his work."

"Which is what, exactly? Minding the store?"

"No," she said, watching his eyes. "I work the stones. I'm a kind of sculptor. Alan, my fiancé, takes care of most of the business. But even so, there's so much to do, I don't have as much time as I'd like for cutting the gems."

"Do you miss them?"

"I suppose so. Sometimes. I do miss the pearls. The pearls are my specialty. You see, there isn't much of a market anymore for natural pearls. When the Japanese perfected cultured pearls, in the 1920s, the market dropped. A natural pearl takes a decade or more to form; a cultured one takes three and a half years. Now just a handful of customers around the world can afford and really care to have a natural pearl. Theoretically, it makes no difference, of course. On the outside, they look exactly the same to most people. But on the inside, you can see with an X ray that a cultured pearl has an implant. It's the idea of a natural pearl that's exciting. To think of the odds against its growing in a hostile sea, the odds against its survival . . . They're called true pearls, or wild pearls. And we pearl doctors—that's what I'm called, a pearl doctor—know, from experience, that an extraordinary jewel may exist beneath a flawed surface. To find it, you have to take a risk by destroying the exterior. If you judge wrongly, of course, you've lost everything. My great-uncle had a special gift for this intuition. He could even tell a natural from a cultured with his eyes. No one can do that. Only a few great masters before him knew how. He told me one day I'd learn to see, too, but that he couldn't teach me yet. It's a matter of time and love, he said. He's a romantic old man."

Lily gripped the tin cup in her hand. "It's very hard work. Mind-breaking work, and you must have steady hands. Pearls are like onions, layer upon layer, and these layers have to be carefully peeled away. It used to be done with spirit of vitriol, and cosmetic touches were added with alabaster powder and white coral. Long ago the pearls were fed to doves, and the birds were killed an hour later—God, I'm going on. Forgive me. Look, there is something I want to ask you about your work. Why is most of it so hideous, and then the women . . ."

He looked at her sardonically. "Afraid of the dark?"

"Yes. I don't understand it. I just try to make beautiful things in my work. We don't cut ugly stones, we don't make ugly jewelry."

Johnny Penthe didn't say anything. He traced circles in the plaster dust at his feet, and the black hair hid his eyes.

That night, Lily spent a few restless hours reading trade journals she had brought home from the office, and several more hours reading novels and dawdling. By the time she decided to reread the pages of the book it was nearly dawn. The faint sounds of morning began: traffic, garbagemen, small herds of huffing joggers below her window in the hazy dark. Normally, these noises aggravated and upset her. She often had insomnia, and these harbingers of the dawn were her enemies. She hated to go to sleep at dawn—often, when she lay awake until the last moment of night, she quickly pulled down her shades after a glance at the pink San Francisco morning. But tonight she barely noticed the petty cacophony outside her window. Finally, pushing away the pages, she yanked the shades and sank into her bed.

She started to fall asleep. There was a wind outside, trying to get in. It was bashing against the house, and then it stopped, starting again suddenly. The periods of stillness frightened her more than the wind. She wanted to hear the trees whipping against each other. She felt a touch in her sleep, like a paw on her thigh. She shifted under the covers, moving to where the sheets were cold and crisp. The feeling of the paw moved with her. It scared her, yet at the same time it was soft and reassuring. She went to sleep with the feeling of the paw against her.

She dreamed as if drunk, or deeply exhausted: everything around her was blank and heavy. When she woke, she had the sensation that she had been far away, or rather deep down, into layers of sleep where, she hazily thought she had read, no dreams occurred, the dreamer abandoned and shut away. This foglike feeling yielded only after she thrust open her window, and reveled in the fresh, cold air. The wind was gone. Lily remembered the feeling of the paw. She wanted to talk to someone about it, but she felt too silly. She attempted to analyze it, but it was no use. Perhaps she felt a touch. Perhaps she was hungry for something, a gentle contact, and so she dreamed of it. Dressing quickly, she fed Curse and walked to her great-uncle's house.

She found Mordecai standing by his bookshelf, lost in contemplation of a row of titles. He jerked away from them when he saw her. Lily spoke first. "I've been reading the pages from the book."

"Yes. Well. I'm sorry I gave them to you. I shouldn't have let you see them. They're morbidly exciting to a young woman's imagination."

Often his baroqueness irritated her, but today it was relaxing. It was comforting that he lived in another world.

"I think I dreamt of a paw. But I'm not sure it's a dream; it was too vivid."

"What? Isn't that odd."

"I thought so. It touched me." She looked down. "It was the day after I had held the Nakamura pearls. I didn't want the owner to have them. I wanted to steal them. And then the next night—this. Do you think it's because I wanted to steal something beautiful that I had a strange dream? It's like I let that dream out of a box."

Mordecai was toying with a small ivory carving of a bird. It was smooth where hands had rubbed it a thousand times. "I have never seen the Nakamura pearls," he said wistfully, ignoring her question. "What did they feel like? Were they cold?"

"Well, yes, they were."

"I thought they would be. Because after all, a necklace with such a history . . . Tell me how you came to touch them."

She told him the story of the pearls, appearing to be absorbed in it, but all the while she eyed him carefully. He didn't look well. And after all, it wasn't a healthy environment. The daylight was shut out, the air was old; only his spirit kept the room alive and tender, giving a gentle life to its objects and to the soft glow of the dusty lamplight.

Slowly, slowly, as she spoke, the premonition of an ague seemed to seize the old man, an inner trembling that was not quite sickness but its halo. Lily stopped speaking and stared at him.

His eyes met hers. "Please go," he said softly. With a small lurch, he leaned against the heavy desk. One moment more and Lily would have called out, but instead she watched him reach for a crystal decanter, which had been there so long she had ceased to notice it. He tipped it against a small glass, and half an inch of ruby liquid dripped out. It gave off a sweet, acrid odor.

He drank it quickly, staggered a little, then fell back in his chair, his lips pressed unnaturally tight. She had never seen him look so ill.

Lily ran, ran up a winding stair and down a passage, frantic, calling for Chen Li. She found him in a small, quiet study flooded with a gentle light, arranging pink peonies in a glass vase.

She was breathless. "Quickly." She meant it to sound urgent and loud, but it emerged hushed, whispered. "I don't know what's wrong. He's, Mordecai is—"

Chen Li turned a flower toward the light. The edge of a peony was browning, and he plucked off the petal deftly. "These peonies," he observed, "are quite rare. They have been specially bred. While they are more beautiful, they are not as hardy as the common varieties."

Lily felt tears of rage burning behind her eyes. Her mouth quivered. "Haven't you heard me? I don't know what's *wrong* with him. Do you know? We must call a doctor, immediately."

Chen Li snipped a stem. "Okay, little ghost." He often called Lily "little ghost," a diminutive left over from her childhood. "I'll call a doctor, little ghost."

"But *now*," she said frantically, casting about for a phone. She had never used a phone here. Perhaps there was no phone at all. She lifted piles and shoved curios, in a rage. Clouds of dust rose, but there was no telephone. Chen Li seemed displeased with his entire arrangement, and began again, removing each pale flower gingerly, its stem leaving a wet spot in the dust on the table.

Lily lunged at him. She beat her fists against his spare shoulders and chest and felt a scream rising in her throat. Chen Li grabbed her by both arms, so sharply and firmly that she gasped.

"Little ghost," he said, "you go on now. He'll be fine. I know."

"Fine? Fine? But he was . . . You didn't see him. You don't know."

"I know. He's sick. For a very long time. He'll be better."

"Sick? With what? He needs a doctor. What is he sick with?"

"Malaria."

"*Malaria?* What are you talking about? I mean, they can cure that! Quinine, and everything. If they can't cure it you die from it. He'd be dead by now."

"Go on, little ghost. He's not dead."

She was being pushed, gently, steadily toward the door. She felt heavy and awkward; her hand brushed the table, she upset the peonies. The pale pinks lay, abandoned in a trickle of water that spilt on them like rain. Chen Li did not look at them; he merely propelled her down the stairs to a door, and out into the blazing light. She stared at the bright street. Looking back into the gloom of the house, she saw Chen Li smiling.

"Little ghost, you come back later." The door slammed.

Lily staggered, numb with feeling. She made her way to a small library not far from the house, one she'd loved as a girl. It was rare that her great-uncle didn't have a book, any book she could think of, but sometimes, sometimes. And sometimes he sent her away to the library even when she knew he had the very book she wanted. He never gave a reason when he sent her away.

At the library, she composed herself, and asked for the books she needed. She went to the encyclopedia.

Malaria. "Although it has nothing to do with 'mal,' or bad, air, it does rise from the waters and spreads across the surface of the land. Heat and cold and the moisture of the air affect its movement, and even twilight, darkness, and dawn mark the rise and fall of this infection in the habitations of man."

The female mosquito takes in malaria parasites by sucking the blood of infected humans. The parasites grow in her stomach in tiny cysts, which burst in three weeks, giving birth to the young, sexual parasites. Her next victim receives them in turn from the mosquito's saliva, which it injects into the human flesh. They multiply in the victim's liver, spilling into the bloodstream in a week or more. There they multiply until they burst out, destroying red blood cells, and repeating the cycle over and over again.

Plasmodium vivax, *P. ovale*, *P. malariae*, *P. falciparum*. Periodicity: quotidian, tertian, quartan. "Treatment is in theory simple." But if the treatment isn't administered properly, immediately, the disease can remain dormant.

Perhaps, she reasoned, he wasn't taking the drugs properly. That would be like him. And he might have contracted it anywhere, at any time, in some acrid jungle, from the poisoned saliva of a female insect, injecting him with sexual parasites. She ran her hand over her brow. Lots of people had it. He seemed to be treating it, with that stuff he drank, whatever it was. But didn't it say here that the treatment was in the form of pills? She had to lose him one day, he was so old. But he'd had it a long time, that's what Chen Li said. She'd just never seen an attack before, that's all. It was awful to see. Even the clinical description was horrible: "Recurring bouts of fever that shake the sufferer with alternating shivering and sweating." But did that account for the death-pale face, the hollow eyes watching a scene far away, the faint tremor that was not a seizure but a warning of loss at the very heart of life? You're morbid, she said to herself. And you always have been. Stop. Stop thinking. Go about your business. Go to work. Go on, little ghost.

Alan brushed a piece of lint from his sweater and poked at one of his cuticles. His craggy face was set in worry, his glasses were slightly askew, and his thick hair was tousled from running his fingers through it. "God, you picked a hell of a day to be late!"

"I'm sorry, Alan. I slept in. I had a headache this morning and I just—"

"Another one of your headaches? I wish you'd get tested thoroughly, Lily. There could be something wrong with you."

"Oh, I know there's something wrong with me."

"That's not funny. Now listen, we've got a problem. It's about the Nakamuras. I haven't had a lot of time to look into it yet, but my initial research hasn't been promising. There might be something for us in London, but I doubt it. I saw one in Los Angeles last year, but it's orient wasn't good enough. It wasn't —What's that term? It wasn't ripe. Perhaps you should go down and look at it, though. It might have to do. Pearls of the quality we want just can't be found. I know you don't like me to talk about it, but—Couldn't you speak to your great-uncle? You know I wouldn't bring this up if I didn't think it was really necessary."

Lily colored. "You know I can't."

"Jesus, Lily! Is this what it's going to be like? I *love* you, you know that, but I'm sick of your family's dark secrets. I know you don't want to hear it, but I'm allergic to cobwebs, and tragedy, and—Why don't you just talk to him?"

"I can't bring this up, and you know it."

"The man was the greatest pearl doctor in recorded history. *Was.* That pearl is sitting in a vault in his house—God only knows if he takes good care of it—"

"You know he does. You have no right to talk like this."

"To talk like what? I'm just calling it as it is. It's sitting there, it's the answer to our entire problem, that pearl is a *legend*. If he won't doctor it, you can do it. Hell, we'll get someone else to do it—I don't care. But there is no pearl in this world like the Celebes pearl. I can't find a thing. And you know how to talk to him."

"Alan, he's not well."

"All the more reason. God, he's *old*. He'll never cut that pearl."

"You're asking me to do the one thing I can't do."

"Oh, really? There's a lot you can't do—move in with me, for example. Oh God, Lily, I'm sorry I said that, there's no hurry. Don't let's fight. Just think about it. We need that pearl. He doesn't. Come here."

He reached for her. He kissed her neck, then her cheek. Then he lifted her hands to his lips.

"Where's your ring?"

"My ring? Oh . . . I took it off. To do dishes, and I left it by the sink. Gosh, a week and I'm already careless."

"Wear it tomorrow. I like to see it on you." He brushed her cheek with his hand.

* * *

The fog had rolled into San Francisco; there was a wet chill on everything. Lily rushed through the streets, too frantic for vehicles, needing the propulsion of her own feet and the sting of the air.

She was breathless when she reached the door on Pacific Street. She banged the iron knocker, feeling the grit of rust on her palm.

The door opened a crack. "It's me, Lily," she called into it.

Chen Li fixed his implacable gaze on her, and it withered her. Of-course-it's-you rested behind his eyes. He remained silent.

"Well," Lily continued awkwardly, "I was worried about Uncle, so I—" She paused, then blurted, "Can I come in? And see him? Because this morning was . . ."

She felt hot tears forming behind her eyes, as if she were a child. The corners of her mouth began to quiver.

There was some inexpressible softening in Chen Li's features: perhaps it was a faint parting of the lips, or an infinitesimal droop to his eyelids. But he merely shook his head, slightly and gravely.

"This is ridiculous!" Lily burst suddenly, more a child than ever, stamping a foot in sudden rage. "I've never been turned away from here! I have every right to be worried, and every right to want to help!" She was going to continue, when Chen Li fixed her with the saddest look she had ever seen. It was a look of complicity, of a comrade fighting on the front lines in a losing war, a last look on a battlefield. Lily stopped, her body deflated by the sight. He didn't smile, but there was an illusion, or the ghost of a smile, and he whispered, "Not today, little ghost." The door shut, the chain rattling behind it. Lily stood in the hazy dark and cried like a baby, like a soldier.

She couldn't bear to go home. And besides, she needed her ring. It would tie her to the rest of her life. She went unannounced, the same way she went to her great-uncle's. She found the door open, as she had the first time. Johnny was sitting on a mattress in a corner of the studio, staring at the statue with her hands. He was dusty, from working, and he held an unlit cigarette in his hand. She marveled at the sight. Even at home, unguarded, he had a charm and an easy grace that followed him like a shadow. He didn't seem surprised to see her.

"I left my ring. Hi."

"Lily." He spoke like a man coming out from underwater.

"I brought you something, too. I come bearing gifts," she said stupidly.

She took a small muslin bag from her purse, and knelt beside him. It was tied with a thin piece of cord. She undid it, letting it rest in her open palm.

"My God, they're beautiful. I don't know that I can afford them."

"No, they're a gift. Really."

They both looked at the shining pile of stones. There were chips of rubies and emeralds, and larger opals and cat's-eyes, hematite, crystal, onyx, and rose quartz.

"They're not worth anything, really. They're flawed."

He leaned over, close to her, and let his arm rest against hers. "We smell the same," he said.

She gave a sudden jerk backwards. The bits of jewel fell out of her hand in a spray across the bed. Bewildered, she reached to gather them up. Johnny stopped her, holding her by the shoulders. She swayed a little in his grip, then lay back softly against his pillow, her hair full of beryl and jet and moonstone.

She expected a fierce gesture from his lush, angry mouth, but instead he kissed her gently, just a brush of his lips over hers. His touch made Lily sick with desire. She ran her fingers through his black hair, and tried to draw his mouth down to hers. He laughed, and whispered in her ear. Blushing, she tried to pull away.

Johnny smiled. "Lily, Lily, I adore you. I'm in love with you."

"You can't be. You don't know me."

He let her go, and stretched his long limbs out on the bed. "That's all right. You'll be back for me."

"You're disgusting. You're arrogant." There was a tiny cut on her hand, where a sharp gem had bruised her. Johnny pressed his lips to the droplets of blood.

"Did that hurt?" He looked at the red flush of her cheeks. "Did you get cut badly?"

"Not too badly."

He kissed her mouth, and ran his hands over her body, until she felt strange and sick, as though an illness were passing into her blood.

"You taste like a flower, Lily. Like my little flower."

"I'm not yours." She struggled against him. "I'm not anybody's."

He smiled a cat's smile. "Don't forget your ring." It lay where he had left it, in the heap of plaster dust. He slipped it on her finger, and she gathered her things in silence.

The following day Lily received admission to her great-uncle's home. Chen Li greeted her politely. He saw her into Mordecai's study, then returned momentarily with two snifters of Mordecai's best Armagnac.

"What are we celebrating?" asked Lily, taking the glass from the tray. The crystal was so thin she was afraid it would shatter if she applied the slightest pressure.

Mordecai had been puttering among his books, as usual, his back to her as he replaced a tattered volume. He turned, smiling, four little books in his hand.

"This is a first edition of *Les Liaisons Dangereuses*. Have you ever read it, my dear? I'm sure I advised you to long ago. When I was a boy, we used to call it a young man's guide to the battlefields of love. Of course, it all depended upon—"

"Uncle," she interrupted. "I don't want to talk about books today."

"But, my dear," he protested with mock gravity, "we always speak about literature. Do you really want to alter our little ritual? I have enjoyed it for all these years . . . And now you want to deprive me of it."

"No, it's not that. You know—Yes, of course I've read it. That very edition. When I was nine. Too young for it."

Mordecai had not touched his brandy. Instead, he poured himself a tiny glass of the liquid from the crystal decanter.

"I remember when you wanted to read about love, for the first time, my dear. I gave you two books, and I said, 'Would you like *Tristan and Iseult*, or Sun Tzu's *Art of War?*' "

Lily smiled faintly. "I want to talk to you. It's about what Chen Li told me. I know what you have."

"He told you?" His voice was suddenly taut and cold.

"I've done some reading. There are things that can be done. Lots of new medicines. If you'll tell me which type you've got, and what you take, well, perhaps there have been advances. It isn't inevitable that you should have these attacks all your life."

"But Lily, Lily, I'm very, very old, aren't I? What difference does it make anymore?" He was ashen, and he drank more rapidly from his glass.

She replied fiercely, pushing herself from her chair, "I don't want you to die! I want you to be well. You don't have to suffer like this. And besides, the older you get, the more these attacks could—"

"Kill me? Yes, I know. Do you think I don't think of it? Are you sure I don't want it?"

Lily frowned. "Why would you want to die?"

"We have no secrets from each other, you and I. It's just that we don't speak of what is obvious. It is," Mordecai said with stiff dignity, "in rather bad taste."

"I don't know what you're talking about," spat Lily. "I don't know what you mean, you know I don't. To want death!" She suddenly felt tired, and deflated. "I'm so sorry, Uncle. I don't know what I'm saying. Let's not argue. Just please, tell me about it. What sort of malaria is it?"

Just then Chen Li appeared in the doorway. Leaning his thin frame close to Mordecai, he whispered a few words into the old man's ear.

Mordecai snapped, "None? Then go quickly!"

Thrusting a small package into Mordecai's hands, Chen Li hastened out the door.

Mordecai poured himself another glass of his potion, and drank it in one gesture. They sat in silence. Slowly, very slowly, his head began to bow, drooping gently over his desk, like a hothouse flower bending on a stalk too thin to support it, his ancient body unable to hold the noble head. His eyes were cloudy as he turned to face his great-niece, his pupils small and far away in his gray eyes.

"My dear?" he murmured. "Let's talk about my half-sister. I want to talk about her . . . She was in the hospital a long time, and—"

"Not now, try not to think about it. Uncle, tell me what you drink. What is it?"

Mordecai shook his head. His right hand clutched the decanter reflexively.

"Let me try it," she demanded.

"That is out of the question."

"Why? Why is it out of the question? I might have it too."

Mordecai's face came alive for a moment, and he stared at her intently. "What do you have?"

"Malaria. Maybe I have malaria." She paused. "Like you. Maybe it's hereditary. Because at night I—"

A look of tenuous relief came into his half-dead eyes. "Of course you don't, my dear. You don't have malaria. I . . . I got it in China, in the jungles there, south of Yunnan. It was so many years ago, and the night was sweltering. Even the netting seemed to enclose us in the impossible heat! We slept with the netting anyway, of course, we had to. But it is not infallible. You see, one of the bearers had slipped on a rock—yes, I believe it was a rock—and the netting ripped, and so there was a rent in it, and because of this, you see—"

Lily got up and touched him. "Uncle. Don't talk any more now. We'll talk about it later. There's something else. I'm ready for more of the book. I finished what you gave me."

"Yes, so you said. But I don't think you should have any more. I see how sensitive you are. Thinking you have a tropical disease! Your imagination is not to be trusted."

"I'm sorry. It's because I'm worried. I do want to read the book."

"When I see your pale face, my dear . . . Perhaps you are not reading enough suitable material, to *balance* you. Are you reading Zola? Haven't I warned you against the Realists? I have often thought . . ."

Lily sighed. He was drifting again. His head was falling to his arm, and she was afraid to wake him. Faint beads of sweat had formed on his brow.

Because he was asleep, or something like it, because Chen Li was away on one of his dubious errands, because an urgency in her prevailed, Lily snuck over to a dark cabinet behind her great-uncle. Cautiously, and with difficulty, she pulled the book free from its niche on the shelf. The musty smell rose from its pages, more intense than she remembered it. Could it have grown so much older in a few days? It was decaying as she held it in her hands.

She heard her great-uncle sigh a little, darkly, and she had a sudden child's fear of being caught with her hand in a jar of candy, bare to shame. She had no time to examine her treasure, only time, like a petty Raskolnikov, to grab it. She reached inside, and her sweaty hand emerged, covered with dust.

She had grabbed at random from the middle of the book. Papers slid to the floor, dust bustled up to the windows, escaping. She scrambled to gather up the pages, and in the process discovered that they were not all old and brittle. Many were typewritten, and the ones she held were written in a small, neat hand on cream-colored stationery. She stopped, studying the sheaf of letters, when she heard the click of the front door hinge, and the soft tap-tap of Chen Li's step in the hall. She thought she heard the rustle of flowers. Pressing the papers into her briefcase, she hastily replaced the book.

She went to the front hall, and Chen Li showed her out. This time she said nothing about Mordecai.

Lily didn't want to be alone with the papers, and she didn't want to go out. She felt trapped, sometimes, in the city, and lonely when she drove to the country. She had a dream of Home, a Norman Rockwell sort of place where kettles hissed on stoves and puppies yipped. It was childish, like a cartoon. Sometimes she thought everyone else had the dream, too, and other times she thought it was hers alone, the result of all that moving around as a child, boarding schools and other people's households, pseudo-parents and a mad aunt in the hospital. She felt herself beginning a familiar litany, a favorite streak of despondency and self-abuse, and as she prepared to settle into it comfortably, the phone rang.

Curse started, and Lily frowned at the machine.

Alan's voice was solicitous. "Honey? It's me. How's that headache? Are you all over it?"

"Oh, it's a lot better. Really. Thanks. I was just going to take a little nap . . ."

"Shall I come over tonight?"

"Sure."

"I'm sorry about what I said. About Mordecai. I just wish you'd let me talk about it with you."

"Okay, but not now, not tonight."

"No, I didn't mean tonight. I'll be over with some Chinese takeout in a few hours, okay?"

"Alan, do you still have that electric blanket? I've been really cold at night."

"Sure, honey. I wish you'd see a doctor. All jokes aside. I don't like it."

In the middle of the night, Lily woke up. She was trembling.

"Alan? I can't sleep."

"Uh? It's because you took that nap."

"No. I mean, yes, I suppose so."

She touched his leg, and he pressed against her. She wanted him to put his arms around her, so that she would be protected against sleep. Instead, he began to caress her. His touch was purposeful and efficient, and he pulled her toward pleasure like a reluctant animal. Afterward Alan fell asleep, holding her tight in his arms. She looked up at the ceiling. It was 2:45. Lily crept out of bed and put on a robe. She fished her briefcase out of its hiding place and removed her stolen treasure. It consisted of chronologically arranged papers—torn-out pages from a woman's diary and a correspondence between two women. The diary was written in the same excited, up-and-down hand as one of the letter writer's.

Lighting a cigarette, and shivering a little in the dark, Lily flicked on a dim light and began to read. The first page bore a firm inscription at the top in yet another hand:

Dorothy's Diary, 1958
London, 10 September—
I've been so awfully bored here. I simply can't cope. We've missed the entire season at Como and I shall never forgive Gerald. It's too annoying that his bloody business should keep him here. Margaret rang me today and asked me if I wanted to go to a seer—clairvoyant, as she calls it—Too silly. But I've nothing else to do, so why not. It's set for Wednesday. She told me to bring a locket, or something "personal." I don't know why I'm bothering to write about this at all. Well, if some old hag wants to charge me a few shillings to read my palm, it's cheaper than tea at Fortnum's for a little clean fun, isn't it? But all this clean fun is so tiresome. I wish James would get back from America. I do so miss our afternoons at the Ritz—those lovely beds. He's working at that louche bar in California, he'll come back with ideas of himself. It would be more fun if I loved James, I thought I did in the beginning, but that was all illusion. I don't know why I keep on doing it, really, it's an awful bore.

And then sometimes—he's terribly *strong*, James, and so good-looking, and his hands—his hands can make me rest. I need that sometimes, truly I do. Oh, there's Aileen, got to run!

14 September—

The most extraordinary thing. I went with Maggie to this awful little flat in Bayswater, up three flights of stairs with bawling children and all the rest. It smelled like urine and onions cooking in grease in the corridor. I had half a mind to turn around and go back. But Margaret had the most irritatingly *knowing* look on her face, and I wasn't about to let her get the better of me on account of a little unpleasantness. Besides, we really must be openminded about the conditions of the poor—perhaps they really can't help it if their flats smell like that. Though all it would take would be a little potpourri. Anyway, up we went, up all those stairs. And when we got to the top, we were greeted at the door by a middle-aged lady. Her hair was all in a dither, coming out of its pins, and the same went for the rolls on her waist— they were just *spilling* out of her corset, like so much jelly! She had a faintly Levantine look about her, rather unpleasant, and there were two society girls of the same extraction sitting on her divan, chattering like magpies.

I thought to myself, I wish I *was* having that tea at Fortnum's! What a bore this is going to be. Her musty old couch —I suppose it was turquoise once—gave out a big poof of dust when I sat on it—all over my bone linen suit. I nearly told Margaret then and there that all this was perfectly ridiculous. Well, finally the two girls stopped gibbering and Madame Betty took them into a back room. I spent 20 minutes waiting in that horrid little parlor, with Maggie trying to distract me. First she told me how marvelous it would be, but when that didn't work she came up with some rather delicious gossip—I suppose she knew it had to be rich or it wouldn't have kept me there. It seems that Lady Otoline has been having the *crudest* little parties—in which all the guests wear naughty costumes, and they invite the servants to join!

In any case, by the time Madame Betty came back in, I'd entirely forgotten about her.

Maggie said, "Just you go, dear. I've had mine yesterday." She stayed behind, and I followed the dumpy creature into a dark room that smelled like incense tinged with perspiration. The Arab ladies were speaking rapidly to each other in hushed tones. They skittered out like little centipedes. James always said I should have been a writer, he said I was very good with metaphors. Perhaps I am.

Madame Betty retreated for a moment into an alcove that I took to be her smelly little kitchen—she came out with a cup of coffee in one of those tiny Turkish cups. I didn't want to drink it; I wasn't sure it was clean. But Madame Betty tapped me on the knee with her fat fingers—which were covered in *rather* expensive rings, I might add—and said, "Drink, drink!" So I did, in one gulp. I've never cared much for that sort of coffee—I used to drink it out of politeness in Egypt when it was a matter of business and I didn't want to annoy Gerald. But this time I liked it. It tasted good, I think there was a touch of orange flower water in it, and an awful lot of sugar. I started to set it down on the tea table when I was done, but Madame Betty grabbed it out of my hands and quick as a flash she turned it over. Well, I thought to myself, what's the point of this? She must be mad, making a mess all over the saucer. She left it like that for a minute, while she stared at the dome of the cracked cup. I thought she was balmy. Then, as quickly as she'd turned it over, she turned it back, and we both stared at the grounds that were left spilt in the saucer. It was too peculiar, and to make matters worse, she seemed to be going into some sort of trance. I suppose Maggie didn't warn me about any of this because she thought I wouldn't come. She was jolly well right, too. But of course, I'm not sorry now, not a bit. Though it *was* terribly unnerving at the time. Her eyes rolled up in her head and the left side of her mouth twitched, smearing her lip rouge onto her teeth. Her fat hands started to tremble, her fingers jiggled like sausages in a pan, her feet lifted off the ground and hovered there over her tatty Persian carpet! I nearly left then and there, but I thought it would make a grand story to tell at the Wentworths' on Thursday.

26 September —
Darling Aileen,

It's not really cheating, is it? I mean, not really. It's so utterly mad. If Gerald knew — but what does Gerald know? It's been fifteen years with Gerald, and he's perfectly competent, of course. But why am I telling *you?* You went around the track with him back when, darling, I know it, I don't mind telling you. The walls have ears. So you know what I mean — and no hard feelings, especially not now, not when I have the Count. It's all too delicious. Really it is. I've dreamed of a touch like his for a million years. Do you think it's marriage, Aileen? Do you think it's built into the institution? That it gets dull? I don't know. I try to remember back to the beginning, with Gerald. I used to get *ready* for him — why, I think you were there one night. It was before the war, and we had plenty of makeup, and everything. I put on my best lingerie, the black satin robe with the lace at the side, and a marvelous pair of maribou pumps, and the most wonderful silk stockings from Dior, they make the loveliest ones. And you and I drank whiskeys with Loreen and we put my makeup on together and you both sat with me while I bathed. Do you remember? It was super, it was lovely. And just loads and loads of French perfume.

Finally Gerald arrived, from the club. I was perfectly wild with anticipation. I sat on his lap and let the robe slip open, so he could see the tops of my stockings and a bit of my thighs. I imagined what it would be like to *be* Gerald, perhaps that excited me more than anything — to have a marvelous, silky woman in your lap, with a highball in her hand and wet, red lips and her hands going everywhere.

And Gerald did not respond. He did not *respond* to me, Aileen! Someday we must speak very frankly and you simply must tell me if it happened that way between you, ever, even

) 43 (

once. I must know. Even if it is in the past. And Gerald sat there, frigid as anything, ice in that man's veins. And I said, "Darling, whatever is it? I'm all yours tonight, Gerrie dear, I've been waiting for you." And he said, "Dorothy, I've had an awfully long night at the club, you know." And I said — I still remember it — "But Gerrie, no night is too long not to go on just a *little* bit longer!" And he said, "Frankly, Dorothy, I don't know how to say this, but it puts me off a bit, this get-up. Makes me think I'm supposed to do a bit of something special, you know. Can't. Bit of pressure, what?"

Well, that just poisoned it, Aileen. Can you imagine? It was never quite like I dreamed of it with Gerald, after that. I did an awful lot of snow to cheer myself up. And of course there was James.

But now I've got the Count, I don't worry.

Kisses and smoochies and hugs,
Doro

29 September —
Dearest Doro,

I was just a little bit shocked to get your letter today. Who's let that old cat out of the bag? It was nothing between Gerald and me, really it wasn't anything. It's not worth your knowing about. But if you must know — we were up at Oxford, and Gerald was entering that rowing competition, do you remember? And I was there as an honorary judge, it was a charity event. Gerald placed, if I recall it correctly, and we had one of those awful sticky punches to drink after the race. And I said, "Gerald, aren't these things awful? What wouldn't you give for a proper rickey!" And he said, "I can arrange that, Aileen, my pet" (do you mind me telling this to you, Doro? He called me that sometimes) — "how about a spot of gin, eh? We'll make our own." And he pulled a flask out of his pocket and we drank it straight. He had a bottle of it in his bag. We went up to his rooms and we didn't even make rickeys at all. We just drank that gin. And for the rest, well, I don't know, dear, I suppose I didn't have the same problems with Gerrie that you did. He did respond rather a lot. Kissed me all over and called me all kinds of things I'd never heard before. But you're so lovely, dear, I can't imagine what could have happened that night, the night with the Dior. He does drink rather a lot, that was probably it. But you know, Doro, to be really *frank* with you about it, you've always been ever so much more of a romantic than I have. I never went out of my way for that sort of thing. I don't need it. Perhaps that's the difficulty between you and Gerald. Do you think so? I wouldn't ordinarily speak so frankly, angel, but we've come to the point of it, don't you think? And besides, I do so want you to tell me the truth about the Count. One hears things, and I'd rather hear them from you. It's really too extraordinary to be believed.

X's,
Aileen

1 October —
Dear Aileen,

I just got your note, dearest. Musette is drawing my bath, and I only have a minute. At the rowing tournament? Well, it must have been going on longer than that, because what *I* heard was all about that ball in Devon. But never mind, it's all too silly, too thoroughly unimportant.

The Count is the only thing on my mind. I'm going to get into my hot bath and soak up perfume getting ready for him! I'm going to wear my blue chiffon with the low neck and the cabochon, the one Gerrie gave me for our anniversary. Though I don't know why I bother, we're always in that dark room. But *I'll* know I'm wearing it, isn't that what jewelry is for? To make a woman feel heavenly inside? Oh, I suppose you're right, Aileen — I *am* a romantic. I don't understand how a woman can be anything else. I think if you felt the Count's body next to yours, you'd be one too. You've probably just never had the experiences to draw it out. I don't mean to be a tease, darling, I just don't have the time to explain it now. Must rush to Regina's.

Big hearts,
Do

Dorothy's diary:

1 October —

Letter from Aileen. If I tell her about the Count (and isn't she just slavering to know!) it will be *all* over town. But she's blackmailing me, the little shrew — if I don't she'll put it all over about her and Gerald and their bloody rickeys-without-soda. I've known for years, but Maggie just heard it for the first time last week. Aileen's been saving it for a moment like this. That bitch.

Of course, no one will understand about the Count, it's something too precious, too special for those hounds in our set. But still, I don't like the way it plays with my name to be cuckolded by that slut. (Can a woman be cuckolded? Why isn't there a proper word for it? Never mind.) I suppose I am better off telling her about the Count. Anyway, I certainly don't want to give Gerrie the satisfaction of knowing I know about Aileen, and the whole town, for that matter.

4 October —

Oh dear diary! I've had the most fabulous time at Madame Betty's — to think that when I first walked into that cramped little flat I'd find heaven! Why, I haven't kept a diary since I was a girl. It was Madame Betty's idea, and a damned good one if you ask me.

Here the account broke off. The remaining dozen pages Lily had grabbed were evidently from another story entirely: they seemed to be a diary account of a pearling expedition in Malay, and they largely concerned technical matters of little interest.

Lily resolved to approach her great-uncle in the morning. She would confess her little theft, and secure the rest of Dorothy's tale.

She crawled back into bed and ran her hands across Alan's chest, and across his broad shoulders. He gave a gentle sigh at the touch of her fingers, and rolled onto his side. His body was warm, and she pressed her hand against his chest, feeling the surge and fall of his breath. Reflexively, in his sleep, he placed his hand over hers, and squeezed it lightly, a talisman.

Everyone approved of their arrangement. Everyone but Mordecai—she saw it in his gray eyes. Everyone thought they understood why she chose him, but only Mordecai really did. He knew what she needed in a man—bright brown eyes, honest, without secrets, a check, a stop, a watcher, a keeper; someone else's normalcy to borrow, someone else's decency to give her an edge against herself. Being broken was a full-time job. She had seen it when she visited her great-aunt in the sanitarium. Her great-aunt hadn't said too much, near the end, but Lily had seen in her eyes how busy she was being crazy. She looked at Alan's quiet face. Maybe, she thought, maybe I can mark a little time, and she kissed him softly on the neck.

Then she tried to go back to sleep. For a while she lay awake, anxiously, waiting for the feel of the paw to return. Although it had come only once, it was already a familiar part of her life. It did not come. She dreamt instead of a bird, caught in a hot fire. Its feathers were so wet that it didn't scorch. Everything around it burnt, but it had mastered the elements. There was another dream about her cat. Curse pressed against her belly, and then he became Johnny, only Johnny had cat's claws. He scratched her breasts until they bled as he made love to her, and feeling him inside her was like being inside the heart of pain, like living inside a throb. His orgasm was cold, as if he had released some elemental substance into her. She stumbled into a dream bathroom, and touched herself. The liquid inside her was mercury, and it slipped, cold and wet, poison in her hot fingers.

Lily woke up and clutched her breasts. She turned on the light and examined them, taking each one in her hands in turn. There were no scratches.

She didn't try to sleep again. She got dressed, scribbled a note to Alan, and slipped outside. In a few minutes she was walking in Chinatown, strolling in the silky dawn. A few vegetable vendors were primping their wares, but otherwise the streets were empty. In a butcher's window, nude ducks dangled by webbed feet, their limp bodies flapping against the glass. Beside them, in the window's eye, she saw the reflection of an ancient Chinese man, with queue and cap.

She turned her head to see such an anachronism more closely. Across the street she saw Chen Li, without queue, without cap, dressed as always in a tailored Italian suit. He was hurrying. Mechanically, she began to follow him.

He moved so swiftly that soon she was breathless, moving down alleys, past shops full of geegaws, dodging the morning's first tourists. Chen Li's breath never came quickly, but he hastened his step in imperceptible increments, until she was almost running to keep up with him.

He turned a corner off Jackson Street into a small alley, and Lily, forty paces behind him, stopped short for fear she would be seen. She hovered around a corner, watching, her breath coming fast from the exertion, her fingers pressed to the rough brick of a building to steady herself.

Chen Li disappeared into a small, low doorway. Above it was an awning decorated with bright yellow characters she could not read, and the faded scales of a red dragon swallowing its tail with fiery breath. There was an unpleasantly sweet smell in the air, like flowers too long gone.

She waited for what seemed an interminable length of time. Long shadows welled up in the streets, and there was a nervous wind in the air. Chen Li did not emerge. Finally she decided on a plan. She would enter the shop, gaily, casually, as if it had a touristic appeal, as if she had discovered it on a lazy promenade through Chinatown.

As she crossed the threshold beneath the dragon awning, her nostrils were struck by a sickly sweet odor, the same one she'd noticed in the alley. It was much stronger here, it pervaded her senses. The light inside was murky, and the walls were lined

floor to ceiling with roots and flowers and ointments and powders, unguents and desiccated mysteries, stored in bottles and
jars and earthenware pots. A pile of antlers lay in a straw basket
beside her, next to a box of graying tubers. Behind a glass case
were dried roots, laid out on a bed of red velvet and tied together
with bits of red thread. She reached out and touched a small
cardboard box with a painting of a bird. It was lichee tea, and
it promised the drinker "joyfulness of life."

After what seemed a long time, a wrinkled Chinese man
emerged from a back room. His face was toothless, and when
he smiled, his gums shone.

"Help you, miss?"

"I . . . was just looking for someone," she blurted. "I thought
I saw a man I knew come in here. I've known him since I was
a little girl," she added lamely.

"No one come in here, miss."

"Well, it had to be here, because there aren't any other shops
along here. It was a while ago, and I—I mean, no one left."

"You like to buy something, miss? Licorice root, very good.
Deer's tail, dragon's blood? Something for your blood, miss?"
He looked at her closely. She flushed under his scrutiny.

He produced a packet of tiny pills, containing ox gallstone,
lymph extract, and lily flowers.

"Good for female condition." He showed his gums.

"What's that smell?"

The shopkeeper pursed his lips, and edged into the shadows
near the back room. He pointed to some dusty boxes of herbs.

"Maybe you like something for mental concentration, miss?
Maybe."

A still more ancient man, tiny as a homunculus, emerged
from the rear doorway. He did not look at Lily. He rummaged
in a deep jar hidden among cobwebs, and brought out two pieces
of Chinese candy. He shuffled from behind the counter toward
her, and pressed them into her palm. His withered fingers felt
like chalk. Lily looked at the candy—the wrapping was incon-

gruously bright. It reminded her of the yellow characters on the awning outside. She felt somehow that she was being ordered to leave, and she obediently walked out into the bright morning, the candy rapidly growing sticky in her palm. Chen Li had not come out.

"I'll follow him again," she said to the candy, a little dizzy from the musty air and the cloying incense. She opened her fingers, and let the gaudy sweets fall to the pavement.

Lily walked from Chinatown to North Beach, where she idled away the rest of the morning, drinking coffee in a café and shopping. She was waiting for the hour when her great-uncle would wake up, which was never before noon. She wanted to go to Johnny, but she exerted a new control over herself: she would let her impulses rise like snakes inside her, stretching toward a bowl of milk. She would watch them, a snake trainer: hypnotize them, subdue them, return them to their basket-homes. In spite of this good resolve, she ached for him. Just knowing he was here in the same city with her made it seem intimate, like a bedroom. His presence made a wound in her life. She thought of her dream. He wasn't far away, he was as close as sleep.

When it was nearly noon she decided to walk in the direction of her great-uncle's home, but somehow she stepped on a bus instead, and somehow it was the wrong bus, and in the end she found herself there, in the Mission, surrounded by afternoon air that hung brown against the shabby buildings. Stepping over an old drunk, she climbed the stairs, and found the door open. Creeping inside she found him, asleep in his bed. She took off her sweater, her shoes, her dress, her stockings, and crawled into bed next to him. The bed was warm where she lay, and she felt the delicate imprint of another body.

She ran her hands over the lean muscles of his chest and shoulders, and traced the veins in his arms with her fingertips. He pressed his leg between hers. He opened his eyes and smiled.

"Johnny? Has someone else been here?"

"Sure."

She nestled closer against him. She was going to say something, make some objection, when his touch pulled against the thoughts.

He spoke gently. "Do you want me to make love to you?"

"I don't want to talk about it."

"Yes you do. Talk to me about it."

"There isn't anything to say."

"There's plenty to say. You have to tell me about it." He turned away from her to the bedside table, and lit a cigarette.

She bit her lip. "Maybe you're all used up from the girl who was here before."

He laughed, and smiled his cat's smile. "Could be."

She pulled the covers close over herself. He put the cigarette between her lips and she pulled on it. "Go on then," he said.

"I want you to kiss me."

"Where?"

He touched the inside of her neck while she spoke, caressing the hollow at her throat with the back of his hand, the way one would stroke an animal. She shivered and touched his fingers. "Just here."

"That's where you want to be kissed?"

She nodded. He ran his fingers in an easy motion down her body, until they reached her thigh. He let his hand rest there, as if it were sleeping.

"And then what?"

"I want you to take me and . . . Make it so I don't have to think about anything. I want to stop thinking about things."

"But you have to keep talking about them, whether you think about them or not." He pulled his hand away and fumbled for another cigarette. Through the flame of the match, he looked at her wounded eyes.

He gently lifted her chin and looked at her. "I suppose you want me to put it back?"

"What?"

"My hand. Are you going to tell me the truth?"

"Yes, of course I do. Jesus. You kill things when you talk about them like this."

"Oh really?"

"Please."

"Well then. If you don't want to talk about it. Just show me where you want me to put my hand. Oh. Uh-huh. You don't really need me then, do you?"

She lunged at him. He caught her hand in the air, and kissed her palm, then licked the dew from her fingertips. She lay back against the pillows in defeat. There was a vicious ache between her legs. He touched her lightly, smiling at the betraying nectar.

"Lily, this is my little flower," he said, stroking her gently, "my little burning flower."

He lowered his lips between her pale thighs, tracing the sap to its blazing source, coaxing the flower's trembling heart, until all her thoughts died in her, her fingers snaking crazily in his hair. First panic rose in her, then sweetness, and then the sting of pleasure. She felt it angrily, an invading force, the enemy of control. She tried to stop it, to stop his despotic tenderness and her response. She pushed him away.

"Johnny, don't. I don't want you to."

He looked at her severely. "You want me to do everything to you, you think about it all the time, but you want to pretend decisions are in my hands. I'll do anything you want, Lily. Everything. Later I'll even do what you want the most. I'll make you please me. Now, where were we?"

"Johnny, stop. Not like that. I don't want to wait anymore —" She reached for him, but he pushed her away.

"Sssh." He pressed two fingers to her lips to quiet her, and holding her hand in his, slipped it gingerly between her legs, guiding her fingers.

"I've never done this in front of anybody, I can't."

"There's nothing you can't do with me, I want to see everything." He gripped her hand more firmly. "Show me your face,

Lily. Open your eyes. Like that — That's right. There . . . everything . . ."

He found the place on her neck that she liked so much. She closed her eyes. They looked like two children, in the dim blue light of the window. Sweat curled and ran between their bellies, between her breasts, until she tasted him in every pore. In the last wave of these tastes she distinguished his tears, slipping down her cheek into her ear, into her mouth. Hurt welled up behind his eyes. She was shocked, she suddenly felt excluded, as if she were already a memory. She was the day after Valentine's Day, all those cards one didn't know whether to keep or throw away. She touched his black hair. Already the touch was very old, the way it was between a married couple. "What's wrong?"

"You're lost to me already, Lily," he whispered into her wet ear, letting the tears curl down her throat, unlacing his body from hers.

"That's stupid," she said. "I love you."

"You love pleasure, girl. Come on, I have to get up. It's late."

Lily put on her clothes quietly. "Johnny," she said softly, "I brought you something."

In the little box were hundreds of seed pearls, a bed for the three pieces of ivory wrapped in tissue. She had carried them in her purse for days, waiting for this moment. "They're illegal," she said.

He took the box, nodded, and put it aside. Then he kissed her softly on the neck.

The next day Lily forced herself on her work. She managed her paperwork, but she couldn't face the little pearls that were waiting for her. She didn't feel like it. She didn't like to trust her hands when they felt like this. She had ignored all the sensations in her body from the moment she walked out Johnny's door, and now she didn't know her own hands. After a few hours she pushed the papers on her desk into little piles, and headed for her great-uncle's house.

Chen Li answered the door. He was wearing the same suit she had seen the day before. They nodded, but exchanged no words.

Mordecai rose at the sound of his great-niece's footsteps in the hall.

"Good evening, dear." He paused, studying her. "You look tired."

"I didn't sleep well. It was something I read."

"And what were you reading?"

She looked down guiltily, staring at her fingers. "I took some pages out of the book. I know I shouldn't have without asking, I just—I was so curious, and you fell asleep. Only the story cut off in the middle, and—"

"I know. I noticed."

Lily stared harder at her fingers. How could he have noticed in that mayhem of papers?

Mordecai sat down, looking a little flushed. He poured himself a small glass of deep red liquid from the decanter.

"And now I suppose you want the rest of the story."

"Well, yes, I do." Lily sat down too, a wave of achiness in her bones. "You know, I don't feel so well. I don't feel well at night, especially. I don't know how to describe it. My head feels so full, and so strange. Reading used to distract me, but not lately." She looked up at Mordecai. "I do like to read the book, our book. I can forget how I feel when I'm reading it. God. I have these headaches." She ran her fingers over her temples. "Uncle, what you said about malaria not being hereditary. I don't know. I just seem to have something." She motioned toward the decanter. "Couldn't I try some of that? Please? Just a sip."

"If you don't have malaria, and you cannot, then this medicine is quite—" He swiped the air with his hand. "Quite inappropriate."

Lily lunged for the crystal bottle. Mordecai's reflexes were quick, and he pulled it away. In the struggle, the decanter tipped. Half the viscous liquid oozed onto the desk.

"I've seen you drink it!" she burst out. "I've seen you calm down, I've seen your sweat dry and your shaking stop! Yes, you do shake—I've seen it—I want this. Don't tell me it's not right!"

She thrust the palm of her hand into the ruby mess, and drew it to her lips, ready to suck the dripping stuff from her fingers. It looked as if she were bleeding from a violent wound. Her great-uncle leaned over and stayed her hand.

"Stop. Stop. What an outburst." He shook his head. "So histrionic. Lily, I will only say this one more time. It is not malaria. Let me mop up this mess." With decorum, he withdrew a silk handkerchief from his vest pocket, and wiped his great-niece's hand. Like a child she submitted, her head bowed in shame, lips trembling. He looked at her gently. "I'll go get a towel to clean this up."

She waited for him to leave the room, then quickly, stealthily, she lifted the heavy decanter to her lips and drank. It had an acrid taste, like cloves and peppercorns mixed. As she tasted the thick liquid, she felt a wave of nausea, sudden and faint. She must have had a dizzy spell, because when she opened her eyes, Mordecai was pressing the sodden handkerchief to her brow. He tried to find a clean corner, but the liquid had inundated the square of silk, leaving damp traces on her skin like purple bruises.

"My Lily," he began. "I'm so sorry . . ."

She smiled up at him. "Sorry? But I feel better now. I'm beginning to feel better." A slow warmth began to suffuse her, making her blood seem to run more tenderly in her veins. It began in her stomach, this warmth, where the potion cloaked everything, and from there it ran out, lining every aching nerve with relief, comforting all the troubled cells that made up her nightmares. A meandering sleepiness lolled inside her, and she smiled, looking up at her great-uncle.

"I feel better now. I feel as if I've been sick for centuries. You won't let me die of being sick, will you?"

"God, no! Child, don't say such things."

"I feel so much better . . . I guess that old saying is true. Joy is the absence of pain. I always hated that saying, but maybe . . ."

"My dear girl, don't ever let me hear you say that." He stroked her damp forehead. "Maybe you love someone."

"No. Just a dream of someone. Which makes no difference. My own dreams don't love me."

"Lily. I want to tell you something. Believe this from an old man who's lived these last decades only to kill a pain, a memory. I know love, and I know visions, and dreams. There's no flesh in dreams. And no comfort in what we love only in the night, in shade. Do you hear, Lily? Do you understand?"

"No, Uncle Mordecai. And I'm so tired now . . . Look, about the book. I'm sorry I took it without asking. I was afraid you'd tell me I couldn't read any more, and I was so curious . . . I can't believe your half-sister would get mixed up in a thing like that, it's so bizarre . . . Séances . . . You know, I feel as if I'd always been cold, all my life, and I came inside and there was a fire going. I'm finally warm . . ."

"Ssshhh . . . Try to sleep. Go to sleep."

He pressed a wrinkled hand to her brow, watching her face as she fell into a soft sleep.

Some hours later, she woke. She felt her great-uncle's eyes, and she shifted under his gaze. He addressed her as if they were already in the middle of a conversation.

"Lily, you were a very strange child. Do you remember all of it? The things you used to do, the odd rituals you used to concoct? You took my jewels, or I gave them to you, and you divided them into little piles. You named them and spoke to them. You didn't like people. You said they hurt too much, and you could feel it. Do you remember?"

"I don't like it when you reminisce about me like that."

"No. You never have. But I like to remind you. You can't pretend you sprung out of nothing, that you have no past."

Lily felt a ripple of defiance. She rubbed her eyes. "But look at you! Secretive. Do you tell me the truth about yourself? Do I know about your past? Do I know anything about it?"

Mordecai regarded her impassively. Then, a little ashamed, he sighed. "I suppose . . . I suppose you're right, I just don't want you to think as I have, to feel as I have, that you moved and burned and loved in a dream, that you never really knew waking . . ."

He looked at her sharply. "And then there were the contracts. I still have them, you know, after all these years. That's right, I do. They were elaborately drawn up. I signed them all. Do you remember the one that demanded that we wouldn't speak for a week? Chen Li was permitted to speak, but only in Chinese. Do you remember?"

"Of course I remember. That was the first time you showed me how to work a pearl. In silence. As if we were two criminals, robbing a bank."

"As if we were two criminals."

They looked at each other then, with a look of vast complicity. After a moment, Mordecai looked down at his nails, and watched them as if they were birds that would fly away.

"And then there were the other contracts. The ones demanding my absolute constancy in matters of religion. One week there was a god, a god who made the stars and the planets, a god whose character we agreed upon. The next week there were animals in the sky instead, and they presided over a tribunal, counting sins like poker chips. Hell came and went, if I recall, and we spent hours and hours discussing its persecutions. Heaven got very little of our time by contrast. I remember your hells, Lily — they were graphic monuments to your childish imagination. Insects that had transgressed were consigned there, to the same hell as people — but they grew, as big as pine trees, with towering probosci. Certain inanimate objects suffered there, as well. There were sick rolling pins, lonely cars . . . and body parts, exiled from bodies. Spleens that sat, helpless; livers, excreting puddles of bile; restless hands and feet.

"Very early you came to a certain frightening understanding — the gnashing of your entrails by sharp-toothed predators, the intrusion of pins into your ears and nose, these were the inferior tortures. You devised a room you called the Shame Room — For hours a day, we, the condemned, were forced to sit on a throne in this terrible room, with machinery strapped to our heads. This instrument took us back, back to the moments of greatest derision and unhappiness in our lives, the moments when people we loved mocked us, the moments when our greatest dreams failed. The time, for example, when you vomited into your sweater on a school bus, and everyone saw it drip; the time the boy you loved kissed your worst rival, slowly, in front of you; the time you tried to fly, but only stumbled and fell.

"And then there were the contracts that pertained to love. These you held most precious, and you were always revising them. There were countless codicils, to be initiated and stamped. You made me sign these in blood, and you were not afraid to prick your own finger and sign with your blood, too.

"The contracts stated that I would always love you, even if you had to go to hell, even if God never forgave you again; and no matter who you hurt, or how badly. I remember asking you if these weren't the very conditions of heaven. But you said no, this was something else, something more important than heaven, and bigger.

"In these contracts I agreed to love you if you were ugly, if you cut off all your hair, or if you lost your lips in an accident. If I were to break this contract . . . Well!" Mordecai threw up his hands. "It took days, no *weeks*, I think, to devise a hell that would accommodate me. And people who loved each other well, and truly, who were kind, who petted each other's bruises with gentle fingers — These people you noticed, you made a list of them and put little gold stars beside their names.

"And the final condition, the most imperative rule: if you failed to love me, I was permitted to scold you; but I mustn't stop loving you in return. And if you came back to loving me, even though you were angry, you gave yourself a star, sticking it on the back of your palm. Some days your hands looked like the heavens."

Mordecai paused, and they sat a moment, in silence. Lily looked stubborn, and inaccessible. Finally she spoke. "Please stop, Uncle. Why are you doing this? It doesn't help anything. I'm tired. I don't like remembering."

"Nor I. Sometimes it's just a task, a necessary task. Now, perhaps you'd like something to read. Jane Bowles is rather good. And Algernon Blackwood would be relaxing for you. Blackwood is a spiritual *kin*, really, and consequently —"

She kissed him lightly on the forehead, took the volumes that he offered, and, still dazed and hazy, let herself out into the light.

Alan knocked gingerly on Lily's door, and when there was no answer, he let himself in. He saw a tousled bed, and a pile of papers spread out on the coverlet.

"Lil?"

From the bathroom he heard gagging sounds, followed by a fierce retching. He peeked in the door and found her on her knees, vomiting into the toilet.

For a moment he stood, staring down at her, then took a towel and patted it tentatively on the back of the girl's damp neck. Her whole body shook with little tremors, and occasionally a thick, racking wave swept through her. He touched her hair carefully, as if it would break. She motioned him away, as if her nausea were shameful; he waited outside, listening for a convincing silence.

At last Lily emerged, shading her eyes with her hands.

"Oh, sorry, babe. I forgot." Alan pulled the shades, and steered her to the bed. "Damn these migraines. Can you get into bed? Good, that's better." He tucked her in with meticulous care. "I'll bring you some tea. Say, what are all these papers?"

She turned sallow eyes on him. "My uncle gave them to me to read. A little family history."

He ignored her reply, seeming to have forgotten his question. He stared at her worriedly. "Lily, you need to think prevention. You're susceptible when you start getting tense. I pressured you about Mordecai, I'm sorry. And the *Bijou* layout, that's a strain, I know. Enough of these factors together, and—"

"It's not a regular migraine. Something I drank didn't agree with me, I think . . ."

"Yeah." Alan absently flicked at the pages of Dorothy's diary. "When we're through with the Nakamura pearls, I swear, I'm going to check you into the Mayo Clinic. I'm not going to marry Camille, you know."

"Alan, I need to talk to you about them. About the papers."

"Well, sure. What is it?"

"There's a diary, and some letters, and they're bothering me. They're to do with my ancestors', um, *problems*. They're bothering me."

"Bothering?"

"They're ominous, somehow. Not bad luck, exactly, but a foreshadowing. You know?"

"Well . . ."

"Like a bad dream makes you feel."

"Forget it, Lily. You've got the old man's imagination, but I'm sure that's where it ends. Now get some sleep. Put things out of your mind."

In a short while, Alan got into bed and fell asleep rapidly, as he always did. Lily pretended to sleep. The nausea had subsided, and now she lay wide awake, thinking about not taking a sleeping pill. It would be unwise, on a delicate stomach, and besides, surely her mind had the strength to think of something, something sweet to send her away. Her mind might atrophy if she didn't let it do its work, if she wasn't kind to her imagination.

She imagined making love to Johnny. She thought she could

feel his fingers, and the sleek pulse of him inside her. She shifted in bed, white with despair. She tried to put these thoughts out of her mind. But it was a temptation and a lure to imagine that she could call Johnny with her sleeping siren song. She had once read a book about autosuggestion and dreams. It advised the dreamer to choose the texture and content of the night's adventure.

"I want to dream of you," she said out loud. And that night she dreamt that Johnny made love to her; she felt the ripple and slice of him, her fingers drummed tense tunes on his phantom scapulae, she felt his slick stomach against hers, his sweat poured down his forehead into her mouth. When she woke up she was tired enough to scream. She didn't know how she would go about the day. As she drew herself up out of bed, weary and full of pain, the thought came to her: Good. Soon I can go to sleep again.

Alan petted her and fussed over her. "Are you okay? You still don't look right. Here, take some vitamin C."

"I don't have a cold."

"Maybe you need a hair of the dog that bit you?"

"Oh. In this case, I don't think so."

"Okay, be mysterious. But get better. I'm worried about you. Besides, we've got that lunch with Mrs. Franstein coming up. Want you to be well for that." He looked at her thoughtfully. "I could postpone it for a while."

She nodded, and ran her fingers through his hair.

"Why don't you rest today, Lil? Stay home. Read or something. That always relaxes you. I'll call you tonight."

Lily made tea and toast and lit a cigarette, brought Curse into bed with her, and looked at the stack of books on the bedside table. A new monograph on the emerald trade, and a history of ornamental brooches. A well-thumbed copy of *The Story of the Eye*, and an equally tattered paperback of *Beauty and Sadness*. An untouched *Crime and Punishment* and a new translation of the *I Ching*. She touched their spines, then reached for the pile of cream-colored pages and, holding the cat close, began to read.

5 October —

Well, dear diary, the sight of Madame Betty's fat little feet lifting in the air was so utterly absurd that I began to laugh. If she'd keeled right over in front of me at that moment, I'd have still been laughing! But then it happened.

A voice issued out of Madame Betty's lips. That is, she started to talk but it wasn't her at all. It was a deep voice. It said, "Dorothy, do not be afraid. Madame Betty is merely the vehicle. You have been chosen — your presence here is no accident. Those of us who are chosen call to one another, whether or not we be incarnate. Do you understand?"

I was a bit giggly, but I was scared as well. I figured if this was a parlour game, I could go right along with it. I nodded, and the voice went on.

"Dorothy, you are a seeker of love. We two have known each other in many lives, and I am here to guide you in this one. We have known each other as brother and sister, father and daughter; but we are always, in our hearts, lovers. Twins. The night and the day. I know how you've tried to satisfy your longings for a truly spiritual love! I know about all of it, and the disappointments you've suffered. Your husband. Your husband is a good being, but he is not an old soul. He was not put on this earth to reach the heights of union — you were joined with him so that you might enjoy life's comforts, those comforts you deserve, and so that you might know me. That is all for the first session. You may ask one question."

I was jolly well frightened, but I said, "Well I have two questions. What's your name?"

"You may call me the Count."

At that moment Madame Betty gave a big twitch, and the folds of fat jiggled against her neck.

"Well, Count," I said, trying to remain calm, "how do I know this isn't a trick?"

"Look to your dreams in the nights to come, Dorothy. There you'll find the truth."

Madame Betty sagged then, just like a pastry when you step on it—all the life went right out of her, and she nearly fell out of her chair. Well, I hadn't a clue what to do, so I jumped up and slapped her face. She wore an awful lot of powder. In a few seconds she gave a big wheezy breath and opened her eyes.

"What happened?" she asked.

I told her about it, and she nodded, her eyes little slits.

"Ah," she said. "This happens to very few. You had better make your next appointment now. I think you will not want to wait."

I made an appointment for Saturday—five days, dear diary!—it would have been sooner but I can't get out of that fundraiser the Etchams are throwing in Chelsea. I paid Madame Betty my five pounds, and when I left that little room there was Maggie, reading a magazine just as normal as can be! Madame Betty tugged at my sleeve and whispered in my ear, "Your friend understands. God be with you." And in a moment we were in our car, and then having tea at Liberty's, just like we always do. Maggie squeezed my arm when I told her about it and said, "Darling, it's so exciting—you've discovered the spiritual life! I wish I could come with you on Saturday but I've got to go up to Granny's. I don't want to spoil any of it for you, so let's not talk about it now!"

I'm inclined to think it's a silly hoax, but I must admit it was extraordinary the way Madame Betty's voice *changed*. In any case, it's all a lot of fun and I need something to do. I've been so bloody bored. I admit I look forward to Saturday.

7 October—

Good Lord, I've just had the most extraordinary dream! I had to write it down immediately.

I fell asleep as usual—I was jittery, but I didn't want to take my veronal, so I could remember my dreams. And in my sleep it seemed I was in a little room, far, far away from anybody. It was very safe there, and there was a window onto a garden, and just a table and a bed and a small shelf of books. It was a room I felt so cozy in, like when I was a little girl. I was looking out the window when I heard the sound of a horse's hooves galloping up the garden path. It was a grey horse, with a man on it. He looked like a Russian soldier, in military clothes and gold epaulets, and a big black moustache. He dismounted, and let the horse roam around the garden, eating the tips off the flowers. And then he came into my room. He had a sword in his belt. I reached over to touch it—it scared me and I wanted him to put it away—and he grabbed my hand and put it on the hilt, and told me, "Go ahead, pull it out, it's magic." I did, and when it was all the way out, I was transformed—I was a beautiful princess, with lovely long hair. I said, "Who are you?" And he said, "My lady, you already know. I am the Count who killed for you." He put me down on the little bed and began to kiss me all over—his moustaches tickled, and I pushed him away, and—O dear diary, thank God no one will ever read this!—he stripped off all my clothes and made love to me, and I had one! I never have before, even when I used to be terribly excited by Gerald. Why, I never knew what it felt like. It feels like you're going to melt in there. After it happened once, I could hear myself screaming for more—I was asleep, but I knew I was dreaming. Then Musette came knocking at the door—I must have screamed aloud—I told her it was just a "petit cauchemar." And now here I am, writing it all down. I tried to go back to sleep. I feel so changed, and I just want to sleep, but I'm too excited. Saturday, dear diary. XXX.

Saturday—

Thank God Gerald is out and I have the time to write all this down in my diary. I have so much to tell. I've been a wreck these last four days, waiting. I haven't even been able to write. I never had another dream like that, and I kept hoping for one. In the end I was so nervous, and I'd slept so little, that I did take some veronal, and of course one doesn't dream.

Then the day came. I dismissed the car a few blocks from

my destination — I wanted to walk those squalid little streets and think things through. When I got there, there was no one else inside, I had Madame Betty all to myself. She looked fatter, though I don't see how a person can put on that much weight in four days. There were bits of food sticking to the side of her mouth. When she saw me, she smiled, and her breath came out garlickly. She took my hands and led me into the back room, mumbling in Turkish and English about "very few, very few." The room was very dark, with only a few candles burning and some sweet incense.

Then it began again, just like the first time. Only it didn't frighten me as much to see her mouth twitch. She began to drool a bit, the crumbs on her lips got caught in the saliva and I wanted to take out my hanky and wipe her off. But I thought I shouldn't interfere.

When the Count finally began to speak, I admit I was trembling. He said, "You have your answer. I came to you in your dream and you felt my power. I have the power to take you to a height of pleasure very few know. The dream was only a beginning. These are not mere sensual debauchings" (Madame Betty can't talk like that! Those are the Count's beautiful words) "these are *inner regions*, where the body is on fire with the flame of the soul. I am going to give you a gift. I am capable of incarnating, but only temporarily — and only here. It is a great strain on Madame Betty — she will pass into another state of consciousness for an hour, and we will be as if alone together. You must close your eyes, you must meditate deeply on my presence, on my essence. Remember how I appeared to you in your dream, remember my sword. Are you prepared to obey me, for the good of your soul?" I nodded, and he went on, "Go to that couch in the corner of the room, and take off your garments — there you will find the sacred robes you are to wear for the ceremony."

I got out of the chair. I suppose I ought to have felt foolish, but I didn't. I stood at the divan, and I took off my blouse first, and then I pulled down my skirt. I wondered if spirits could see, but I felt sure it didn't matter. It crossed my mind that he really *did* know my dream, the sword — it was real.

I took off my brassiere, and I wondered if it was spiritual to leave on my peach silk suspender belt, the one with the little ribbons. As if in answer to my thought, a voice said, "That is enough." I stood there a little nervously, I could feel the silk of my stockings rubbing together. I still had on my rope of pearls, I meant to take them off, but—I didn't want to disobey. There was a robe on the divan, if you could call it that. Just a flimsy piece of charmeuse really. A bit tatty, but —it felt like a holy mantle. I put it on and it didn't cover my breasts properly, and I had to tug it to cover myself in the back. Oh, dear diary, everything is so changed now— the sacred and the profane seem to be each other's twins. Well, that's how the Count put it.

Anyway, the room grew darker—I looked over to see if Madame Betty had put out the candles, but she was still slouched in a heap by the chair, she seemed quite unconscious. I lay down. I had to wait forever—that's how it felt, forever, and then finally it happened. I heard the Count's voice.

"I am here, sacred vessel. Give yourself to this glorious union—it is a union of two spirits, who use the poor flesh to express their highest vision. The sacred and the profane —they are each other's twins."

I didn't know what he was talking about. I was holding my breath in excitement—and all at once I felt hands on me, real hands! They were almost as real as the ones in my dream. They moved up and down my body, they pulled away the sacred robes, I felt the tickle of moustaches between my legs and then against my buttocks. The Count talked incessantly, he never stopped, I can't remember it all, I was in a cloud, but it was about us, and our divine reunion, about the celebration of our love. His voice intoxicated me, and I felt him introduce his "sacred lingam" inside of me—it didn't feel at all like Gerald, or James—I was mad for it. I reached the top of everything, again and again, I said the most awful things, I did things I've never thought of doing. All the while he kept talking. He told me I was making love to God and nothing was evil between two beings of light, those were his very words. Oh, blast! I hear Gerald, I must run.

12 November—

I've had *no* time for writing, I've only got a moment.

I go as often as I can now, without appearing conspicuous. I went three times this week. The Count told me that the cost was very high on Madame Betty's health, and to be together even this much might send her to the surgery! She has agreed to suffer it for a higher purpose, but I must help to pay her bills. I'm afraid Gerald will notice something, so I've pawned a few things—I should feel ashamed, I know, but it gave me an awful thrill to do it. Gerald wouldn't know the difference between the real thing and paste anyway. I can't touch him anymore, really I can't. We've always done it every Thursday, Gerald insisted upon it, but I've made excuses these last two weeks. I'm afraid he's noticed some change in me. At first people told me I had color, but now they're starting to say I've got bags under my eyes. I don't wonder. I still have the dreams as well, and when I do, it's not like sleeping at all. I wake up and the sheets are positively damp—I wonder whatever Gerald will think about it. I feel quite ill in the mornings after I've had them—sick to my stomach. The Count tells me that deep inner change sometimes causes "eruptions in the body," as the soul adjusts to the higher plane.

The Count has told me to do all kinds of things—to put the "sacred lingam" in my mouth and taste "the seed of life and heaven," and to kiss him at the back—he says what other people call degradation is truly harmony, that truth can be found through the sensations of the body. Oh, dear diary, it's all so astonishing—some days I have bruises and scratches, I have to cover them so Gerald won't see, or Aileen, that nosy parker. But to think that the spirit world can leave its mark on my body! How simply wondrous.

From Aileen to Maggie

Dear Maggie,

I've been meaning to jot you a note for some time, and after running into you last night I decided not to put it off any longer. It's about Dorothy—you've been ever so much closer to her these last few months than I have—I hardly feel she's my friend anymore. There was a certain personal matter between us—I think you know what I'm referring to—that may have caused some bad blood. But I do still have, and always will have, a loving friend's concern.

Let me be blunt: I heard from old Tattlelips that Doro was having an affair—with a person of nobility! And that she was terribly in love. The silly thing can be such a romantic, and I didn't want to think of her being hurt, so I wrote and asked her to tell me all about it. She's always been perfectly frank with me, of course—even to the point of telling me about James's *special interests*. And in this new matter, she has told me a little, but in the main she's been so—evasive. Something about meeting him at a *séance*. Well, my dear, who *is* he? I know these sorts of things amuse you and I thought I'd ask you straight out. To be perfectly frank, she's behaving strangely. She's gone off a bit. She talks about the spiritual life, as she calls it, when she talks to me at all. What are we to do? Do you think Gerald ought to be informed?

Most sincerely,
Aileen

Dear Maggie,

You won't believe what I've just heard—it's too incredible. It isn't public knowledge yet, but it will be any minute. I heard from an inside source. Your little séance parlour is a hoax! Oh, I'm sure *you* knew it, my dear, I'm sure you just went for a lark, but Dorothy, well, she got in completely over her head! She was found—*during a police raid*—in the arms of a certain Italian gentleman—and he was no Count, let me assure you! The place was raided Friday. It seems these so-called "occultists" employed chambermaids to snoop on their mistresses' diaries, after said mistresses were ordered by the spirits to keep diaries in the first place. That's how they got the personal details that impressed the clients, and you can guess the rest. Musette was one of them. But apparently she had second thoughts when she began to notice Doro's state of mind, and she went to the police.

Anyway, the police just barged in and turned on the lights

and caught them going at it like a pair of rabbits—I even *heard*—mind, I don't know if it's true—that she was having "un petit mort" at the very moment the police cameras clicked! No one can reach Gerald, and Dorothy, of course, is entirely incommunicado. I sent a basket of fruit round. Maggie dear, I'm glad you weren't in this awful mess.

Tons of love,
Aileen

Darling,

Got your note. I understand perfectly—you can't have your name mixed up in this, so you can't ask anyone anything. Don't worry—I'll give you all the news. This is the latest: When they brought her in for questioning—they had to do it, my dear, Gerald simply wasn't there to prevent it—she kept muttering the strangest things. I heard this from Mr. MacIntyre, the police inspector—she was babbling about "the joyful union with God," and "reaching beyond the limits of the flesh." Lord only knows what kind of gibberish those monsters have been feeding her. It's frightening to think of.

And Maggie, we're having a little tea this Wednesday— just the Daltons and Harold and Miss Cruikshank. Do you think you can drop by? We'd so love to see you both. Ta, darling—

A.

A tattered clipping slipped out of Lily's hand and wafted to the floor. It was thin with years of reading and handling.

SOCIETY BEAUTY CAUGHT
IN SÉANCE SCANDAL

Lady Dorothy Ardmore, wife of Sir Gerald Ardmore and heiress to the van Velsen fortune, was apprehended yesterday at the home of Tanya Pillinini, aka "Madame Betty," and Antonio Pillinini, also known as "Willie Jones" and "The Count of Aman." The Pillininis have been operating a traveling "séance ring," with Mrs. Pillinini posing as a spiritualist and entering "mediumistic trances." Their victims, wealthy society matrons, succumbed to Mr. Pillinini's seductions while under the influence of his hypnotic powers. They donated large sums of money to the Pillininis, who posed as "messengers of a higher being," in the words of Mrs. Alice Shaw, one of their victims.

Yesterday at 2:00 P.M., the Pillininis were apprehended when Dorothy Ardmore's maid, Musette Desseux, reported the couple's ring to the local police. She and other chambermaids were in the employ of the Pillininis, hired to read the diaries and papers of their mistresses and report the details found therein to their employers. Lady Ardmore, who was reportedly found in flagrante with Mr. Pillinini, is being held in police custody for further questioning. According to inside reports, the Pillininis operated their ring in cities throughout the provinces.

A second clipping was attached to the first.

THE MAYFAIR TATTLE
BY A. NON

When you think you've heard it all . . . What o-so-beautiful darling of the Mayfair set, known for her white complexion and her grey pearls, gave horns of plenty to her o-so-distinguished husband in a tiny Bayswater love-nest? Well, as we all know, that sort of thing happens every day . . . What makes this story so rare is that our beauty claims she gave her favors to a ghost! No, don't adjust those lorgnettes—instead, picture this: the room was dark, our heroine was lonely (her husband was away on business) . . . She went for a séance, only this time the ectoplasm had a mind of its own! When the lights dimmed, the ghost, who gave himself the moniker of "The Count," showed her he knew a thing or two about the material plane. He must have known a few etheric tricks, because our fair lady kept on going back, until the strong arm of the law intervened. It seems she not only gave up her charms—her husband's bank account went with them! Can her rich relations help her out of *this* scrape — or this time, has she gone too far?

Gerald to Aileen:

Aileen, I want you to keep these papers, at least for a time. I can't have them in the house. I tried to burn them, but— They're hers, you see. I couldn't. These last days have been some of the most terrible of my life. I have to tell someone.

I went to collect her at the police station. I didn't know a thing, I never knew where she went afternoons — I thought she was doing charity work, or shopping with you — else why was she withdrawing so much cash? There was a message from the Inspector waiting for me when I got back from Spain. I had no idea what the matter was. When I saw her — she was babbling, the strangest things. They frightened me. I brought her home, but her delirium only got worse and I called Dr. Browne. He told me she was very unwell, having a fever for that long. He told me she needed a few days in hospital, and then, well, he said if she didn't recover her mind, that she ought to be sent away for a time. I gathered her things to send her to St. Jude's. I packed her case myself. Musette was gone, and I suppose I wanted to do it anyway. I came across the diary. I didn't know she kept one, she never has before. I shouldn't have read it, but of course, now . . . Aileen, Doro is pregnant. By that animal. I know, because she hasn't let me touch her in a long time. It's too late to do anything about it, and even if it weren't, Browne says she couldn't bear up under the strain. She'll have to have it. If she's well enough, we'll go to a place in the country somewhere.

Gerald

Doro's diary, undated:

It's been a long time now since I've had my monthlies, it can't mean anything else. Oh dear God, I really am to have the Count's child! I'm not going to tell him yet, I want to be terribly certain. It will be an avatar. I *am* the Count now, dear diary, we're one person. I'm always thinking of him, people tell me my face is flushed, but it's just the thinking of him.

How wonderful to feel my belly begin to swell a little. I don't want Gerald to see the size of my bosom, not that he'd notice anyway, the pig — but the Count exults in my "vessel," as he calls it. He says I am the soul of the feminine.

I told the Count today. He told me it was a matter of the greatest urgency that I have sex with Gerald as soon as he comes back from Madrid. He says we must pretend it's Gerald's, that the child's mission on earth depends on it. He made me swear to it at the height of my passion. He didn't need to — if he tells me our beautiful baby's karma depends upon it — upon *anything* — I'll obey his wishes. It won't be easy to let Gerald profane my flesh now, but I must obey the Count.

Gerald to Aileen (fragment of a letter):

to see that she's well provided for. I don't know what to tell you about your visit — it was typical, I suppose. She's always like that now. The child has been placed with relatives. I can't bear to see it. I find myself somewhat reduced by the cost of its upkeep, as well as the price of the sanitarium — it's the best one in England — and so I shall have to go on a long trip to the Far East to manage. Her uncle, of course, has made every attempt to help financially, but I will not accept.

Lily folded the papers neatly and put them in a pile. She thought she should take a nap. She pulled the shades down against the morning light and looked at the bed. It was threatening, as were the pillows: she saw Johnny's head against them. The moment before sleep, which she once loved, terrified her now. It was the vulnerable moment, when the rigors of daily battle were relaxed, when the horrors came pouring in. She could not sleep in a lighted room, but she was afraid of the dark. She hated the noise of the city, but silence was terrifying.

She found a vial of sleeping pills, broke one in half, and swallowed it. The pills were very unsatisfactory. They made her feel more frightened, in the interval before they took effect, when she began to lose control. It was a horrible feeling, as if all the night monsters and demons would tear her apart in her sleep, and claw at her dreams. She drew the cat into bed with her, for safety.

It wasn't long before she woke. A scream caught in her throat, making her gag. Something foreign pressed against her. Sweat soaked her, and made the sleeping cat's fur cold and slick. She pried Curse away from her body. He rustled uncertainly, then settled himself into the crook of her waist, his damp flank resting against her belly. After a few moments he drifted back into sleep. His ears lost their vigilance, and his breathing deepened. Carefully, she took his paw in her hand. He flinched a little, involuntarily, then relaxed in her grasp. She let the tiny pads fall limp into the center of her palm. He was a big cat, thirteen or fourteen pounds, but still his paw was small. Smaller than whatever had touched her. But who could know, in sleep? She gave him a familiar pat, then reached her hand up to her face. It was damp. She often woke up sweating now, and the inside of her spine was cold. The sleeping pill left a metallic taste in her mouth. She swallowed the other half, and slept into the night.

She woke up screaming. Bad dream, she thought. Something came toward me in that dream, I know it did, and it was taking over, I know that it was. But I liked it, I *liked* it that way; at least I wasn't alone in that dream. I've got to get out of here. She dressed quickly, ignoring the leaden feel of her drugged limbs, and rushed to her great-uncle's.

Pushing past Chen Li, Lily burst into the study. Mordecai arched his eyebrows when he saw her, but he said nothing. She began to speak in a frantic voice, still standing and gesturing as she spoke.

"I met someone. I met him, you know, and then it just—oh God, I'm going to cry—we made love, and I told myself I was just doing something crazy, things were a little wrong with Alan, maybe, but then, his touch . . ." Lily moved closer to Mordecai and squeezed his arm, too tightly. "It was new. It was new, I never felt like that before, not with anybody. He *fit* me, Uncle, his whole body fit mine. I feel like a jigsaw puzzle, and somebody found the piece that was missing, the piece that was always lost, the one that fell on the floor and without it something was always wrong . . . But it's bad, Uncle. I need to have him. I'm greedy. I never felt like this before, I want him all the time, I'm so ashamed. He's not that way about me, there are other women. I don't see how one person can feel like this and not the other one, it's not fair. I don't understand, but I can't stop it. I want to go to him, I have to stop myself from going to him. You don't know how ashamed I am. And the worst part is, I'm so *jealous*, even though I hardly know him. I never get jealous of Alan, not like this. But I don't want Johnny to have anyone else, I don't want him to be hungry for anyone else. Uncle, I'll die, I will. I'm hungry all the time for him, even when he's holding me, even when he's inside of me, I think about when it will be over, and I'll want him again. Why does he want other women, Uncle? The way we fit . . . How did I get this way? I don't remember myself, I need to know, I—" She stopped, suddenly embarrassed.

Mordecai shook his head slowly. "You've always had certain qualities, Lily, qualities others found alarming, but that I understood. A barbarous curiosity, for example, a kind of savage fascination for details about other people. For the most part, you cared about no one—I saw that early on. But on the odd occasions when someone touched your heart, when you loved, you became a demon, pelting them with your inquiries: What do you think of the sky? Are you lonely in hot weather? What was the most terrible itch you ever had? Even I, who so shared your temperament, used to wonder what you expected to acquire, to achieve, with these inquisitions.

"I remember the Dobson boy. Don't look away, Lily, I remember all of it. He was a small boy, and scrappy, a little jaunty and recklessly handsome. One day he challenged an older boy to a fight, and the whole school, it seemed, gathered around to watch. The Dobson boy was small, but he fought hard, and urgently. I remember all you told me about it, later — how the blood ran from his nose into his mouth, and how the older boy fell down once but didn't bleed. The school principal broke up the contest before it reached its conclusion, but you felt instinctively that the Dobson boy had won. The principal made the two of them shake hands. As he reached out, intense and contained, you saw in Danny Dobson a thrilling defiance, you read it in the cast of his jaw, the color of the drying blood.

"You asked questions about him — absurd questions that none of us adults could answer: Did the blood taste different when it was dry? Did he think about getting taller every day? How did he get brave?

"You developed an extravagant crush on this boy. No, don't look at me like that — I'm not trying to be cruel, though I know it seems that way. It points to things, things it's best to see. Urges that matter terribly. I always warned you not to overlook them, not to treat them casually. They swell if you turn against them, these urges, they do violent things to your heart. But as I was saying . . . You began to long for Danny, a longing that your aunt and uncle tolerated, then ridiculed, then tried to cajole you out of—"

"Uncle, I was just stupid. Let's drop it."

"No. Let's not. You were afraid to speak to Danny, and since he was a hero after the fight, he was even more unapproachable. One day he complimented you on a picture or a poem, something that the teacher had pinned to the wall. Something to do with an escaping kite, wasn't it? After that, you went deep into your desire, you curled up in a big leather chair in my study, and you thought, and you hoped. I feared for you, when I saw you there. Other adults teased you, but I was solemn, I understood. These were the signs.

"And as for Danny, perhaps he liked you well enough. Perhaps not. This was never established. There was so much to lose if you found out what he felt, perhaps a whole world of dreaming. I used to watch you, sitting in my study, as you pretended to read, but dreamed of him. Your long brown hair hung over the pages; you held a little, purring cat in your thin arms, scratching her ear with half-bitten nails . . . And when the Dobson boy took a steady girl, you fell ill. You had to see him every day in school, and the agony of it made you sick. The nights were the worst—you developed somnambulism, of all things. What a baroque ailment, especially for a child! I thought perhaps sleeping here would help, and so you tried it for a night. But I found you in the leather chair, just before dawn. You didn't remember leaving your bed. Lily. I'm sorry, dear. I'm trying to say something to you, something about—"

"Yes. But that's enough. It's morning now, I'll try to come back soon." They embraced, and as Lily left the house, Chen Li watched her carefully. How curious, she thought. He's worried about me.

Even this early in the morning the traffic was heavy on Pacific Street. She didn't take her usual route, and she found herself stuck in a long line of cars in Chinatown. "It's a parking lot. Should've walked," she said out loud, talking to herself. She pulled off into a dead-end side street. "I'll just park here, got to stop at that Chinese jeweler's, anyway, see about those clasps from Hong Kong." She was very near the little dragon alley. She got out of the car and walked, slowly, window-shopping. She was not surprised when she saw Chen Li ahead of her, moving briskly through the crowd.

She meant to confront him when they reached the little alley where the flaking dragon loomed. But before she had time to compose herself, he had darted into the herb shop. She hesitated a moment, then crossed the threshold.

She was greeted by the same old man she had seen two days earlier. With a small, indelicate push, she moved past him, following the light sound of Chen Li's footsteps. There was a low, dark hall, and beyond it, a doorway barred by a beaded curtain. The beads clattered against one another as they fell away from her shoulders.

The smell was so strong that she instinctively jerked her head. A wave of nausea curled over her, and she felt the cold sickness in the back of her knees. Holding her breath, she peered into dim light. Figures moved slowly and heavily, kneeling at glowing lamps on low tables. A few cushions were scattered about, but otherwise the room was bare except for a half dozen wooden bunks. She told herself to start breathing again. There were seven or eight Chinese men seated around the tables. They looked up at her languidly, indifferently. There was a dense, molasses-like air to their movements. No one spoke until a thin, elegant man emerged from a doorway in the far corner of the room. In the dim light Lily saw Chen Li's eyebrows arch in surprise. "Lily?"

"I followed you," she announced stupidly. He didn't reply, so she continued. "I saw you in the street, so I followed you." She wished he would move closer, so she wouldn't have to speak in full voice. She could not traverse the barrier of the kneeling, torpid men. "I was window-shopping, and I saw you. And I don't know why I followed you. I didn't know what else to do." She couldn't understand why she'd said that. The smell in the room made her eyes burn, like some troubling incense.

She took a few steps nearer to the center of the room. The bluish scent bubbled up to her, hitting her nostrils, sweet and stunning. There was a soft thrill in the air. For a moment she forgot the heavy pulse of her heart in her chest.

Chen Li cast her a sad, beaten look, and moved to take her

arm. "I've seen your great-uncle's eyes like that," he said, propelling her to a cushion.

Her eyes adjusted to the dim light, and she began to make out the figures of the old men, squatting sloe-eyed, with long, thin pipes perched between their lips. Lily gagged once more, a last impulse against the malicious odor of an Oriental flower. Chen Li appeared not to notice, though she knew he noticed everything. She thought of the peonies. The men in the room looked at her idly, lifting heads like swamp plants. The little lamps blazed, holding fuming black balls that bubbled like tar. Opium's canny odor.

An attendant scurried to them and muttered a few words in Chinese. He disappeared. Lily stared, free of fear now, through the seamy light at the smoke, at the men. Though she was the only woman present, it was a sexless atmosphere — she could have bared her breasts to them, these dead-eyed men, and not have touched their dreams. "I'll be like them," she intoned to herself, "everything from a distance."

She whispered to Chen Li. "I had no idea one could still . . . in this day and age."

He smiled wistfully. The attendant returned with a lump of black clay. Chen Li motioned him away.

"I'll prepare this pipe myself," he said. Placing the pellet between two long, thin needles, he molded it deftly until it thickened like taffy. When it was the proper consistency, he removed it to a small porcelain bowl. This he affixed to a bamboo pipe, which he balanced above the lamp flame.

At the first puff of the sweet, poisonous gum, Lily felt a lulling. It was only after the fourth that the image of Johnny began to recede. She lay back against the cushions. There was an old man beside her, crabbed and invisible, gray with years of smoking. He reached over and clawed her idly, almost indifferently, feeling beneath her skirt for the white flesh of her thigh. Chen Li batted him away as if he were swatting an unruly insect. The old man sank back into the shadow of his bunk.

Lily watched, from a distance, this languid violation. The smoke tasted comforting, and the odor no longer made her sick.

Chen Li watched carefully for her reaction. Seeing the natural ease with which she sucked in the opium, her lashes lying against her cheek in happiness, he shook his head faintly.

"Surely you have the illness, Lily," he whispered. "The medicine does not turn against you."

Lily smiled up at him. "Chen Li, how did you know how to fix that pipeful? Have you ever done that before?"

He remained silent, and stared at her fixedly.

"What, is that a silly question? I don't think so," she added, reflectively.

He had not smoked himself, but now he motioned to the attendant. A pipe was prepared. He smoked it in one easy, rapid inhalation, and when he was finished, he looked at Lily. "I have often made such pipes."

"For yourself?"

"No. Not often. For your great-uncle."

Lily's eyes widened. "For Uncle? Did you bring him here?"

"Only in emergencies. We made the pipes at home. Before that, we made them in Shanghai. That was where he fell ill for the first time. The doctors tried many things, it looked as if he might die. But I—I knew what medicine was best. I was very sad to give him this medicine, but he was worse, always worse. After the first time, he demanded it. It is a very ancient medicine."

"It's a pity he can't take quinine," she said hazily.

"But, little ghost," he said, "quinine is for malaria. This is something else."

"It makes your nose itch," she said, rubbing abstractedly at her face. "Chen Li. I have something to ask you. Ordinarily I wouldn't inquire, but—I don't understand why you serve him. Don't you find it demeaning? Chinese houseboys, Chinese servants—they're from another era. A man of your . . . God, I itch all over, really . . . Where did you meet him, anyway?"

He tapped the cone of ashes out of the pipe, and gazed at the embers in the lamp.

"I sold him pearls in Shanghai, in 1925. He was traveling with your grandfather, Leo. They always traveled together, they were a striking pair. Leo had a strong character, one liked him, everyone liked him. Your great-uncle was quieter, more serious. We took to each other immediately. We did a good deal of business, we became quite good friends. That autumn, we were completing an exchange. It was on a Friday, I remember, when they disappeared. I heard later that they'd had a letter, some bad news, and left immediately. Years later, Mordecai reappeared alone. He looked completely changed. Haggard, drained of life. No *chi*. Do you understand? I saw the first gray in his hair. He complained of not sleeping at night, and clearly he did not eat. He would not talk about what had happened, or what had become of your grandfather.

"In those bad years, I was imprisoned falsely, imprisoned for things I did not do. I lost everything. I was dying in my cell, dying of sickness and grief and starvation. Your great-uncle was unwise to return to China—he had dangerous allegiances, and I begged him to leave. But he wouldn't, he didn't. He stayed and he made a bargain, and this was not an easy thing to do. He traded something for my life. It was a pearl blister this big"—he motioned with his fingers, making a circle one inch in diameter. "It was the biggest I had ever seen in my life. He traveled with it, it never left his person. He brought it to China to be cut by a master who lived in the Shansi province. It would have made him inconceivably rich, this pearl, and he didn't dare to cut it himself. He gave it to my jailers. When I asked him why he had done such a thing, he just laughed, and said it was better to be rid of it. It was the first time I had seen him laugh since his return to China. Did you know, little ghost, that when you come to the house—when you walk through the door—it's the only time he smiles?

"He told me he would see me safe passage to America, he

said he would help me start in business here. But we were not able to leave immediately, I was too sick from my time in prison.

"And then something curious happened. I was more or less a free man now, you understand—I was under informal house arrest until I could leave the mainland. One day I heard a knock at my door, and there, of all people, was Zhao himself, one of my jailers, one of my persecutors. I was sure it was the end for me, that I was to be taken back to prison. Zhao looked shaken as he stared at me across the threshold, and this is what he said:

" 'Chen Li, you must take this back'—he thrust a little package into my hands, something crumpled up in a bit of newspaper. I started to unwrap it, but he stayed my hand. 'No. I don't want to look at it again. Take it. It's the pearl we took in trade for you. No, Chen Li, don't be afraid, we don't want you back . . .' He spat on the ground. 'Or your cursed friend. Leave. Leave quickly. Why? It's bad luck, all of it. My wife, she knows *feng shui*, she has the second sight. I know that such beliefs are outmoded, but she has it. Years ago my wife saw the death of our second son, and it happened just as she saw it. When she saw this pearl, she said, "Take it away from here. It will harm us all if it is carved." She made me promise to deliver it into your hands myself. Go away soon, Chen Li. You are not wanted here. It would be best for you if you left quickly.' And so the blister came back to us.

"I was recovering rapidly, but your great-uncle grew sicker. Whatever he had tried to hide from me began to show. I thought he would die, Lily. He would have died, I think, if I had not begun to care for him. The doctors gave him all sorts of medicines, but only opium calmed him, let him sleep, let him eat. We stayed in China eight months—the doctors told him if he traveled, he would die. Opium saved him, in the end, in a way. He lived. And by the time we boarded our boat for America, I had to carry a large supply. Very large. And the cost of the bribery! It was not easy, once we got here, to find what he needed. There were bad nights, bad weeks. I tried to wean him off it, of course. A hundred times. But always, in the end . . ." He set down the pipe. "I couldn't leave him like that. And, well, the symptoms are rather like those of malaria. So that is what we say."

"No quinine, then," she said hazily.

"No."

"You know," she said, "I feel just a little sick."

Chen Li looked relieved. He thrust some money into the attendant's hands, received a small packet in return, and within minutes he was leading her past the jars of bear claws and the jellied squid and the dried starfishes, into the dazzling sun. He hailed a taxi on Grant Avenue, thrust her through the gaggle of tourists, and took her back to her great-uncle's house.

Mordecai was still asleep. It was late afternoon. They had passed the whole day in the opium den. Gripping her firmly by the arm, Chen Li led her downstairs to the basement. At the foot of the stairs was a small bathroom. She had not been to the basement in years. She allowed him to lead her to the toilet, where she vomited. He wiped her mouth with a towel, and patted her brow with cold water. Then he pulled her into an adjoining room.

Chen Li set the little package from the opium den on a counter, and reached into a cupboard. He extracted one of a dozen small, amber-tinted bottles. Carefully removing the glass stopper, he stuck his little finger inside, and held it up to her lips.

"Taste it." She was shocked at this familiarity, but she obeyed. The tip of her tongue darted out and licked his finger. It was Mordecai's medicine, their nighttime drink.

"Laudanum, not quinine. I make it here, out of opium. We cannot go anywhere without it," he added. He shook her thin shoulders gently. "Please don't be sick, little ghost. Don't be."

"Get me a glass of water, please, Chen Li."

"Of course." As he turned away, she reached into the cupboard and took two of the little vials, slipping them into her pocket.

In the weeks that followed, Lily found frequent excuses to return to the little alley. Soon she was making daily visits. The old men nodded when they saw her at the door, and made the little black pyramids for her to smoke. Contrary to what she had always heard, opium did not entirely stop her life, or prevent her from working altogether. Rather, it slowed things, and regulated them, and gave a rhythm to her suffering and her attempt to conquer it.

She waited a week before returning to Johnny. She didn't call, and again she found him at home. That night, as she lolled in his arms after making love, she told him all about the necklace, about Mrs. Franstein, about Alan, and about her uncle's pearl. He listened carefully, quietly. Embarrassed, she changed the subject. "How is *Lethe* coming? What's in the chalice, anyway?"

"I was going to put some little jewels in. But it would be more powerful to have a single, beautiful jewel. It's entirely outside of my budget, of course." He smiled. "Maybe someday."

"It would be more beautiful like that. I see what you're saying."

"Well, it's a moot point."

"Yes."

She kissed him, little feathery kisses down his chest to his navel. He leaned away from her to get a cigarette.

"That's terrible, that stuff about Alan. To think of a pearl like that going into some old witch's tiara or something. Ugh. What are you going to do about it?"

"It's not up to me. It's up to my great-uncle. It's not up to me."

"Oh? I guess not."

He turned his back to her, reached behind and gave her a pat. She saw his cigarette pulse a few times in the dark.

She wanted to go to him every night, but she was afraid to,

and afraid to ask for it. She avoided Alan as much as possible, making excuses, and instead appeared at Johnny's door as often as she thought he would allow it. He told her that he loved her, and that she was special to him, but she suspected that special was something that happened every day, that one woman was special just like another. She suspected that he could never be filled. But none of this guessing and wisdom changed the wanting, and in any case, she could not truly justify it — wasn't he always there to receive her, wasn't he always at home? She gave him her phone number, and he did call her, from time to time, but there was no pattern to it, so that she could never plan. It was not hard for her to imagine a life of total bondage to the telephone. Two months passed.

One night, in this period, Lily dreamt of Chen Li. He was tampering with a long pipe, but instead of oily balls of opium, the two of them were smoking dew. It did not seem strange. Perhaps the dew had been trapped in vials, or the vials had attracted and captured the dew. She didn't know, but there it was. After he had smoked his fill, Chen Li reached over to her and laid his hand on the inside of her knee. She felt that this was a very private place to be touched, but she permitted it. His fingers were adept, tapping and drumming and stroking the flesh around her knee, the top of her calf, and the lower thigh. But while he stroked, he never moved his hand — his fingers seemed to be very long, like antennae. There was tremendous tension between them as she wondered if his hand would wander farther. She began to tremble under his touch, as if she were succumbing to a masculine force, masked by apparent indifference. The angrier she became at his control, his indifference, the more her trembling increased. As if that same hand were two hands, it reached up and touched her forehead maternally, the flesh pressing against her skin. "But you have a fever," he said. And she woke up.

Going back to sleep, she dreamed of Johnny. She dreamed that he was pale and sick and she had to go to him. It was very difficult to arrive at his studio, which no longer seemed to exist in the temporal world. Somehow she reached it, but there were no sculptures inside. Now there was an empty room, and Johnny was molding clay with his fingers, pressing it around an armature of a naked woman. The woman was giving birth, and Johnny wrapped layer after layer of papier-mâché around the lumpen mass that was the infant. Over and over again he destroyed it, dissatisfied with his creation. She burst in, and he told her to finish the sculpture. He was busy, he told her, he had to make love.

She woke for the second time, her palms pressed to her eyes in horror. She could feel the sweat on her back, and her gown clung to her skin. She told herself to stop dreaming about him, to stop thinking about him, and then she laughed bitterly at this exercise: try not to think of a canary, and you have a hurricane of yellow birds. She knew that she would never stop. It was in the very nature of her suffering to know that it would prevail, a relentless suicide against the self, while her body went on and on, mechanical, a rote machine, vassal to duties and small pleasures.

Lily got up, dressed, and stumbled out the door, heading to her great-uncle's house. She was uncertain what she would find. She was afraid it would be something horrible — Mordecai in a posture of suicide, some grotesque comedia of death: he would be standing in a chair, tying the knot on a noose suspended from a chandelier, wearing a Punchinello mask. The smell of gas, and the old man splayed out on the floor, violently, all his erstwhile elegance a mockery. Chen Li arranging irises in the foyer while Great-uncle died on the floor. She cursed her morbidity, but she couldn't stop it.

As she walked, a few drops of rain shuddered out of the gauzy gray sky. She felt one fall on her neck, slipping, somehow, through all her clothes to one bare spot. It felt like something living. She did not wipe it away. She caught sight of her face in a window, and she barely knew herself. She was gaunt, her cheekbones were taut, and there was a ghostly beauty in the color of her skin. It was the wrong color for skin, she thought, but maybe it's just this window, this light. She looked very beautiful. Her pupils were small points in her green eyes, ringed by thick lashes. Backing away from her reflection, she quickened her pace, until she arrived at Mordecai's house.

Lily found him at his bookshelf, absorbed in making some new arrangement of titles. He started at the sight of her. "Lily!" He seemed almost buoyant. "I'm happy to see you. What's the matter? You don't look well."

"I can't sleep."

"No? You can't sleep?"

"I've been taking sleeping pills."

Mordecai did not say anything, he just looked at her.

"Well," she said, a little aggressively, "I don't think I should."

"No, I suppose not."

"Do you ever take them?"

He looked surprised. "No, not really. There was a time when all the doctors prescribed veronal, but that was ages ago."

"I would think you would."

"Well, only the dull are a friend to sleep," he said inanely. They were playing a cat-and-mouse game. He was master in this house, the elder, her host; but she was the predator, after his dark secrets. He regarded her carefully. "Is it this man? The one you met? You haven't mentioned him, not for some time."

"No, no, no. Never mind that." She waved her hand in the air between them. "I've finished about Aunt Dorothy. My God."

Now Mordecai averted his eyes.

Lily went on. "What happened after that? Is there more to read?"

"No, not after that . . . She just—Well, you saw her."

"She never said a word about it to me, all the years I visited her in the nuthouse."

"No, she wouldn't."

"And her baby? What happened to the baby?"

"The baby died. Very soon after."

"Oh. That's just as well, isn't it? . . . There's a lot of death in this family."

Mordecai raised his eyebrows. "In every family. Our family is no different in that respect."

"Uncle, do you have any more? Any more stories?" She let the greed show in her voice. "I won't ask you again for the medicine. I know you don't want me to take it. Although I still need it. Can't sleep."

He ignored her last remarks. "There is another portion you might read, yes. It's not long. You can read it here. It's somewhat out of context—It's part of a larger story, but—it can stand on its own."

He took the book from the shelf. Again the smell—of dust and jewels and particles of mystery. Fishing through it, he extracted a number of parchment sheets enclosed in a silk case. The handwriting was large and elegant.

"This is the original. Very delicate, very old. And these"—he pulled some more papers out of the book—"are my translations from the French." He held a dozen neatly typed pages.

He walked around the desk to give them to her. Touching her shoulder, he stopped. "You're shivering." She didn't reply, but let him wrap her in a shawl.

"Better?"

She began to cry. "No. I don't know why. I still can't get warm."

Silently, he poured her a glass of brandy. When she was warm enough, she began to read.

It is with some small sense of misgiving that I make the following account of the events of the winter of 1782. It is not that I have done anything to regret—I was just a bystander. But it is as though I have had two lives—the first, one of sorrow, and now, a life of some small joy. To entertain memories of the former time is exceedingly painful—I am frightened of my memories—but I shall not go into them here, this is not my tale. I console myself by thinking that the events of this period signified my great Transition, from grief to contentment.

The twin blisters were found in a single oyster in a bed in the Celebes. They were each the size of a very large walnut, and grayish-black in color. "Gambling blisters," as they are called in the trade, result when a fully formed pearl is thickly overlaid by shell nacre, and nothing can be seen of the contents. A large blister may command extravagant prices, and in the end may yield nothing. It was the Vicomte de Vigny who first acquired these two, and carried them back to Europe, where they came into the possession of the Duc de X—.

The character of the Duc de X— was well known to be harsh. While every pearl doctor in Europe wanted a chance at the blisters, at the same time no one wanted to incur the Duc's wrath if he did not meet with perfect success. The story of Fourier and the fate of the Valestinis serve to remind what terrible consequences could result from such a transgression.

Furthermore, the pearls arrived with an elaborate curse. Pearls, as a rule, do not carry curses the way other gems do. But the bed from which they were plucked was held to be sacred to an Indonesian goddess, the equivalent of Aphrodite.

The curse was this: any blemish on these pearls would affect the man who set eyes on it. Whatever the true condition of his heart, it would be magnified, such that his inner flaws, which all trouble to keep hidden, would become visible. It would be better to die. This transformation could take any of a number of forms: sudden exterior deformity, madness, or grossly aberrant behavior. Conversely, it was said that if a soul was really beautiful, and a heart was truly pure, he who looked upon the issue of this oyster would be healed of his darkest sorrows. The curse of his birth would be lifted from him, and his heart's deepest wish would come true. After viewing the defect upon the pearl, one would change in either direction, but could not expect to remain the same. No one wanted to take the chance. Most of the natives had fallen into the habit of throwing the oysters from this bed back into the sea, lest they find a pearl which might disturb the balance of their lives.

The adventurous took this risk and sold to traders. What began as a local superstition grew to such proportions that it became a well-known curse.

Apparently even the great Boucheron refused to handle the blisters. Thus it appeared that the Duc de X— was going to endanger his reputation. Such confidence had he in the stones that he had promised them as a pair of earrings to Madame B—. His honor was now at stake.

And so the Duc de X— did an extraordinary thing. He pardoned from prison the notorious murderer Lamer, who was also the greatest pearl doctor France had ever known. Lamer had committed a crime of passion but two years before, when he found his young wife in flagrante with his brother. What made the matter infamous was the method Lamer chose to execute his victim. I will refrain from furnishing the details.

Not only was Lamer the finest of workmen, but it was assumed that no further blight could befall such a wicked heart, and so — he had nothing to fear. As for the Duc, he did not believe in superstitions and feared nothing for himself. However, Lamer was to be permanently pardoned only on the condition that he deliver to the Duc de X— two perfect pearls. Failing this, he was to be executed in the same horrible manner as his bride.

By the time he was making his arrangements with Lamer, the Duc was in a highly overwrought condition. He was a very unattractive man, who suffered acutely from a scrofulous condition, and the pearls were his only opportunity for winning Madame B—. He ranted and raved at Lamer: "I want them to be beautiful! I want them to be the finest! I want them to be . . . superb! They will grace her little shell-like ears! I want—"

And then Lamer made his famous reply — "Monsieur," he said, "I will take from you a pearl — I will give you back the moon."

And so the preparations began. Lamer, who had been living on black bread and water and a little gruel, was to be fattened up. The Duc had his chefs prepare special meals, and every night Lamer was invited to dine with the Duc himself. But Lamer turned away the ortolans and the rich sauces and the amber-colored sauternes. He dined, each night, on a small roasted chicken and a bottle of burgundy.

The Duc wanted to put his captive guest in good spirits, so he brought the best whores in all of France to his château, but each night Lamer declined them. He had vowed never to take another woman after the lamentable moment when he had discovered his wife. And so they were sent away. Even the old Duc seemed to have fallen under some spell in Lamer's presence. Where once his lustful appetites had kept the whores of Paris rich and busy, he now seemed to think only of Madame B—, and he too turned the ladies away. This caused much comment among the Duc's servants, and word of it reached his friends. It was muttered that Lamer, bewitched by love, emanated a dark night glow — "the embers of the moon," it was called — that bewitched men into constancy. But I digress. After two weeks of attempting to relax the pearl doctor, the Duc saw that it was impossible — his man was as ready as he would ever be to attack the jewels.

Then, of course, there was a terrible problem. While no one likes to admit to believing in a foolish superstition, it was nonetheless difficult to get anyone to assist at the doctoring of the first pearl. Difficult! No one would do it. And Lamer needed helpers to act as his surgeon's assistants — to hand him his files and knife blades, to mix the pumice of olive oil and ruby powder that he used for the polishing. Finally he made a wry suggestion to the Duc — why not choose men who were so brokenhearted that they could not be further cursed? Men like Lamer himself. At first this sounded like a fairy tale to the unromantic Duc, but as I have said, he had lately been softening. And so a search began: a comic, melancholy search for the most wretched, the most lachrymose men in the country. The men with nothing to lose, in this life or the life beyond. I suppose one would think that hundreds, nay thousands, lined up. But in fact, it was hard

to find a man whose heart was completely purged of hope—
a man with not a dream of love left, not a trace. The Duc
found five, who were employed to work in shifts. These poor
wretches assisted at the skinning of the first pearl, and I was
one of them.

When the day arrived, Lamer seemed strangely at peace.
His former agitation appeared to have passed off entirely.
The Duc took this as a sign of the murderer's confidence.
One sees what one wishes to see.

The work began. Using a fine chisel, Lamer took his first
chips at the blister. They availed nothing. Calling for a stur-
dier instrument, he took a hard stab at the ugly shell. It
yielded, splitting like the husk of a walnut. A dull, blackish
pearl was revealed underneath. It was oblong. The Duc
looked uncomfortable. Evidently he was not prepared for the
tedium of the task, as if he had expected Athena to spring
full-blown from the head of Zeus.

The next penetration revealed a soft, rosy tint—a color
with the hint of the shadow of a Burmese ruby. This is a
color much prized, of course, and Lamer seemed deeply
moved by it. When he had sculpted a pink hole the size of a
lentil peeking through the black skin—it looked like the
breast of a Nubian—he looked up at his employer. The Duc
was restlessly pacing, drinking goblet after goblet of wine
and eating oysters. He offered them to Lamer, who astounded
the Duc by for once sitting down with him, and taking a
hearty repast. The two men exchanged few words, and in
any case, Lamer was eating with such vigor that he could
scarcely have spoken. His mouth was constantly full of oysters. It was, in fact, rather disgusting. He ate as if he had
not eaten in months, in years. The Duc, reduced to silence
by this display, found himself unable to eat.

When Lamer returned to his task, there was a sated look
about him. The sharp edges of his hawklike face seemed
dulled and softened. With the steady perseverance of a machine, he chipped and polished at the orb for four straight
hours. When he had finished, he revealed a pink globe of
perfect roundness and a most uncommon hue.

Lamer looked up at last. The Duc coughed nervously,

adjusting the sputum in his throat. At last he hacked up a piece, and delivered it into an embroidered handkerchief.

"Very nice, very nice," he muttered, glaring at the pearl. "But—we'll have to go further with it. It's awfully . . . red."

And so it was. A most extraordinary rosiness had come over it. I thought it irresistible. But the Duc evidently had something on his mind. He was a gambler.

"I want you to go on."

Lamer paused, gazing at the air two inches above the pearl. At last he spoke. "Monsieur, if I continue . . . we may lose her, and who knows what we will find?"

"I'll take the risk. Now, my gout is bothering me. Must have been the oysters. Have my man call for me when you have what I want." The Duc seemed anxious to get away from Lamer.

With the Duc gone, and just we five sad men and Lamer, the atmosphere changed. There was an understanding.

The pearl doctor set to work in earnest. His hands were remarkable. They were old, and the purple veins pushed beneath the skin's surface, but the tips of his fingers were finely shaped. There was a particular elegance to the thumb of his left hand.

The work was impossibly tedious. Scraping, chipping, polishing, he worked with a terrible patience. I had nothing to do but mix olive oil with powdered rubies, and contemplate the murderer's hands. In the space of an hour, another layer had been revealed. It was softly green, with the melancholy viridescence of faded moss. I have never seen a lustre to compare with it. After many hours, the rosy skin was entirely removed, and in its stead was a sea-colored marvel.

Quietly, we sat and ate together, the six of us. We did not discuss the pearl. Lamer permitted himself a little wine, and fell into a gentle sleep.

When he awoke, he pressed on. We said nothing. If this man of genius saw another pearl beneath, we believed in it. And indeed, the next slice of the chisel revealed an amazing color: a pearl gray with a shimmer and glow such as I have never seen before or since in this world. May I see it in the next one! It was alive. There had never been a pearl like it. Lamer worked for six hours, with the ardor of a man disrobing a mistress he has waited years to conquer. Though we had gone most of the night without sleep, none of us could have rested. What a queen that pearl was! How she glowed in that dusky chamber, and with what a melancholy fire!

Lamer was quiet now, wrung out with the strain of it. He seemed shelled, completed. We sad men understood. His interior was on display. He nodded to me, and I went to one of the servants outside the room and told him to send for the Duc.

When the Duc arrived, he was in a state of excitation. Lamer unveiled the pearl. The Duc looked at it, and glared. He walked around it, muttered a few words, and flung at Lamer,

"*Comme ça?*"

Lamer, appalled, could only nod.

"Out of the question."

Lamer replied softly, "Monsieur, it is the most beautiful pearl in all the world."

The Duc frowned. "Yes, yes. It is beautiful, yes."

"I gave you the moon."

"But the moon is *white*, you fool! White!"

The Duc was growing redder and redder in the face, his famous choler showing. Lamer said nothing. The Duc continued, at even higher decibels, "I can't possibly give this to Madame B—! What would she think? She is a woman who should wear only the whitest pearl around her exquisite throat, against her shell-like ears!" He said it in the manner of a man who has rehearsed a speech. Evidently he meant to speak these very words to Madame B—, but they had leapt out, unbidden, before Lamer and the assemblage. At last we perceived the nature of his objection. Madame B— had lived a life that was less than reserved. Her past had been scarlet. The Duc, who did not wish to see what was before his eyes, liked to think of her as a virgin. Only a white pearl, the symbol of an unblemished Aphrodite, would do.

There was nothing more for the notorious murderer to say. He had to attempt to deliver to the red-faced Duc a pearl to suit a virgin. It was a shameful task. The Duc left the room, sputtering about whiteness and purity and the beauty of Madame B—'s soul.

Lamer shook his head. "My first murder was very small. Now I am killing the moon." With that, he set to work, even more slowly and carefully than he had before. It was an extraordinarily difficult affair. We did not know what lay beneath. The risk was great. After an hour, we had an astonishing surprise. A speck of white peeped from beneath the skin of opal-gray. It had a light to it that . . . Well, we men said nothing. Perhaps we ceased to breathe. Except for Duval, who was gasping now, heavily and steadily. It was not until Lamer was three-quarters through that the tragedy was revealed. There was a ring in the pearl, a defect in its purity. Lamer did not seem surprised. Perhaps he was beyond feeling. He nodded to me again, and I fetched the Duc.

It appeared that the Duc had been restored to his old self. He had been roused from the arms of a concubine, and he was stupid with wine. He looked at the pearl.

"There, old man!" he exclaimed. "That's it! White for virginity," he burbled happily.

"Sir," said Lamer, "she has a defect. There is a ring around the heart of this pearl. We should not have cut to the marrow of the thing."

"Nonsense!" roared the Duc. "Keep on, man! Chip around it! It's just a layer, I'm sure!"

He lurched toward the dais, he began to fall toward it. We had to subdue him and remove him from the room. Although Lamer worked into the next night, it was folly, and we all knew it. He merely obeyed the Duc's orders. By the dawn of the next morning, the Moon of the Celebes was a pile of dust, the excrement of a sea animal.

Lamer was not surprised to learn that he was to be executed. It struck the other men as curious that he showed no sorrow, only a little relief. I understood, however — he would rejoin his beloved in death. The Duc gave Madame B— a cabochon sapphire of 17 carats. She spurned him shortly thereafter for a Portuguese count.

Since the Duc was a man of so little sensitivity, we did not expect the loss of the pearl, or Madame B—, to cause him any great imbalance. Consequently, we were deeply surprised when we learned of his suicide attempt in the Oriental fashion. He did not succeed; his hand was not steady, and the consequence of his attempt was great disfigurement and incapacity. Perhaps it was bad luck; perhaps it was the viewing of the ring around the heart of the pearl. I don't know. The rest of us sustained no further traumas as a result of the event. The remaining blister passed into other hands.

Lily looked up from the manuscript.

Mordecai's head was drooping now, he had lost his former buoyancy. He looked at her with clouded eyes.

"The second blister belongs to me. Someone gave it to me, a long time ago."

"The Moon of the Celebes . . . that's your hidden pearl?"

"Don't talk nonsense, child. One would think you were simple. Do I have to repeat it?" He rarely spoke to her like this, and it stung. He was scraping over an old scar, she was merely in the room.

Lily looked down at her hands and spoke softly to her fingers. "People want it."

"People have always wanted it. What people?"

"Alan. For Mrs. Franstein's necklace. To retain the integrity of the Nakamura pearls."

Mordecai snorted. "And what other people?"

"Someone I know. Someone else might want it."

He looked at her carefully. "I don't think I wish to skin that pearl."

"I didn't ask you to, did I? I just talked about people."

"No. Of course you didn't ask."

"Uncle, is there more to the book? Something else for me to read?"

"Oh, I don't think so. Not right now. You've read most of the important parts."

"But I don't understand."

"Still getting on well with Alan? Everything all right? Your other young man? What about that?"

"Huh? What? Alan's fine, of course. My other . . . Oh, that turned out to be nothing." She shrugged. "Why? Don't change the subject."

Mordecai smiled. "Well, there is more to the book. I'm writing a chapter of it myself. But I'm not finished yet. When I'm ready, you can read it. Now, you'd better go. I have work to do . . ." He waved vaguely to the shelf of books behind him. "And besides, you look tired. I want you to get some rest." He peered at her. "Being newly engaged is a strain. I understand that. Good night, my dear."

Lily left, kissing her great-uncle on the forehead. His eyes were faraway seas.

Dawn was cracking over the city, and she decided to go in to work early, to make up for her neglect, to surprise Alan.

She hadn't been to work in days. She sat alone in the shop, her desk piled with notes and papers, telephone messages, letters, and bills. She pecked at them for a while, methodically, and then she got up to make coffee. On her way she stopped and fished through some boxes. She pulled handfuls of jet from a bag, and some Nepalese turquoise that had the dark sea-gray green of—of what? Of her great-uncle's eyes. There was a strand of Burmese rubies, uncut, that had recently arrived. It would be missed, she thought idly, putting it in her purse.

She moved to the safe and clicked its combination, then rummaged inside for a moment, and withdrew the Nakamura pearls. She had not held them in her hand since the day they arrived. She rubbed the orbs against her throat. Methodically she unbuttoned her blouse and slipped it off. She ran the pearls over her breasts, and her nipples hardened against their cold skin. She pressed the strand of tiny moons to her lips, sucking gently, then roped them around her neck. When they lay against her throat and chest, she snaked her hand beneath her skirt. A few restless motions of her fingers, an intake of breath, the sensation of the cold, wet jewels against her skin. She heard a click at the door below. Gathering herself together, she pulled on her blouse and stuffed the pearls into her bag.

It was Alan. He was shocked to see her. "Honey!" he said, his face breaking into a grin. Then concern. "You still don't look good. You're sweating. Should you be here?"

"Oh, I'm fine. I thought I'd make up for some lost time."

"What're you doing in the safe?"

"I wanted to have a look at those diamonds for Mr. Patsquara. I'm not sure they're the cut he asked for."

Alan looked at her curiously. "But we settled that up with him, don't you remember? We talked about it." He rubbed his forefinger against his chin. "Well, maybe you're right. Let's see." He went to the safe, and returned with two small boxes. "Here."

They looked at the diamonds together. "They're perfect," proclaimed Alan, and Lily nodded. "While we've got it open, Lil, let me show you the Nakamura pearls again. I think we've got a contender. I don't know, but we might. I have some photographs of it. I didn't want to bother you when you weren't well, but I need your judgment." He nuzzled her neck. "I hate to be without your judgment. God, your skin is hot."

He returned to the safe. He was gone a long time. "Where are they? Come here and help me look, would you? I had them yesterday. I put them right . . ."

They looked together.

"Alan, they're not here. Are you sure you put them away safely?"

He gave her a shocked look. "Of course I put them away

safely. Lily, you know, things have been missing. Someone— But this I can't believe. This is impossible." He was biting one of his cuticles, so close to the moon of his nail that Lily had to look away.

"Oh, Alan, I didn't know. I should be around more, I'm responsible, I—"

"Ouch. Shit." He had bitten his cuticle hard, there was a hot spurt of blood.

"How disgusting," he muttered, looking at his bleeding finger. "Where's my handkerchief? Oh, hell—" He looked around for something to staunch the flow, sucking heartily on the wounded digit all the while. With his free hand, he reached for Lily's purse. "Um," he mumbled, "you always keep one in here—"

She lunged for the bag. Startled, he pulled away, and as he did so, the pearls tumbled onto the floor. He stared down at them.

"For God's sake," he said, withdrawing his finger from his mouth. "What on earth is the meaning of this? I don't even know what to say to you. What are you thinking?"

"I don't know . . . I don't know." She shook her head back and forth in the cradle of her arms, and her brown hair tumbled free of its clasp.

"This is outrageous." He held the pearls as if they were a distasteful, faintly contaminated object. "Stealing from yourself." It was not a question, or an accusation, but a flat statement of puzzlement and disbelief. He repeated the words, as if to see how they tasted. "Stealing from yourself."

"Alan," she pleaded. "The pearls were getting, I don't know, *foul*. I was only going to borrow them."

"Foul?"

"They took on her tone. Mrs. Franstein's. It's the way pearls have."

"Took on her tone? What are you, nuts? That's nothing but a ridiculous superstition. Pearls don't take on anyone's mood or aura or anything. I cannot *believe* I am saying this to *you*. Pearls respond to the oils and secretions in the skin." He paused, looking down at the pearls curled in his palm. "I admit, they may be slightly yellow, but perhaps Mrs. Franstein has . . . very . . . skin with a lot of secretions. You know," he finished lamely.

Lily looked up at him and began to bite back a smile. Alan bit his lip, and laughed.

"Okay, okay, Mrs. Franstein is uncommonly oily. Her spirit is sebaceous. Hey, what does that prove?" But they were both laughing. Then, suddenly, his smile faded.

"This is ridiculous. This is serious. You are in very bad shape." He glared at her. "Do you want to wind up like your aunt? Do you? In one of those places?"

Lily seemed to deflate, tiredness weaving through her. She examined her knee for bruises.

"Did you hear what I said?" Alan set the pearls gingerly on the table. "I want you to get some help. You're never here. I don't know what's going on with you. You could have caused a major scandal. Worse."

"What's worse than a major scandal?"

"Stop it. You know what I mean. Christ. Maybe you should take some time off. Maybe *we* should. We'll go skiing."

"No. I hate skiing."

"You never told me that."

"Never mind. I'll be all right."

"What would I have told Mrs. Franstein?"

"That one of our employees stole the pearls. That with enormous diligence we hope to uncover the culprit. That we don't understand how such a person could have infiltrated our ranks, but that we will be ever vigilant. We understand if she wishes to take her business elsewhere."

"Are you sleeping nights?"

"Oh yes. A lot."

"Go home. I'll forget what happened. Nothing happened. I'll

see to the rest of the *Bijou* layout. It's no problem. The shoot
went fine yesterday, and—"

"What shoot?"

"Yesterday was the first shoot with Penthe's statuary. It went
fine. The guy from *Bijou* had an interesting angle, they changed
the format. Penthe brought four of the models, and they'll be
shot wearing the same pieces the statues are wearing." Alan
made an okay sign with thumb and forefinger. "Side by side.
It's going to be very effective. My God, you should see his
women! I don't know what the guy's got, but he has them
trained. He was making out with one of them like there was no
tomorrow. I thought those girls were going to tear each other's
eyes out. Well, actually"—he rifled his pockets—"I've got
some Polaroids right here. See . . . There's the ruby brooch,
you can hardly see it in this shot, but—Yeah, that's the one he
was kissing. Had to keep fixing her makeup. And this one
practically had her hand in his pants. The life of an artist," he
said dryly. "Anyway. He's just finishing a sculpture now, he
wants it to appear with the jade pendant and a ring, said he's
especially proud of the hands. Says it's his best piece yet. Calls
it *Lethe*. Weird guy," Alan concluded. He was silent a moment
as he straightened up the office.

"Lily," he began. He touched her tentatively. "I should be
mad at you. But you look sick. I want you to go home and rest,
and then I want you to go to the doctor. Promise me? Okay.
Did you walk to work? I'll call a cab."

That night, as so often happened now, she woke with a start.
She dreamed she had fallen asleep wearing the Nakamura pearls,
and that they stuck to her skin, lying bunched between her
breasts. She had heard it was bad luck to fall asleep wearing
pearls, even in a dream. The covers stuck to her, and her breasts
felt soft and full. It was the heat, she imagined. It must be hot,
the sheets were damp. She pushed the covers away, like a pettish
child, and padded, nude and sticky, to the window to let in air,

expecting to be greeted by a humid gust. Pushing it open, she felt a blast of icy wind and a splatter of chilling rain. She checked the thermostat, but it was off. All the heat was inside her. She had a fever.

Pressing the heel of her palm to her forehead, she reflected that she was behaving hysterically. This was a meaningless symptom, and she was a hypochondriac. As she thought this, she made her way to the bathroom. In her anxiety to find the aspirin, she pushed aside boxes of tablets, aging bottles of perfume, and half-crushed lipsticks. When she finally found the bottle of aspirin, it was empty. She could not endure this fever. It was 2:30 in the morning. She dressed and rushed outside, thinking frantically of finding an all-night drugstore. There was none in her neighborhood, but she didn't want to drive. She was hot, and she wanted to be in the cool air.

She walked steadily for nearly an hour. Inevitably she found herself in the Mission. It seemed to her, with all due logic, that this was an area in which one might reasonably find an all-night drugstore. It occurred to her for the first time that she might have something to fear: she was a young woman walking alone in the cadaverous dark, in a bad neighborhood. However, she felt no fear. None at all. She realized it was because she felt herself to be under Johnny's protection, under his hovering aura.

She soon found herself on Valencia Street. It continued to rain. She saw a cab, once, in the street's dim light, but she certainly was close enough now to an all-night drugstore; she had no need of a cab. She remembered that she had once seen a drugstore in this neighborhood, the first time she had visited Johnny. It seemed like a long time ago now. She remembered thinking, I'm going to get to know all this so well—I'll know the all-night drugstore, I'll know the corner liquor store, with the scowling Persian man, I'll know that seamy bar, I'll know the all-night drugstore. Perhaps it was no longer there, she allowed. Things change. Things do not remain stable. We imagine ourselves in a world of luxury, where a smile or a scar will be ours to examine for decades, for a lifetime. And then all that is taken away from us, and we only have a memory of the scar, of a brilliant smile. It was impossible for her to imagine that she had left others with the memory of her own scars.

She arrived, finally, at the drugstore. A few junkies shrank into the shadows under its eaves, trembling a little in the rain. No one else was in sight. She went in. The fluorescence would ordinarily have startled her, but now it seemed mundane, this coming out of the dim into the nude light. She suddenly felt tired, as if she had taken a long, arduous journey. She glanced at the junkies out in the cold, and then at the drugstore's gray proprietor, fiddling with insurance forms in the back of the pharmacy.

"I'd like some aspirin, please."

The owner looked up, mild irritation on his face. The drugstore was not large, and the aisles were clearly marked.

"Halfway down D."

She chose a generic brand. She was wet from the rain, and didn't know if her fever had broken or not. Probably not. She was still very hot. Hot and anxious to get outside, back into the rain, back to the shivering addicts. But when she passed them on her way out, they seemed foreign and unfamiliar, like creatures from another race.

Lily knocked on the door. The light was on in the studio. He was home. She was certain he was awake—It had not occurred to her that she might be waking him at 3:30 in the morning. She had to ring the bell twice. A head poked out of the upstairs window.

"Who is it?"

"It's Lily. Oh . . . did I wake you?"

"Sort of. What are you doing here? Are you all right?"

"I'm fine. I had to go to the all-night drugstore."

He looked puzzled, and he paused for a moment before turning from the window. "I'll be right down." His voice floated down to her.

Johnny arrived at the door, pale from sleep, his dark hair mussed. His lips stood out against his pallor.

"Lily, it's late. I'm sort of asleep. I think you should go."

"I left something here. I left my purse. It's really important."

"Oh—" He looked faintly surprised, as if this were a ploy he had not anticipated. "Of course."

She followed him upstairs. He stood, rubbing his eyes with the heel of his hand. He made no move to sit down, or to motion her into the bedroom. She stood awkwardly, looking at the glowing tip of his cigarette. "Johnny—"

He just looked at her.

"Let me stay, Johnny. Please. I don't want to go home."

"Lily, you have to go. I don't want you here tonight."

"But why not? Why don't you want me here?"

"It's late. You should have called."

"But after everything you said. You promised—"

"I can't help you tonight, Lily. You should go now."

"Can't help me? Can't help me? But you said—Remember in the beginning, what you said? You said you always wanted to see me, no matter when. You promised to always love me."

"I didn't say that. It was you who said that."

"No. There was the time . . ." She recited it all meticulously, a list of vows.

Johnny shuddered, suddenly childish and confused.

"Oh," he said. His lips and mouth were set hard against her; she read everything in his mouth.

Lily looked wildly around the studio. Lethe stood, as she had before, by the window. Another statue was growing next to her, another woman's body, stretched out long and languorously, her face a picture of lazy mirth. Lily recognized her as one of the models for *Bijou*. She lacked Lily's tension, but she had a lax beauty in its place. Topazes glittered at her throat.

"What's that, what are you doing?"

"Do you think you're my only model? Besides, my new patron, the good Mrs. Franstein, wants two statues."

"Two? What two?"

"Well, *Lethe* would do as one — and *Untitled* here makes two."

"I thought *Lethe* wasn't for sale."

"I guess she is. Why not?"

"Oh baby," she said, reaching for him, trying to touch his face. He pushed her away, repulsed, and she began to cry. He stepped back and stared at her, aching and livid from her pain and her questions. She wanted to scream from not knowing their answers. What is a promise? What is a broken promise? How do you break them? Do they have fault lines, which eventually grow weak and crack apart, or do they crumble? Can you smash a promise? Can another person break the other one's promise? "And everything I gave you, Johnny? All the jewels?"

"I thought they were gifts, I never asked for anything."

"No! You didn't! Of course you didn't. I didn't mean it that way. I only meant . . . the meaning behind my giving them, your accepting them, I . . ." She looked up at him, grabbing on to a thought. "There's one jewel more beautiful than all the rest, you know all about it. For *Lethe*. You'd know, if you had that, how I really feel. Do you think —"

"I could never ask you to give me that. It's too much."

"But if I did? If I could?"

"I don't want it."

"Oh, Johnny." She pulled on his arm, trying to tug him into the bedroom. She sat down on the bed, dizzy with hope. The sheets were warm and mussed where he'd been sleeping. The bed smelt of him.

Johnny came after her, grinding out his cigarette and standing over her. "Lily, leave. I'll call a taxi."

"No. You can't make me. I'm staying."

She collapsed on the floor and began to rock back and forth, sobbing. Tears ran down her angry face, and her nose filled with phlegm.

Johnny touched her foot, stupidly, tentatively. He looked appalled and bewildered.

She continued to rock and sob, the snot dripping into her

mouth. She felt ugly, her hair felt greasy, but she didn't care anymore. It didn't matter. She had clung to him and he had peeled her away like a scab, a dying skin. Then she saw it. There were fresh-cut daisies in a vase by the bed, a posy only a girl could have picked. She was startled by her pain, like a person who has a terrible accident, and feels an unexpected depth of agony. You look innocently at your own body, she thought, where a landmine has blown off your hand, and you say, "Is it me? Do I feel such a thing?" And you look at the stump where your hand was, and you think, "Now I have a whole life ahead of me, without a hand, without my hand. Nothing will be the same at all."

He was speaking, from a mist. "If you won't go, then I will."

Was he calling her bluff? She thought of spending the night alone in his bed, beside these flowers. She inclined her head to the side, and gave him a skewed little smile. "All right," she said very softly. "You win."

He reached for her elbow. "Come on back in the other room. I'll get you a taxi."

She gave him a wild look. "But my purse . . . it's around here somewhere . . ."

"Forget it. You have to leave now."

Johnny was pulling her now, bodily, toward the kitchen, but a sound pulled her back the other way. She strained in both directions, until the sound of a woman's voice snapped her out of his grasp.

"Johnny? Are you coming in? Did you fall asleep? Who was at the door at this hour? I'm gonna come get you. The water's nice and hot — You know I love to do it in the shower, let's —" The sight of Lily stopped her.

The girl was a model for *Bijou*, Lily had seen her picture. She pulled the towel around herself, covering her breasts, letting water pour off her. Lily shrank back slowly, edging her body toward the door, the bile rising in her stomach. Johnny shrank back too, into shadows, contracting into the room's hollows.

Only the girl moved rapidly, her mouth open, leaving a trail of water behind her.

When Lily woke the next morning, her mouth tasted of horror. Acid brown and stale, like too many cigarettes smoked and whiskeys drunk. She ran her tongue over her teeth, feeling a thin film of filth. It wasn't the foul flavor of barbiturates, it was the memory of Johnny's implacable face. It lay thick and greasy over her eyes.

She made a pot of coffee, and drank until her nerves jangled with false energy, a parody of wakefulness. She dressed slowly and carefully, and fed Curse, who lay swollen and sleeping in a patch of hot sunlight.

When she arrived at the store, she found Alan already at his desk. He did not embrace her, but looked at her with scrutiny.

"I called and called. I was going to come over, but then I was afraid to wake you."

"I unplugged the phone."

"How do you feel? Did you make an appointment with the doctor?"

"Much better. Oh, yes."

"I was just going to open up quickly, but then I've got to run. I'll be back for lunch." He hesitated. "That is, I have that lunch date with Mrs. Franstein, at La Luna. I'm going to show her a pearl we might use. But as soon as that's over, we'll talk, we'll go out."

"I saw the lunch date on your calendar. I'm going to join you. I really should be there."

"If you think—"

"Don't be silly. Just some crazy flu. Getting back to work is the best thing. Alan. About my . . . about my stealing. You understand that I didn't mean it. I was going to return them right away. I just wanted to pretend, for a little while, that I could have something that beautiful. Do you understand?"

"I don't know. I guess so. When I said doctor, I didn't mean only an ordinary doctor. You might want to—"

She laughed. "Sure. It runs in the family. Keep me off the streets. Kleptomaniacs Anonymous."

"Please." He looked pained.

She replied softly, "Of course I will. I know there's something wrong. It's a problem. I'm going to put it right."

He embraced her. "That's my girl. Anything I can do . . ."

"No. Nothing." She put a "sssshhhh" finger to his lips. "I'll meet you at La Luna."

When he had left, she turned to her neglected work. When she felt tired, she took a sip from the little vial of laudanum she had stolen. She made phone calls, examined balance sheets and invoices, dictated to her secretary. When she was alone at lunch-time, she went to one of the small cabinets in the back of the store. The Paxton ruby had been there a long time. Every effort to sell it had failed, though it was a beautiful stone. Lily slipped it into her purse and left for downtown.

The interior of La Luna was moon blue and austere, a temple to food. Waiters glided by with cold grace, bearing spartan entrées on thin silver platters. There were blue foods and pale blue drinks.

Lily spotted Mrs. Franstein by the back of her neck—a faint dowager's hump rose beneath a head of gray-blue hair, whose rinse had been left on minutes too long, so that she unwittingly matched the food.

She was alone at the table, a pink lady resting between crabbed fingers. A cherry bobbed in her drink, setting off the enormous emerald she wore on her right hand. Diamond pendant earrings wobbled beneath the blue hair, and a matching necklace hung in her vast cleavage.

Approaching the table, Lily smiled and introduced herself, extending her hand.

Mrs. Franstein paused a moment too long before reaching out, while the maître d' waited anxiously for the handshake to be consummated, so that he could push the chair behind Lily. At that moment Alan appeared, grinning broadly, elegantly dressed in a gray linen suit. In the flurry of introductions, the two hands never touched.

Alan carried the conversation neatly through the breast of quail and the aperitifs, blue like the summer sky. Mrs. Franstein said little, and rooted heavily in the bread basket.

While Alan prattled gracefully about the charms of San Francisco (Mrs. Franstein was well acquainted with them), the peculiarities of modern cuisine (Mrs. Franstein gave a low-pitched sniff), and the vagaries of a gem buyer's life (silence), Lily poked at the singed bird splayed out before her. It glared back at her. Alan addressed himself to her frequently, and she nodded and smiled in his direction. After a time, his manner grew more serious.

"Mrs. Franstein," he announced. "I've brought a pearl to show you. I believe you'll agree with me that it's a replacement for the one you've lost. Better."

Mrs. Franstein reached across the table for the bread basket, and in the process upset her glass of cabernet. The wine dripped into Lily's lap, soaking her napkin through to her dress, swamping the yellow silk in a red stain. Alan grabbed his napkin and snapped for a waiter in one quick motion, clucking "Now don't you worry" to Mrs. Franstein and mopping frantically at Lily. Mrs. Franstein made not a move toward her own napkin, but tsk-tsked as if the wine had spilled itself. Lily fumbled for her handkerchief in her little purse. As she pulled it out, a spark of bright red tumbled from its folds. It was the Paxton ruby.

When Alan saw it, he ceased his daubing and fussing. His patter died out, and he sat, stupefied, staring at it.

"Ah, Mrs. Franstein," Lily began. "And I was going to save it for the dessert, the denouement! This is . . . yours, from Van Velsen's. It's the Paxton ruby. We wanted you to have something special, a token of our esteem, of our appreciation. With hopes that we'll enjoy many more such luncheons."

Mrs. Franstein looked at her suspiciously, then gave the ruby a hard stare. "I've never cared for rubies," she said.

"Well." Alan coughed. "Well, of course. We didn't know. Something else might do. A surprise is always a risk!" he added stupidly. He cast Lily a wild glance.

"Of course, Mrs. Franstein," said Lily. She began to wrap the ruby in the wine-soaked handkerchief.

"Oh no, I'll keep that. Let me," said Alan.

Mrs. Franstein did not care for the new pearl, which was displayed after the tablecloth was changed and the liqueurs ordered. She disliked the lustre, she found fault with the orient. She knew her subject. She demanded a superior product.

After they had seen Mrs. Franstein into a cab, Alan grabbed Lily by the arm. "I'll forget this, all of this, if you get that pearl. Do you understand me?"

"Sure."

Lily went directly to the opium den. Her skin had begun to ache. She had planned to go to Johnny's with the Paxton ruby, but it was impossible, now that Alan had it. She traced the familiar route from downtown to Chinatown, easing her pain with the anticipation of languor.

Arriving in the shadowy alley, she stopped a moment to savor her entrance, to plan it. She felt the same way in this alley as she felt at Johnny's door. The same sense of nervous anticipation, of excitement, of relief and fear. Over time, the alley had become safer, more reassuring. She had dismissed the danger of opium.

Crossing the threshold beneath the gatekeeper dragon, she entered the outer room, waiting for the shadowy footfall of the old man. There was no sound. The room was empty, and so was the room beyond it. The shelves had been cleared, where only yesterday they stank of Oriental herbs. A few empty boxes of jelly fungus and Seahorse Tonifier lay strewn on the floor. Shards of bark crumbled beneath her feet. Stumbling over a cracked abacus, she hurried to the back room. It was bare, except for the bunks. The pillows were gone, as were the braziers.

There were no locks on the doors, but there was nothing to steal. It was a shell.

A wave of sickness crackled through her. She made a frantic run for the tiny bathroom, and vomited into the sink. Her spine chilled as she ran the water into the filthy bowl, and starbursts of panic broke behind her eyes. She crumpled a moment, against the wall, her eyes adjusting to the gloom. She cast about in the frightened dark for some familiar thing, some neglected ball of opium, a sign of a practical joke: she imagined old Chinese bursting through the door — Ha-ha! We scared you? — but nothing happened. A few gusts of wind from the street disturbed the still air of the little room. She splashed cold water into her mouth, trying to rinse away the acrid taste; then she hurried to her great-uncle's.

He was writing when she arrived. His spidery scrawl covered the pages spread out before him. When he saw her, he gave a thin smile, and pushed the papers together. He wrote with a fountain pen. She'd heard the scratch of the nib all her life, the *scrik-scrik* of its tip against the creamy bond. The book was out on the desk.

"Hello, Uncle." She kissed his brow.

"Hello, my dear. Is something wrong?"

"I'm really cold. I can't sleep. I need some medicine."

"My malaria preparation? I'm out, for the moment. You're not sleeping well? It's only the afternoon—"

"Out?"

"Chen Li is mixing up the next batch. It'll be along in a few hours. It's not for you," he added severely.

"A few hours? Don't you have any?" She cast about frantically for the decanter.

Mordecai's eyes narrowed into slits. "My God, Lily," he said, as if seeing her for the first time. "Just a few drops . . . just this once. I see, I didn't realize." He reached behind him, and managed to extract a trickle of blood-black liquid from the bottom of the decanter.

She drank with desperation. When she looked up at him, she saw tears crouching behind his eyes as he watched her.

"So it's come to this?"

"You know I can't sleep."

"Ah."

"And I know what this is. I know you don't have malaria. And neither do I." She licked the edge of the glass, pressing her tongue inside of it. "You're addicted to this. It's opium. You might as well be some old junkie on the street."

"Oh, my poor child," he said, because she was crying now, curled up and crying, the pain eddying inside her. He hugged her close until the spasms stopped. "You can talk to me, dear. I'm an old man, and I've seen so much that you can tell me anything. What is it you want to say?"

"Oh, I'm so ashamed, Uncle, please, I need the pearl."

She felt the quiver in his touch, but he still held her tightly to him.

"If you need it, of course, it's yours." Old fingers curled her damp hair behind her ears. "Let's talk about something else until Chen Li comes, with the medicine." His fingers feel so cool, she thought, like pieces of jade. He wiped away the streaks of tears.

There, she thought, I've said it. He might have sent me away. It's the one thing no one ever brings up. Bring it up, and he might never speak to you again.

He was patting her with his handkerchief. It smelled delicious, linen-clean. "And have you been reading?" he asked.

She sniffled, too ashamed and sick to speak. He went on. "Ah, I have. I've been reading Rilke. I'll wager you haven't read Rilke in years. Of course, you don't have German, do you? It's a shame that you don't. It's not enough to have French and restaurant Italian . . . Of course, your stepparents never saw properly to these things. In my travels, I found German to be of enormous importance; you will too. And if nothing else, you can read Rilke. Shall I read you a little? Here we go, it's just here, beside me, I'll start in the middle. It's one of my favorite parts."

How we squander our hours of pain.
How we gaze beyond them into the bitter duration
to see if they have an end. Though they are really
seasons of us, our winter—
enduring foliage, ponds, meadows, our inborn landscape,
where birds and reed-dwelling creatures are at home.

High overhead, isn't half of the night sky standing
above the sorrow in us, the disquieted garden?
Imagine that you no longer walked through your grief
    grown wild,
no longer looked at the stars through the jagged leaves
of the dark tree of pain, and the enlarging moonlight
no longer exalted fate's ruins so high
that among them you felt like the last of some ancient race.

"There, you see? It's restful, when you're waiting, to be read to. I almost know how to wait, now. You have to learn it, the way you learn to conjugate verbs, or to tie knots . . ." He talked on and on, his beautiful, old voice soothing her.

When Chen Li arrived, Mordecai let her pour a small glass of the laudanum. He sat in silence, waiting for her cells to compose themselves, and finally he spoke. "And what do you want with the pearl?"

"I told you, someone needs it. I need it, for that someone. I can't justify it. I just—"

"If you say you do, of course. Only, Lily—you know I can no longer skin a pearl. It's been years, my hands are too old. And I have too many memories. Not that pearl. And you, you're not well. Your hands shake. When did you last touch an important pearl?"

"You want me to do it?"

"You have to do it. You have to get well first, and then you must do it. I'll tell you its legacy. I thought I might write it all down, I made a few notes . . . but I'll tell you instead."

"Uncle, I can't cut the Moon of the Celebes."

"Then who's going to?"

"Help me."

"I can give you my pearl-doctor's eyes, that's all."

"That's everything."

He snorted a laugh. "I see. All right. But you must listen, listen carefully. I have a story to tell you. See if you still want the old moon when I'm done." With great decorum, he got up to walk to his safe.

The pearl blister was huge, an inch in diameter. It was bigger than any she had ever seen. Flecked with the scars and ordure of the sea, it possessed an ugly majesty. Mordecai gave it to her to hold, and settling back in his chair, he began to speak.

PART II

The Moon of the Celebes

*It is enlightened rest, neither fever nor languor, on the bed
    or on the grass.*
It is the friend, who is neither strong nor weak. The friend.
It is the beloved, not tormenting nor tormented. The beloved.
The air and the world not sought after. Life.
—Was it this then?
—And the dream brought coolness.

— ARTHUR RIMBAUD, *"Vigils"*

You've heard so many stories about your grandfather, Lily. It's not necessary for me to repeat them all. You know about his bravery, his charm, his appetites — that's the stuff of family legend. So were our exploits together, our travels, the stories of the gems we smuggled — you've heard all that. What no one has ever told you — because no one else knows the truth — began, for me, in 1920.

Leo and I had traveled together since we were very young men, buying, trading, and smuggling. We left America and made our base in London — at that time, of course, Hatton Garden was the heart of the international pearling trade, and we dealt in pearls and all variety of stones. Leo had no special love of gem cutting, as I had; and as the years went on, my interest in the art deepened. I hadn't much money — neither had he — but we agreed to go our separate ways, at least for a time. I left for Paris to pursue what had become a profound ambition. Leo continued to buy and sell, and more often than not the stones I cut were acquired from him. We both made a modest success in our endeavors, but as the years went by I grew bored with my gems, with their occlusions and their facets. Slowly, I came to love pearls. I let others handle the other jewels, the kings and queens, the diamonds and emeralds — I wanted to handle the king's concubines — the pearls.

In 1920, Paris was the other great capital in the pearl trade. I haunted the elegant shops on the Rue Lafayette and the Rue Cadet, seeking employment. I worked here and there, but it was a long time before I found my teacher. He was an elderly gentleman—Monsieur Lemaître. He was at an advanced age when we met—eighty-two. I saw him at a demonstration on the Rue de Rivoli. I had heard of him, of course—his name quietly dominated the field, even beyond those of Duparc, Thillier, and Payen. It was said that when a pearl doctor had reached what he imagined to be complete mastery of his art—when he no longer made mistakes, or so it seemed; when he was at the height of his powers; when he was admired, praised, and rewarded—that then he might go to Lemaître, and then he might begin to learn. That then, like a child, he might begin the arduous task of beginning, and stumbling, and beginning again. Oh, Lily, I was already good! I was very good, and very bored, and beginning to be a little bit rich. But it was from Lemaître that I learned to *see*, that I learned the clairvoyance of pearls.

I remember very well the first sight of him—he was a slight man, with a hooked nose, a firm mouth, and strong, fine hands. He wore a little beard. He was a dandy, too, and the ladies adored him.

He was surrounded by them, that winter day on the Rue de Rivoli. The ladies sipped chocolate, and the smell of it permeated the room, mixing with their perfumes and clinging to the heavy burgundy curtains that lined the walls. The women, in their best jewelry and furs, giggled as they approached the master at his little table. His students mingled with the elegant crowd—here and there one could spot jewelers and pearl artists whose names had once been well known in society. Each and every one had withdrawn from the social whirl when he became Lemaître's pupil. It was not that Lemaître requested it—it seemed the apprenticeship was so demanding that a man had to choose between his task and his habits. Many began and quit after weeks, or months, or even years, not having developed the sight.

When I cast my eyes on the little man, I felt a thrill run through me, the way one feels on a roller coaster before the first dive. We were introduced. Lemaître clasped my arm firmly, looked into my eyes, smiled broadly, and said, "*Et voilà! Un americain . . . Voulez-vous étudier?* You will teach me English in return, eh? American English! *Et aussi, si vous voulez étudier avec moi . . .* You are too thin! *Il faut manger, monsieur!*" He plucked a petit four from a nearby cart and pressed it into my hands. "*Ici, ils font des bons patisseries . . .* I like especially the marzipan . . . *Mon cher monsieur, il faut manger!*"

He laughed and walked away. I excused myself to my companion, and stepped outside for a moment. I walked until I was certain I was alone. I had left my coat inside, and it was raining and very cold, but I didn't care. I had found Lemaître.

And so I began my apprenticeship, in the tiny basement of a house in the Sixième. He made us sit day after day watching pearls without touching them, as I've taught you to do. In these long meditations, lasting many hours, we were to try not to think, only to receive the pearl itself. Lemaître came in sometimes and stood at the door, watching us. Occasionally he would smile, and gently adjust the positions of our heads, directing our gazes this way and that, or he would point to the pearl and talk about it, saying,

"This one belongs to the night. Do you see that? On the outside, she is white ivory, but if you were to unveil her heart, you would find a shimmering blue. *Vous le voyez? Non? Il faut attendre, il faut attendre longtemps.* When you have learned the secret of waiting, Monsieur van Velsen, *je vous assure*, you will be a great artist. Hah! And this one—" So saying, he extracted a little pearl from his pocket. "This pearl is entirely different. From Constantinople, you know. She has a very light heart. Is she finished or not? I will leave you to decide." He laid the little pearl next to its nighttime cousin, and left the room smiling, and muttering in French and English.

It was exacting, this training, which called for stillness and sight. It was hard on the students, and for myself, I saw nothing, those first years. I was ready to give up hope many, many times, but sometimes when I looked at Lemaître, as he sipped his morning coffee or fussed with his cravat, I felt that first dizzy rush again, and so I stayed. Often he stood and watched me, shaking his head. He said, "*Vous le faites mal, monsieur. Je vous en prie—Look* at her." And so saying he took a cloth, and rubbed the pearl as I watched, then placed the jewel in the palm of his hand.

"A lot of money, eh, monsieur? And more if the inside is superior . . . And if not, oh monsieur, how many francs would you lose if you destroyed her? Don't think too hard about it, monsieur, be very stupid, like Père Lemaître."

And so we watched, day after day, in the little room on the Rue des Beaux Arts. And we ate. Lemaître loved to eat, and he was especially fond of pastries. The little *mille-feuilles* from Angelina's were his favorites, or sometimes éclairs. On special occasions he made *pots de crème*. His wife had died some years before, and it was her recipe; he was very proud of it. I remember what it was like to sink my spoon through the firm layer at the top, and to feel the bed of soft custard beneath.

In my training, I learned to wait. Lemaître used to say, "Women wait. Cats wait. Children wait. Seasons wait. Until you've learned waiting, what good will you be as a pearl doctor? Your work will suffer, your digestion will suffer. You will begin again and again, never climbing a single step on the ladder, though you may be rich, and you may have fame.

"When you meet a woman who will wear your pearls, wait for her beauty. Maybe she will show it slowly. When you've seen it emerge from behind her eyes, behind her skin, only then can you match her with the right stones. A woman's skin and hair will ask for colors—you all know this, of course. Fair-skinned wants rose, dark skin wants golden, brunette wants cream-colored. But what color does her beauty want? What size, what tone, what orient, what lustre? If she is ugly, gentlemen, more's the pity. But if you've learned waiting, perhaps you'll find her beauty.

"Let me tell you a story about my first wife, messieurs. She was a beautiful girl. All the men in Paris wanted her, she had the face of a little angel. I courted her, and I won her, and this was not easy to do. Her little angel's face . . . bright, deep eyes, a delicate nose, and such a mouth! All the men in Paris wanted her mouth. And her neck . . . I was mad for her neck, which peeked out of her lace bodice. I used to give her pearls, of every description, to adorn her neck. Men envied me her neck.

"On our wedding night, I took her back to an inn in the country. In the candlelight I kissed her, and I began with her neck. And then I kissed her mouth, and her adorable curls, and those eyes! At last I began to remove her clothes, peeling away the layers of crinoline and velvet, petticoats and corset, the ruffles and the silk. As I began to remove the last, delicate barriers, she turned away from me, and reached for the candles with her fingertips, snuffing out their light.

" 'No, *petite*,' I said. 'Let me see your adorable body.'

" '*Non, je t'en prie*,' she replied.

"A woman's shyness on her wedding night, gentlemen. Entirely understandable. But the moon shone through the window, in such a way as to make all visible. And when I had her nude, what did I see, gentlemen? White skin, yes, a slim waist and very nice here"—he pointed to his hips—"but here"—and now he pointed to his chest and wagged his finger—"her breasts, messieurs, they hung down, how do you say? They sagged. Very much. She must have seen the dismay on my face, for she began to cry. I could not conceal my own disappointment—after all, I had courted her, I had won her, and her face was so lovely—to think that it was not all I had dreamt! I'm like any man, messieurs—I like to kiss a woman's breast, to hold it, firm and round. I had married a woman who looked like a Venus, but when I took the wrapping off the package . . . A sensitive man, you will say, doesn't care much about such things, he loves his wife, and that is good enough. But I felt betrayed by the ugliness of her breasts. And she felt it, too, in the way I touched her, though it was a long time before she spoke of it. When she finally said, "I'm not pretty enough for you. I know it,' I replied foolishly. I said, "*Petite*, perhaps they aren't your best feature, but how I love your hips, and your skin, and your hair.' That was my mistake, messieurs. I ought to have taken her breasts in my hands and kissed them, and told her how I loved her, and how I loved their beauty. I ought to have worshiped them, messieurs—for you see, it was the *body of my wife*. Do you understand? But I didn't see. And I didn't know how to wait for their beauty, for her beauty, which shone in her pendulous breasts, as it shone in her lovely hips. I knew nothing about loving, and nothing about waiting.

"My little wife stopped loving me then. Her love died because she felt so much shame. One day I came home and she had gone away. I did not remarry for many years, gentlemen, and I did not touch another woman for more years than I care to tell you. I made a very great mistake, gentlemen, because I knew nothing at all about beauty."

He pushed at a pastry with his fingers, and then he smiled. "Now back to work, messieurs, there is much to see."

Lemaître's students came from all over the world. There were a good number of Parisians, of course, but for every Frenchman there was an American, an Englishman, an Indian, an African, and so on. There was only one Lemaître, and the scent of his genius emanated around the globe, drawing his students to him.

While we shared a common goal, of sorts, I did not feel a great affinity with most of my fellow students, and I kept to myself. But there was one whom I befriended. His name was Desmond McConnell, and he was of Scots-Irish descent. He arrived one day at Lemaître's door, dead drunk, demanding to be let in. We were sitting quietly at the time, with our work, when we heard the violent thumping outside. Lemaître rose, and answered it, and there was McConnell. He was a dead handsome man—tall and lean, with black hair and fierce blue eyes, rimmed red with drinking. There was something weak in his mouth, I saw it at once, but one forgot it when one saw the mad and irresistible lust in those blue eyes.

Lemaître was completely unperturbed. He simply asked, "*Monsieur, que voulez-vous?*"

McConnell looked as if he would spit, but he coughed instead. "I've come about pearls. I'm looking for a teacher. A Mister Lemaître. He's supposed to be the bleedin' best. Bleedin' hell," he added contemplatively.

"*C'est moi, le père Lemaître.*"

McConnell seemed stretched between a gentle pugnacity and a terrible collapse. I saw then what the weakness was in his mouth: he had never in his life surrendered to anything or anyone. He looked away from Lemaître's bright eyes, and when he spoke again, it was to let out a string of curses in his thick brogue, a string of expletives so vile, so exacting, and so profound that in all my travels I had never heard the like. The words raked the air of our quiet salon, stinging the interior and flying around the pearls.

Lemaître enjoyed this very much. Leaning close to McConnell's beery breath, the old Frenchman clapped him hard on the back.

"*Très bien;* good, good. Only two things, monsieur, you must remember. Pay me now, and pay me promptly each month. And remember to eat regularly. *Si l'on ne mange pas* . . . There is no fire inside." The old man shook his head and smiled, waving his hand through the air. "Come back tomorrow morning."

McConnell had no money. He paid Lemaître for his first months in pearls, freshwater pearls from the rivers of Scotland. He took a job mopping floors at a small bistro, until Lemaître employed him around his home, fixing things and managing what an old man could no longer do.

McConnell had done some work in the fisheries of Bahrain, and he had worked the freshwater rivers near Glasgow. He was tired, he said, of being taken by every two-bit hustler who touched a pearl. His profit, he said, was cut in half every time. He was a fiery man, with a hot Irish temper and a gentle heart, who moved with a terse grace, as if he were pent up inside his body. "I'm not afraid of pain," he used to say. "I once took a bullet here." And he showed me the puckered wound on his right biceps. Above the scar was a tattoo—a tiger's livid face, homage to a fighting art he had mastered in Singapore. On his left arm there bloomed an opium poppy, the key to a story he refused to tell.

We often went drinking together after our studies, sitting till late at night at the Café de la Paix, drinking *vin rouge* and talking until the soft morning rains washed away the chalk portraits that covered the sidewalks. Customarily, Desmond was silent at first, and listened patiently while I spoke of my travels and adventures with Leo, and of what I planned to accomplish under Lemaître's tutelage. We felt a little foolish in the old man's service, sometimes—two grown men, two adventurers, sitting quietly for most of every day—but I could see in my friend's eyes that he too had felt the glorious pull of the old man's soul the day he walked in the door.

But there was a hurt in McConnell, a point of damage, that I did not fully understand. After four glasses of wine, he began to talk about Ireland, about politics, about the crimes of the church, and so on. At first it all seemed natural—McConnell was something of a freethinker, and he had emerged from his conventional Catholic upbringing with the air of a long-penned animal who had at last been freed. He had never lost this air. But as he went on, drinking and raving, I saw something alarming in his angry blue eyes, and in the slight weakness of his mouth.

"The hell with God," McConnell was fond of saying. "The hell with bleedin' God."

But in the presence of Lemaître, McConnell softened, and we could all see that the surrender was painful to him. He showed great promise from the first; he flowered rapidly in his studies, and he was swifter than any of us at working a pearl. He had a natural hand for drilling and stringing, and he knew the good from the bad with a sharper's instinct. We felt he would surpass us all, with his fierce dedication and his great ability. All that marred his progress were his drinking spells, which carried him away for days, sometimes weeks at a time. After one of these, he would crawl back, surly and closed. Lemaître never reprimanded him in front of us, but only set him harder and harder tasks.

One night, as we sat drinking, watching the rain coming down in a fine mist, McConnell fixed his blue eyes upon me. There was a mad look in them, and something obdurate about the corners of his mouth.

"I don't care that much about women," he said. "No, Mordecai, I don't. It doesn't matter to me. What matters is getting ahead, that's the thing, whatever you have to do, whatever it means to you. I loved a girl once, I suppose — She was a cold girl, aloof, really, and she went away. It took me a time to get over it, but of course I did."

He paused, looking at the dregs in his cup of coffee. He pushed it away and ordered another brandy.

"There was another girl, too. It was something else with her, I never understood it. She was a friend of mine, actually." He looked up at me suddenly, embarrassed. "That's not it, actually. It's Alyce. Alyce."

I was shocked, and I tried desperately not to let it show. Alyce was one of Lemaître's students, an American girl, who had been a jeweler in the States. She was small and intense, with a fierce will, a mop of black curls, and dazzling green eyes. I was friendly with her, since we were both Americans. I realized that Alyce knew things about people, she had an intrinsic brightness that I liked — but she had an offputting intensity, too, and wild moods that she could not hide. It was on account of these that I did not let myself grow too close to her; I was intent on my work, and there was something seductive about Alyce, seductive and distracting, and I didn't want to be swept up in it. We soon established a level of pleasant camaraderie. Lemaître had a special fondness for her, as if she were an errant, beloved daughter. He scolded her gently and often, and there were times when I suspected that Alyce was his favorite.

We all knew she liked McConnell—that was clear from the first. The day he arrived she noticed him, and took him aside, instructing him and flirting, charming him and laughing. They struck an easy rapport. McConnell never spoke of her, not in any particular way. The only thing I noticed out of the ordinary was that on some days they seemed subject to a peculiar estrangement, as if they had quarreled—and this after they'd been their most teasing and playful together. I stared at McConnell, I truly couldn't think of a thing to say.

"I know, I know," he said, gruff and awkward. "I know." It was an extraordinary sight, but McConnell was blushing. "Don't know what I'm telling you for. I don't love her, if that's what you think. It's not like that. But she fancies me, you know that, don't you, Mordecai? She made a spectacle of herself when we were alone, told me how fond she was of me and all that. Americans," he concluded.

There was a long silence, during which I waited, searching madly for something to ask, something to say. There was an alarming quality in McConnell's protestations. I suspected something had been touched inside him that he hated to reveal, to himself or to me.

"I've had her, you know. Little animal. American girls," he repeated. I could tell that he wanted to say something more. Finally he spoke.

"It feels wrong to me, when I'm with her. I don't know what it is. She's dangerous. It distracts me, affects my mind." He tapped his forehead significantly. "But there was one night when I was at her flat, as I often was, talking and drinking, and something in her smile, her manner—" He stopped, frustrated.

"I don't know. I grabbed her and—it couldn't be helped. Oh, she wanted it—never saw a woman want it more. I don't think a woman ought to want it like that . . . She pressed her body against mine, and—men are very weak about these things. I said I'd never do it again, and I told Alyce. She took it hard, Mordecai. I didn't like to hurt her. And I meant it, I swear I did. But it happened again, and again, with long intervals between. I don't want it to go on. I've got no guilts about sex. Why should I? Yet after we've been together, I always feel wrong, I don't know why. I avoid her. But Mordecai"—and here he leaned close to me—"it's like the devil sent her. The last time we were up until dawn."

I could see that he was done with his speech. He looked at me bitterly, as if I'd forced him to make this confession. Then he sat back in his chair. "I've got a scheme to make a bit of money, Mordecai," he said. "If you want to go in on it with me, I can find a way. There's a boat leaving for the Ceylon fisheries next Tuesday, and they need some mates, in a hurry." He withdrew a crumpled bit of newspaper from his pocket and stabbed at it with his finger. "See here, I've found an ad." He read it to me.

THE CEYLON COMPANY OF PEARL FISHERS LIMITED

NOTICE

It is hereby given that a Pearl Fishery will take place at Marichukkaddi, on the island of Ceylon, on or about February 18, 1922.

The banks to be fished are:—

(1) The Karativu, Dutch Moderagam and Alanturai Pars, estimated to contain 17,000,000 oysters, sufficient to employ 100 boats for twenty-one days with average loads of 10,000 per day. The North-West and Mid-West Cheval, estimated to contain 2,000,000 oysters, sufficient to employ 100 boats for two days with average

loads of 10,000 oysters; each boat being fully manned with divers.

(2) Marichukkaddi is on the mainland, eight miles by sea south of Sillavaturai, and good supplies of water and provisions can be obtained there.

(3) It is notified that fishing will begin on the first favourable day after February 19. The oysters will be put up for sale in such lots as may be deemed expedient.

(4) The Ceylon Company of Pearl Fishers is presently hiring crew and divers. Particulars can be obtained at The Government Agent, Northern Province, Saffira, Ceylon.

"There's good money in that," he announced with some satisfaction. "I've looked into it. What do you say, then?"

"It's not the right time for me. I'm beginning to learn, here. And Lemaître is old. Listen, Desmond, if you left now, who knows when you'd be back . . . It's dangerous."

"You sound like an old woman, Mordecai."

"You're just getting really good, Desmond. You're better than any of us." I added, with sudden passion, "You'd be a fool to leave, for God's sake."

"For *God's* sake?" he spat, returning to a favorite theme. "The bleedin' hell with bleedin' God."

There was an awkward silence, and finally he said, "That's enough talking about it." I felt a moment of challenge pass between us. He shifted a little in his seat, and I could hear the creaking of the chair legs. The rain had stopped, and there was a damp smell in the air.

McConnell was looking off into the night, at the couples strolling on the wet boulevard. Do you remember what I told you about his eyes? That they were an unnatural blue. And there was something else about them. A look he had at times, as if a wall came down between his soul and those eyes. I saw the coldness come into them, then, as I watched his face—I was used to it, this ominous closing, and I always wondered if he heard it in his own head, like an audible click.

"Say, Mordecai." McConnell spoke without looking at me. He pointed to a corner opposite us. "Do you fancy that one?"

There were two women there, girls really, standing against the flat air, talking quietly to each other. "They've got pretty-looking whores in Paris, I'll miss them. Never mind. Mordecai, I fancy the little blonde. A bit tarted up, but you can see by her mouth . . . You can always tell by a woman's mouth, did you know that? Never wrong." He said this last with an air of finality. Slapping a few francs on the table, he grabbed my elbow and prodded me across the street. I was in no mood for it. But when Desmond's eyes grew closed, closed against his heart, I found him strangely hard to refuse.

The girls were from the country, by Reims, but they had been in Paris several years. The small blonde was named Marcelle. After she and McConnell had fixed a price, she moved very close to him, as if she were a piece of apparel. He was a little distant with her, and I could tell she found this frustrating. She let her breast brush against his arm, but he showed no reaction, and continued talking to her politely, just as if they were at the opera.

My girl had red-brown hair, a hat, and thin, pale cheeks. They took us back to their rooms on the Rue Mazarine. I let my girl—Barbara, that was her name—how odd that I remember their names!—I let my girl caress me, efficiently and thoughtfully. I watched her hands and her thin cheeks, but all the time I listened to McConnell, on the other side of the thin wall that separated us. In those days, in those places . . . you could hear everything. Marcelle had begun to moan, in a practiced way, and to make small, professional cries, almost like the yips of a little dog. Then the sound changed; it became a shallow, heaving breath. My girl stopped, mesmerized; she had never heard this sound from her friend. Where before I was bored, I began to burn under my whore's touch, her lips and hands rippled around me, lighting my quiet ache into fire. I touched the perspiration on her pale forehead, and traced my wet finger around the moving O of her mouth.

In the room beyond ours, Marcelle was thrashing on the bed, and small, maddened sobs clashed with words in her throat. I pictured her, splayed out, and severed beneath him, reduced by him, her limbs spread and welcoming, the sweat streaming on her warm breasts . . . Perhaps she clutched at his back and clawed him, clawed at the red tiger on his arm, and bit, enraged and lost, against its fiery mouth. She groaned a little, then, urgently, and from deep inside; and at last I heard McConnell's breath, full and heated, moving between their sliding bodies, flying into her, and ending.

Barbara quivered at this sound, and grabbed desperately for my hand, until I found her, wet and sleek, wanton, like a queen. I heard my own cries, faint, beginning, as the girl slid and pressed against my fingers, bursting at last with a glorious, reeling shudder. At once I heard the other girl — one last, ravening cry that mingled with my own, and with the ancient sound of McConnell's quieting breath.

On Tuesday he was gone. He'd left me a note, which read, "Mordecai — Hate good-byes. Will write — Desmond."

I did not have the courage to discuss it with Lemaître, or with Alyce.

One day, a few weeks after McConnell had gone, I went into the back room and found Alyce sitting alone. She'd been crying, and her head was still bowed between her hands. Her black curls tumbled over her fingers, and she hid her eyes. Beside her were a small bowl of ruby pumice, and a few cracked pearls. I touched her shoulder, very lightly, and she looked up at me. Her green eyes were shining.

"He's not coming back, is he, Mordecai?" She looked like a child, innocent and astonished.

I sat down beside her, and looked at her small hands. The palms were wet from her crying. "No, I don't suppose so."

I saw the helplessness in her, then; the animal bewilderment. For just a moment I hated McConnell, as one would hate a monster.

"It's a secret, Mordecai. A secret that everybody probably knows." She shook her head, and the pretty curls brushed against her cheeks. Some strands of black hair caught in the wet streaks on her face.

"Mordecai." She looked away from me as she spoke. "I always felt undressed next to him. And I couldn't stand near him in a room without seeing his naked body, his chest, his legs. When we sat together, looking at the pearls, of course we didn't speak. But I could hear him breathing next to me, a low, relaxed sound . . . and then I remembered his breath as he slept, and the warm feel of his skin. I could sense the air between us, as if it were alive. I always knew when he stood behind me in a room, the air was always thick between us . . . I always wondered if the old man knew. Do you think he did?"

"I don't know what he knows."

"Mordecai, I've lost myself. Do you know what that means? I must find myself again. I surrendered because — it was like a force of nature, it was like eating when you're hungry. I never felt" — and here she faltered, as if the words were going to hurt her — "I never felt so like a woman as I did with him. I was only a girl before. But it made me a whore to him, Mordecai. And nothing more."

I touched my fingers to her soft, red mouth to stop her, but she had finished speaking. I lifted her face, so that she would meet my gaze. "No. Something more."

She looked up at me, her eyes bright. "He has a lock of my hair. I gave it to him when he left." She paused then, her shoulders sagging. "He didn't kiss me good-bye. Not even that."

"No. Alyce. If you can ever come to understand . . . That's your work." I took this woman in my arms, as McConnell had taken her, and for a moment I felt the trembling in her as if it were my own. When she finished crying she pulled herself away, and I knew we would never speak about it again.

As for Lemaître, the old man said nothing, and for a while I didn't like to look into those eyes—I hated to see sadness there. Weeks passed, and then months, and there was no word from Desmond. I sat alone in cafés at night, drinking. One morning Lemaître approached me as I was cleaning some files.

"Monsieur van Velsen, *le voilà*." He looked happy, and relieved, as he reached into his pocket and handed me an envelope. It was from Ceylon. It read:

Mordecai,

It's been a bit rough here. But it's magnificent as well. I can't describe it. I'm keeping a diary. One day you'll read it all. I've got to go back to Dublin for a bit, and raise some money. I've got a plan to make a big fortune here in Ceylon —you can still get in on it with me if you like. When it's all done I'll come back to Paris. Give my best to old Lemaître. Tell him I've got some fine pearls to bring him. I'll bring you something too.

Your,
Desmond

That was the only letter I ever had from Desmond. A package came seven months later, from Ceylon, but without even a note. Inside were two small sacks. On one was written "For Père Lemaître, from the Ceylon Sea." It contained seven black pearls. Black pearls of this quality were such a rarity, and worth such a fortune, that I cannot tell you. The other sack had my name written on it, and the words "from the Dublin Sea." It contained a single, pale blue pearl. Lemaître and I stared quietly at these treasures, until finally the old man spoke.

"He is a good man, Monsieur McConnell, *il a un bon coeur*, but I am afraid for him. He ran from this"—Lemaître tapped his heart—"but it is always trapped inside us, *n'est-çe pas?* Where will he go?"

I didn't know what to say, and I looked down at the pale

blue orb in my palm. Lemaître looked at me gravely, then he touched the pearl lightly. "Wait, Monsieur van Velsen, be able to wait. *Vous comprenez? Soyez sage avec elle.* Beautiful as she is, there is more inside. Do not be impatient for her. There is, how do you say? A transformation to be done. Wait until you are very good to open her. *Et maintenant . . . Vous avez faim? Moi, j'ai une grande envie de manger.* Have I told you about Lanval's new bistro? No? Well, then . . ." And that was the last time we spoke of Desmond.

I tried to reach him many times, I tried to write to him at his return address in Ceylon, to trace his whereabouts in Ireland, but it was useless. There were rumors, later, that McConnell had disappeared at sea. I suppose it was true, though I hate to think so. Sometimes I wonder, still, if I'll hear his knock at the door. If I'll see those blue eyes again . . .

The last time I saw Lemaître he was sitting at his kitchen table. It was morning, not long after Desmond's pearls had arrived, and the sun was streaming in. He drank his coffee out of a big blue bowl, and a plate sat on the table, heaped with brioches and golden croissants. Fresh butter and a pot of jam sat next to it. Lemaître beamed at me.

"You must eat, Mordecai! *Il faut manger!*"

He made me coffee, and we sat quietly together, like two little boys, heaping our croissants with butter and jam. Lemaître smiled, and broke the silence.

"Mordecai, I must tell you"—he tapped his chest—"my heart is not well. Very old, *tu comprends?* I'm going away to my sister's until the end. No, no, no—*ça va!* I can go because you're ready to see—I waited for you . . . *Viens avec moi.* Come. Besides"—he turned and smiled—"you have taught me English very well."

We walked into the attic, where he showed me a little box.

"Inside is a pearl worth half a million francs. I believe there is another inside it worth twice that. It belongs to Mademoiselle Bellecoeur, and has been in her family for generations, so of

course it is a great risk. I'm too old, and of course, my heart"
—again he tapped his chest. "But you, you are in fine health.
Come, let us sit together and see what we can see."

I took my usual seat, and prepared to observe Mademoiselle
Bellecoeur's pearl. But Lemaître took the jewel and placed
it in the center of my palm, curling my fingers around it. I
was so surprised at this uncharacteristic gesture that at first I
didn't notice that he rested his right hand on the top of my
head.

"Think of the sun and the moon, Monsieur van Velsen. Think
of how big they are. Think of how big the universe is, and
when you want to stop thinking about it, keep on. When I was
a child, I thought of it often—most adults give up thinking
about it. When the stars end, the sky goes on and on."

As he spoke, he let his hand rest lightly on top of my head,
and a curious feeling began inside of me. A warmth suffused
me, a fire inside—I swear to you, a small bead of sweat broke
out on every pore in my body.

"Are you warm, Mordecai?" he asked me. "Yes, I think so.
Close your eyes, and think of the sun inside you. That's right.
When you have the sun inside you, think of the little moon in
your hand."

At that moment, I saw, like a picture inside my head—I saw
the little pearl, and I saw concentric layers inside it, like an
onion. I saw where the glow was brightest—two millimeters
in. When I opened my eyes, Lemaître was gone. He had closed
the door behind him, and left his own set of carving tools on
the table. None of us students had ever been permitted to use
them.

I cut her, and she was perfect inside. I made a small fortune
that morning, and I made my reputation. I never saw Lemaître
again. He went by train to his sister's, and died within the
week. He left me those tools—you've never seen them before,
have you? These blades and files, this little scale, and an ivory
bowl for the pumice—look here, they're very beautiful, very
old—this file has a jade handle.

After that, I could always see into the heart of a pearl. But it never made my work dull—the process is difficult, and it calls for constant attention, and, if I may say it, love. I have always fallen more and more in love with their beauty, and with the mysteries I see inside of them. There is only one pearl I have come across that I could not see inside, and that is the Moon of the Celebes. Sometimes, where our passions rise highest, our sight is obscured. That must be the case, for there is no other explanation.

My career as a pearl doctor was dazzling. You know all these stories, too, the stories of my years of glory. I will not repeat them.

During this time, Leo was building an empire, importing diamonds and rubies and emeralds. He had developed a magnificent reputation for his bravery, his dash, and his exploits with women. He had fathered half a dozen bastards, one of whom, of course, was to become your father. It's a shame you never knew him.

In 1923, Leo fell in love. He met the girl in London, at a society affair. Her family were Hungarian aristocrats who had left their native land with their jewels and begun a highly profitable retail gem business on South Moulton Street. The Petófis were an important and prestigious family who, twice a year, migrated between their enormous house in Belgravia and their palazzo in Venice. They relished the idea of marrying their daughter to a flamboyant adventurer, provided he was as wealthy and desirable a suitor as your grandfather. I believe Maria's own father—that was her name, Maria—had once had a few experiences of his own on the dark continent. What's more, it seemed to be a sensible liaison—it was business, wasn't it? The family could acquire superb stones, and Leo would see his conquests—that's what he called his gems—pass into the hands of European gentry. It was a fine arrangement for everybody. But Lily, you must not misunderstand me—there was nothing mercenary in Leo's intentions—he was enchanted by his bride. That really is the word. He had been, as I have said, a playboy — the very picture of a man who was loved by women but did not stop to love. He had never loved before, and it touched him as it would have a child, receiving a toy more beautiful than he had ever dreamed existed. He was young again, foolish and shy when he spoke of her. The other men in our circle often ribbed him — it was an easy game to make Leo blush, just by saying her name. I never made light of it, I never spoke of it. And so it was to me he turned, to speak of her.

He was a virile, dashing man — he was not an articulate one. He tried, in his crude way, to speak of her charms, of her graces. There was an awkward poetry in these expressions, these reveries. We sat at our club, over our cigars and brandies, and I watched, full of wonder, as his eyes took on a distant look that only came when he talked of the greatest, most faraway diamonds, the most dangerous obstacles and triumphs. He spoke of her then, of the things she said, the clothes she wore, the sound of her laughter. You cannot imagine the strangeness of it, the incongruity, from my brother's lips.

He spoke of her beauty, also. In time, out of his halting words, I formed a picture of her in all her loveliness. I listened to him. He was feeling rapture for the first time in his life. He asked me, one murky London afternoon, as we toasted our feet at a blazing hearth and drank our ales, to come to Venice with him. He wanted me to meet her, of course — I was his brother and his best friend — but, in a moment of awkwardness, he hardly knew how to ask me. It was good business, he announced, for me to meet her family — they wanted to invest in some superior pearls. As a nervous aside, he burst out, "And you can meet Maria! There's going to be a ball, and then a dinner for us — we're engaged!"

I knew my brother, so I only nodded. These balls were dreary affairs; one was often invited to them. But it was to please your grandfather, and I would not have disappointed him for the world. He said nothing more about it, he loudly called for two more beers, and he began to discuss his plans for dispatching the latest batch of lapis from India.

It was three weeks later, at a palazzo on the Grand Canal, that I first saw her.

She was waltzing, beneath a vast glass chandelier, the crystal beads falling like drops of light into the center of that great room. She whirled in the midst of hundreds of creatures who spun, swathed in a thousand colors and rays of light — but I saw only one soul. It was Maria, in an azure gown, cascades of chiffon and a violent light in her hair. She was dancing with a tall, stern man, he held her as one would a piece of precious porcelain. There was a glow that issued from her. She was not the most beautiful woman in the room, or the most fashionable. But she had an incandescence, such as one rarely sees. I wanted to step inside of her, to inhabit that light, to burn, to glow. If darkness needs radiance, so does brightness need shadows.

Your grandfather stared proudly and pointed, saying, "Do you see that pretty girl in the blue dress? That's her." Bulging with pride, half a child and half a man, Leo waited until the dancers had stopped. He whisked me through the opulent crowd to his fiancée's side, dismissing her partner with a military nod.

"May I present," he said, "my brother Mordecai, of whom I have spoken so frequently?" He addressed her with an odd formality, as if he was afraid to break some fragile shell that encased her.

Her eyes met mine briefly, held them for a swift spell, and lighted on my brother's face.

"It's a pleasure," she said to him, and to me, averting her eyes. "I have heard so much about you."

The strains of the next waltz had begun, and fairly glowing with pride, Leo insisted we dance together. I slipped my arm around her tiny waist, and took her hand in mine. Her hand was very small, and the fingers very fine. A single Tanganyika diamond glowed balefully on her left hand — Leo had given her the Ehrlich as an engagement ring. It was a diamond with a certain history, and what it cost him, I could scarcely imagine. I wondered that he had not given her a stone from our own collection — after all, he had hunted, and I had cut, some of the finest in the world! But when I saw the Ehrlich on her finger, I realized what he had been thinking. Truly, nothing less would have done for her.

We waltzed quite formally. Her eyes were set somewhere distant, far from me, and I, I gazed upon her honey hair, swept up and back with an emerald-studded comb. Occasionally, she turned her face to mine — her eyes were solemn, but she smiled with a brilliance such as I had rarely seen. She was very, very light. I felt, at times, that I was dancing with light in my hands. And she seemed to bend to me, to ache to me, even, following my every move with a thoroughbred grace.

I don't know how many dances we danced. On and on, light and air in my arms, the gauzy feel of blue chiffon and her honey scent. In time she bent her long neck, and rested her apricot hair on my shoulder. I saw its strands wisping away from the gleaming emerald comb, like runaway animals escaping from a trap.

Leo was dancing with the many women present who demanded his favors, a number of them former conquests. He was gracious and elegant, in his stiff way, and he beamed and smiled and nodded in our direction, urging me to go on dancing with Maria.

When it was nearly time for the last dance, I steered her toward him, and making a show of interest in his partner, I let the warm light of Maria slip through my hands. As I released her she started, as if waking out of a narcotic spell, and shook her head with a quick jerk. The emerald comb came undone, and tumbled to the ground. Leo bent to retrieve it, while her amber hair split down around her shoulders. Untamed, she cast me a sudden fierce look, eyes wild and vicious. And then, all was decorum, the comb restored, the last dance begun, Maria in my brother's arms and my partner in mine.

I could hardly tolerate my desire to ravish her. I had never thought of violence as a part of my nature, and I despised it. Perhaps my urges to conquer and rend were no more than some vestigial brute impulse that lingers around love, and hovers around lust. But from that moment, when I released her beneath the crystal chandelier, and watched Maria in my brother's arms, morality ceased to guide me. From that moment on, I had no code. I was an arrow shot from a quiver — the quiver was desire, the arrow the sheer force of my will. I did not truly understand why I wanted her, or whom I loved, or what limits I could possibly place on the urgency of my desire. Don't look at me like that, Lily. I despise pity. I wish to be loathed, not to be understood, and it is all that I deserved, for what I was about to do.

And besides, what is a person in love, in our century? A curiosity, a kind of circus freak. The victim of a tedious and stupid disorder. Everyone wants to cure him — with psychotherapy, meditation, and worst of all, good advice — people rush to bludgeon him with common sense. His state is a pitiable one, and we laugh or shake our heads behind his back. Bodies join without the slightest remorse on the part of their owners, bacchanalian ruttings, ending in little spasms . . . For example, if two friends meet, and one says he cannot control his urge to promiscuity, he is treated with a sympathetic nod, a cluck, and a few homely words of advice about social diseases. And if the same friend says that he cannot make love to anyone but the woman he adores, and she will not have him! Or that he loves hopelessly, from afar, that many months are passing, and the image of the beloved aches within him — let that friend speak, and he will be greeted with worry, perhaps disdain, and treated as the victim of a hysterical illness. Nothing hurts the lover so much as the fatuous pity of the "healthy" man — "What, aren't you over it yet?" "Her, still? She isn't worth it." "You can do much better. Wait until you really fall in love." Or that most vicious of slurs, "There are plenty of fish in the sea."

We lovers, we are the misfits, the old-fashioneds, the neurotics who do not heal apace. No one tells us how long we are free to yearn and mourn, but we are always over the limit.

For a moment, I stood on a precipice. I excused myself to my bewildered partner, in the middle of the dance. I went and stood on the balcony and watched the ripple of the gondolas on the canal. I seemed to see Maria's comb in the peaks of the water. I looked away from it, up at the sky. But only the moon hung there, a fat, reproachful moon.

I felt a hand clap me hard on the back. It was Leo. He looked at me with satisfaction. He was very drunk.

"Come on, then," he crowed. "We're all of us going round to Harry's Bar—a big party, big party. Come on."

Leo pulled at my elbow, and in the space of half an hour I was seated at his side in the midst of a drunken, joyous bustle. Maria sat on the other side of him. Our table stretched from one end of the room to the other—there were jewel dealers and traders, society women, financiers, and artists. A contessa sat at my other side, and leaned close to me. A smell of scent rose from between her breasts and her hand brushed against my thigh. It irritated me as if an insect had intruded upon me.

The waiters brought us plump green figs, draped with translucent slices of prosciutto. I loved this dish, but I couldn't eat it. Maria and I did not look at each other. Leo filled my glass again and again, and I drank, but nothing soothed me. It gave me no relief. The meal went on and on—grilled sole from the Adriatic Sea, steaming fresh pasta, and thick slabs of osso buco. I pretended to eat. The contessa, discouraged, now left me alone with my thoughts. Everyone chattered madly. I pretended to speak. At the end of the meal, we were served sweet mounds of zabaglione, and dark little cups of espresso. Liqueurs and brandy made their appearance, and there was more champagne for the ladies.

The conversation at the table was full of scandal. Women rolled venom in their mouths like delicious candies, and men bragged of their conquests in business and in love. The guests lost their decorum in bottle after bottle of wine. I stole the odd look at Maria. She was always engaged in a conversation. She too pretended to eat. The talk turned to politics, and finally to jewels. There was a mine in South Africa that was being worked for diamonds, and rubies had been discovered on the Mississippi River.

The Duke of Argyll, well lubricated with drink, allowed that he wanted something very fine for his mistress — he was going to propose, and he wanted a superior ring.

Leo turned to me and said, too loudly, "Well, Mordecai, what do you say? The Paxton ruby would do nicely."

"I think the Nepalese sapphire would do better," I replied. "You can show it to the Duke next week."

"No, Mordecai. The ruby. That's a beautiful stone. It's one of the best you cut for me. It's grades above the sapphire, and you know it." He kicked me under the table. The ruby would fetch far more.

I looked at the timid face of the Duke. "The sapphire."

Leo filled his glass and stared at me. Then he addressed the table at large.

"My brother is superstitious." He belched loudly, and excused himself. "He is. The Paxton ruby has a curse on it, though I don't know why people call it a curse at all. Do you know what it is? That its owner should get his heart's desire. I call that a blessing! I've got mine," he said, and squeezed Maria.

The whole table laughed, and fell to telling tales of curses. Maria and I did not laugh; we looked at each other for the first time since our dance.

Leo went on. "Mordecai, why not? Why shouldn't the Duke have what he desires? And shouldn't we all?"

"In my opinion," I replied, "that is a very dangerous curse."

Leo just guffawed loudly, and called for more brandy. He was dangerously drunk, and perhaps the wine was affecting me, too. A sharp pain had begun to gnaw at my temples.

Maria's father proposed a toast. A toast to the bride and

groom! Leo glowed with pride, and took his fiancée's hand. He handled her cautiously, as if she were made of glass. As she turned to look up at her father, I saw her tensed scapulae. A few strands of her hair escaped from their comb.

"Speaking of curses," he began, "and of blessings . . ." He, too, was terribly drunk. "My lovely daughter," he continued. "Yes, she is lovely. And I want to give her the loveliest jewels, the loveliest and the *rarest* . . . Everyone present who is in the profession knows what I speak of. There is no greater mystery in all the world of gems, and since there is no greater mystery than woman, it is fitting that I should give to my daughter, on this, her great day—" He nudged Louis van der Hofstra, the great Dutch banker who dozed at his side. The old man started, received a few whispered words from Maria's father, and fished from his pocket a small blue velvet box. "The Moon of the Celebes!" he continued triumphantly.

There were gasps and murmurs. The guests had not suspected it—no one believed he could ever part with it. Maria's eyes were hooded, I could not fathom them. Leo was frankly astounded. His mouth dropped open, below his mustache, and he bit his lower lip.

Maria's father was pleased at the effect. "Yes, it is truly the thing. You all know the story of it. Its twin was carved by that great master, Lamer. After the tragedies attendant upon that cutting . . ." He paused here, but we all faced the horrible images, they were well known in the trade. "After all that, no one wanted to carve its brother. I think it's foolishness. I don't believe in curses, and I have not raised my children to be superstitious. This lovely pearl will be hers, one day Europe's finest pearl doctor will carve it for her, it will stay in the family forever!"

He opened the blue box and placed it in his palm, which he held out before the assemblage. Everyone arced their necks, and clamored around the ugly gray blister.

Maria and Leo received the box. Leo seemed afraid to touch

it. For all the fabulous jewels he had handled, none represented a greater risk, or a greater potential sum of money. Maria had no such hesitation. She lifted it from its soft bed, ran her fingers over it, and pressed its cool skin to her cheek.

"Thank you, Father," she said, and kissed him. The box was returned to van der Hofstra's pocket for safekeeping, and the party continued.

At the end of the feast, Leo was bright with his triumph. Glowing with the knowledge of the jewel that was to be his, the bride that was to be his, the life in society he had always wanted, he accepted his prospective father-in-law's invitation to take brandies with him and a few of the elder gentlemen at Florian's. Stumbling a little, still red with drink and excitement, he asked me if I would take Maria for a gondola ride — he had meant to do it, she so wanted to see Venice at night, and now he had this damned familial obligation. Well, he paused, teetering a little, it wasn't so damned now, was it? There was, after all, a fat future in it, he was beginning to see that. And plenty of time later to show Maria the city's lights. He winked a little too broadly. I did not like my brother when he was this drunk. So would I, then? Yes, of course.

The gondola floated through eerie canals, the gondolier shouting his "Aoy!" in the strange dialect of that city, until we were lost in arcs and shadows of light. Maria seemed strangely calm, as if umbraed Venice, with its dark passages, was something already familiar to her.

"Do you love this city?" she asked me. "I understand you know it."

"I know it very well. It's not that I love it as much as I require it. If I go too long without seeing it . . ."

"Ah, of course," she replied, and smiled at me for the first time.

It was a smile so brilliant . . . Lily, do you know how we starve to speak our own languages? Most people babble, or rant, or dabble with their words, expecting to be understood, irritated if they're not, or oblivious. I always knew, always, that I spoke alone, to no one, in a tongue of my own devising. But to be understood, and to see in her smile that I truly was . . . It was the one dream I never dreamed, the only dream that hurt me too much to have.

I could face sorrows, and losses, and disappointments — I'd borne a great many, in my life. But never that one, I never let myself hope for it. I knew with a terrible certainty that I'd die hearing my own voice, that I would die without having been *known*. That Maria understood, her smile and solemn nod, broke the ice of centuries inside me, I felt something crumble.

Like many men, I looked for fatal moments, for points reached that are heights or desolations. Now I stood at an exquisite cliff, with a view to the heavens and down to hell. I felt myself sinking and falling for an endless time; I felt myself flying. Something died inside of me, Lily. Solitude died. I had reconciled to solitude, I did not regret it. And now I had lost it. She had entered into my world, with her luminous eyes, and I was lost forever. I looked at those eyes, at the way she gazed at the quivering oar, the silken, dirty water, the bricks and stones of that grave, magical city.

She did not turn to me when she spoke. "I have never required anything, actually. I have always wanted to."

She looked down at her gloved hands, at the fur that lay against her wrists. There was a shaking, a trembling, at the edge of her lips. Her eyes were tearless, but the strength it required to keep them on her hands was enormous. She could barely speak. When she turned to face me, those eyes were incandescent, hypnotic.

"I think," she said softly, "that at last I do require something."

"Maria" — I bent to her — "Maria, I am no friend to you. I'm in love with you — at least."

I bent to those lips, my draught. Her kiss felt like a brand. And then I took her small hand in both of mine, and I pressed it to my heart.

The moonlight hung on the water of the Grand Canal, which lapped at the stones of the *calle*. Little bits of seaweed floated among the specks of light.

I called to the gondolier to stop, slipped a wadded bill into the Venetian's palm, and lifted Maria out onto the wet stones of the *calle*. Taking her hand, I led her to the steps of the Academia Bridge. It was a great, bright moon that hung in a murky sky, and we watched it as we walked. I heard the gentle rustle of Maria's gown as we left the slick pavement behind us and ascended the steps. We did not look at each other: we watched the moon. At the top of the bridge, we looked out over the magnificent snake of water splayed before us, the writhing canal.

"I want to give you all the water in the world, all the seas, and every heavy cloud, and this canal . . ." I told her.

She laughed. Her laughter bit the air, and her breath made puffs in the night. I could tell she was flushed.

"Maria," I said. I barely knew my voice, there was a foreign sound between my lips. "Maria, stay with me."

"Leo is going away tomorrow, on business. I'll come in the early evening." She curled her hands deeper into her stole, her fingertips touching inside it. It was very cold.

"I'll take you home now. It's late; your mother will be worrying."

"Yes." She finally turned to look at me, pulling her gaze from the arcing canal. "I'll call for you at the Danieli. At six."

She arched her head a little, like an innocent animal waiting to be struck. I closed my hot eyes, and pressed them to her neck. I felt the pulse of her throat against my eyelids.

When I was alone again, at my hotel, I stood and stared out over the water. From the balcony of the Danieli, I gazed at a glimmer of dawn that shimmered in the sky over San Georgio Island. A few vendors hauled carts in the hazy dark, and from somewhere I smelled coffee. I didn't sleep. I told the concierge that I would receive no one, and I tried to rest, but phantoms came into my dreams. Phantoms with white necks and wrists lined with fur.

Leo arrived at 1:00 the following day. Over the protests of the concierge, he barged into my room, and his big laugh filled the dark chamber.

"Got a head on you, have you, Mordecai? We'll soon fix that!" He was waving a bottle of Prosecco. "Come on, lad, have a drink!"

He babbled about his success of the night before—the commissions that would be his, and ours, the worlds of money and prestige that would open to us. In the middle of his diatribe he looked at me strangely.

"I say, Mordecai, you do look peaky." He glared at me disapprovingly, and pressed another glass of wine on me. "I ought to look after you, but I've got to go to Salzburg in three hours, you know. Maria's staying on a day or two, to be with her family. Look after her, will you? And I'll see you this weekend at the club."

It was the week before the wedding, which was Sunday next. That night, I met Maria. I took her to dinner at a tiny restaurant on the Giudecca, where no one knew us, and then I took her waltzing in the Piazza. Orchestras used to play there, and the great square swelled with music. I spun her around, her feet tapping the stones, and the crush of happy couples was all around us. We stopped for a *grappa*, and we danced again. I hoped that dawn would come and we would be spared the true taste of each other. We could still escape.

In the end, I decided to take her to a little hotel on the Riva dei Assasinni, where I knew the concierge. We walked, like dreamers, past a little *campo* with its few lingering patrons. Very close to our destination, I felt a hand reach for my elbow. It was van der Hofstra, the Dutch banker.

"Ah, children!" he exulted. He was thick with wine. "Where are you going at this hour? Ah, it's the lovely Maria! The jewel of Venezia! Where are you going?"

"Mordecai is showing me the little *calles* of Venice. To see how the Venetians live, to get away from the Piazza for a bit . . ."

Van der Hofstra tugged fretfully at my sleeve. "Have a *grappa* with me!" He turned to Maria. "I've just left your father. We discussed the wedding — it's only a few days away, isn't it, my dear? Ah, you must be a nervous bride. I remember the eve of my wedding, my wife . . ."

We stood in the cold, in the little *campo*, while van der Hofstra told us about the bride's nerves, his own fears and anticipations.

"The woman," he said, guiding us forcefully toward the table of a café, "is all nervousness and fear, her blood has not yet awakened. The man is a conquering hero, who knows he will be the first to storm the fortress. And yet he is a little sad — he knows he must give up worldly pleasures for this greater love." He winked at me broadly, alluding to Leo's reputation. He appeared to have forgotten Maria's presence. "For a man to have a ruined bride . . ." He gave a disapproving little cluck, shook his head, then hailed a passing waiter and ordered a round of *grappas*. "A tragedy," van der Hofstra concluded. He seemed to awaken again to Maria's presence, and he cluck-clucked once more, annoyed with himself.

"But never mind this masculine babble, my dear. I have something to say that will interest you, that I shouldn't be telling you, really I shouldn't. I promised not to speak a word of it, but — Venice, the night . . . I have just come from your father. We dined at Harry's Bar, on those little tortellini. They were stuffed with a ricotta cheese, I think, and — yes, your father. We discussed your fiancé's prospects — and allow me to say, my dear, that with your father's firm hand to guide him, and the support of my own company, your husband will become one of the richest men in Europe. I have little reason to doubt it. We have certain plans, the working capital can be doubled in no time at all. Leo is already well known for his courage; now he will add immense fortune to the crown in which he wears his fame!" Enormously satisfied with this last metaphor, van der Hofstra lapsed into silence. We drank our *grappas* hurriedly, I cast about for a way to leave.

Licking his lower lip, the portly banker began his last salvo. "It's like this. Your father, that esteemed man, your father, is going to leave his business to Leo—not on his deathbed, but now! He's going to retire, to take the waters . . ." He waved his hand vaguely at the waters. "Leo will begin running the office in London, immediately, and you, Mordecai—but I imagine you will run the international operations." He turned to Maria once more. "The pearl, the great pearl . . . it was just the beginning. You will live like a queen. There's nothing you could dream of that you won't have. Tell me, tell me, my dear, what it is that you want most in the world, that you secretly long for—I'll tell you it's yours!"

I pulled Maria away from this terrible display of intimacy. I helped her out of her seat and bowed to van der Hofstra.

"I promised to show Miss Petófi a statue of San Marco. You will excuse us."

We rose, but the besotted Dutchman rose with us, throwing a few thousand lire on the table, and nearly upsetting his chair.

"I'll join you! I love a walk at dawn! In Holland . . ."

He waddled with us to the door of Maria's palazzo. He wanted to see her in, but I said, "No, excuse us, please, I have something to discuss with Miss Petófi. It concerns a surprise for my brother. It's a private matter."

He left us at last. I pulled her into a nearby doorway. I took her in my arms, I felt the warmth of her hips beneath her gown. Running my fingers through her hair, I held her head in my hands, trying to crush her smell between my fingers, to take it away with me. Lifting her up to bring her face level with mine, I kissed her throat, then her breasts. She struggled a little against me, and I heard her stockings tear as they scratched against stone. Tears made shining stains on her cheeks.

"We'll go away," I whispered, into her white neck. "Come away."

"My boat leaves in a few hours, I must catch the train. My mother, she'll be up in an hour. And my sisters are waiting in London, I . . ." The tears were catching in her eyelids, fireflies in a net. They wet the bodice of her gown, staining the silk.

"Meet me, meet me Sunday morning, very early, at Saint Mary's church, I'll be there," Maria said. She ripped at the necklace around her neck. A small ivory bird hung on a chain. Yanking hard at it, she broke the chain and pressed the girlish charm into my hand.

"Sunday," she whispered, and turned and ran into the palazzo.

I stayed in Venice as long as I could—I only had two days before I had to return to London for Leo's bachelor party on Saturday. The wedding would take place the following afternoon.

I rested a little, drinking cappuccinos in the chilly mornings and walking on the Lido beach, empty of tourists. At night I ate alone, declining all social engagements and invitations, pleading preoccupation with business matters. The cliché of a lover, I saw Maria everywhere; I smelled her and tasted her. I slept badly, though I had always been a sound sleeper. Are you surprised, Lily? There was a time when sleep came to me . . . but now I saw shades and had restless dreams.

On the train to London, I read the papers. The society pages announced that the best hotels were bulging with the wedding guests. It was said that the most beautiful women in the world were there for the occasion, but that the most beautiful one of all was the bride. I arrived just in time to dress and rush to the dinner in Leo's honor.

It was held at the Café Royale. I'd hardly seen anything to equal it in opulence and splendor. We took the entire restaurant, it was the bachelor party of the season. Champagne flowed into every glass, we ate oysters, and Leo's favorite dish, game pies. The men ate and drank and laughed and roared and swapped wild lies. The absence of ladies was painfully felt, as the hours passed, but of course, all that had been arranged for. At midnight, we piled into cabs and made our way to Madame Eleanora's, London's finest brothel.

Such girls! Little tarts to suit some tastes, and the most soignée for others. I dandled a cream-colored girl on my knee, and tried to appear as occupied as the rest of the revelers. Now and then one of the fellows noticed my lack of progress, and the wench in my lap teased and coaxed me, but I blamed my clumsiness and impotence on the liquor. The debauch went on all night, and there were entertainments from the ladies to revive flagging spirits. I pretended to drink, but after a time gave up even pretending to fondle the girls—they wrote me off for a poof and amused the other men. I slipped out without being noticed, and as I left the house, I caught a sight of Leo in a vast armchair, his head thrown back in transport, one hand buried between the thighs of a cocoa-skinned tart, his lips at the breast of another, and a third, her own eyes half closed in bliss, writhing astride him, while his fingers kneaded rhythmically at her hips.

The next morning, the day of the wedding, Leo and I lay in a Turkish bath, wrapped in hot towels. We quietly sipped at our ales, with eggs cracked in them. Leo spoke first.

"You know, Mordecai . . . You know, I've never had her. What do you think of that?"

"I quite understand."

"You do? Then explain it to me. I could have, I imagine. She's a very modern girl. I know how it is with aristocratic women. The odd thing is, *I* never tried. Isn't that a funny thing?"

"I suppose."

"It's something about her, about wanting to make it special. Different. She's a virgin, you know." He shook his head, and damp drops flew off his mustache. His chest was wet with steam.

"Don't take me wrong!" he added hastily. "It's not for want

of desire. That bosom! And that waist — Have you noticed? Well, every man in London has noticed! Many's the time when I've been off on my travels, and it's put me in a hell of a condition to think of it. But when I'm with her . . . It's rather odd, actually," he finished lamely. He didn't seem the slightest bit repentant about the previous night.

I stood up. "Don't you think we should be going? You've got a lot to do today, I expect."

"Oh, not so much, really. It's the busybody women that are flapping about!" He seemed reluctant to let me go, and I began to wonder if he wasn't just a bit afraid of Maria. But Leo wasn't afraid of anything. I don't know if I could recognize fear in him at all. But it was some foreign emotion, playing in his eyes.

I clapped him on the back.

"Wedding jitters, old man!" I said. He smiled up at me, his eyes full of simple trust.

Maria had asked for an hour to be alone before the wedding. She told her mother that she wanted to pray. This announcement caused considerable surprise among the wedding party, and they whispered among themselves.

"How thoroughly unlike Maria! I've never heard her say such a thing before."

"Perhaps Leo has been talking to her."

"Leo! He isn't exactly a religious man!"

"Well, perhaps he is now, to please her father."

Maria made her instructions clear — she was not to be disturbed. She would walk, and find an empty church.

She waited for me in a pew at the back. I came up beside her, and touched her hair. She wore a small hat with a veil.

"There's a little room here, off the side," she whispered.

I followed her, mute, watching the honey of her hair trapped in pins, and the long white neck beneath. The room was tiny and bare, it had once been a monk's cell. I grabbed her by the shoulders, a little roughly. She swayed slightly, and seemed to totter backward. I caught her, and lowered her to a rough bench. Kneeling beside her, I pressed my mouth to the cleft between her breasts: her heart was inside. I loosed the bodice of her suit, she shivered as my hair brushed her nipples.

I meant to be very gentle with her . . . I meant to try. After all—but she pulled me to her savagely, whispering words that dripped into my ear like lava.

Maybe it wasn't so much blood. But it seemed . . . afterward, she licked it off my fingers, and kissed her own hot blood from my lips.

"Darling," she whispered, "if I die—"

"Hush."

"But if I do, I'll come and be with you. I don't believe in a god, but—if we have immortal souls, I'll consign mine to you. I'll never leave you alone."

A breeze was blowing into the church, extinguishing the lights from the altar. We could smell the wax of the candles. It was as if I felt her hot animal heart pumping wildly in my own body.

"Promise me, then."

"What? Promise you what?"

"That you'll accept my soul. That you want it."

"Oh dear God." I brushed at the blood and tears on my face. "But I already have it."

"Yes," she said, and her fingers clutched hard at my hair.

After the wedding I saw Maria very often. We arranged places to meet—my flat, the odd hotel, sometimes we just walked the streets of London together. But I always felt a raw hunger when I was beside her, that never subsided until I had possessed her. She seemed to feel it too, and the days we tried to spend together without making love were strained and unnatural. Sometimes I wanted to cut off the finger that wore the little gold band. I wanted to mark her, too, by biting her, or leaving bruises on her thighs. I never had the courage to ask her about Leo. But my imagination made me ill. I was poisoned with the image of him pressing between her legs, turning her doe's body this way and that. Or I imagined her like the silky whore of Madame Eleanora's brothel, sloe-eyed with pleasure, head thrown back, as his big hands kneaded her burning flesh.

One day while making love, I was seized by this vision. In my rage, I slapped her across the face, as she quivered beneath me.

"Little bitch, little whore!" I hissed, as my hand went down. Her head turned with the blow, her cheek reddened, all in the second of her spasm. She began to sob, silently at first, and then more loudly. I lay beside her a long time, holding her as she cried.

Two months passed. Two months of meetings and haunted ecstasies. I avoided Leo, gently, but he didn't seem to notice. He seemed preoccupied. I thought perhaps it was his new position in the Petófi firm, perhaps he missed his adventuring ways. Perhaps Maria's fire was burning him, too, and taking away his marrow. Lily, it's terrible to have said this, but—I had begun to feel that way about her. I wanted her so badly that my life began to shatter around me. No one noticed it at first, I kept my duties light, I declined invitations on the pretext of being preoccupied with some important pearls. It was as if she were some kind of living succubus. The more often I took her, the more often I wanted her, until we lay, damp and sick with each other. I can see her now, breathing, her hair slick against her throat, her sleek haunches trembling, the splash of amber between her thighs . . .

One day Leo knocked on the door of my office. I was working on an Irish pearl from the sea near Dublin, but I had not begun to cut it. I thought I saw a beautiful blue hue inside it, of a rare incandescence, but I could not be sure. My mind was clouded; I resigned myself to studying it. I spent long afternoons alone with it. Leo found me on one such afternoon. He had never had patience for my pearl-doctor's meditations, and ordinarily he would have interrupted me noisily. That day he slipped in quietly, and stood a little while in the room's shadows, watching the pearl. I looked up at him expectantly. I found I had little difficulty ordering my face now, it conformed to the lie as if by instinct. I had even invented the pretext of a certain elusive actress, who, I let it be known, was tiring me with her acrobatic attentions.

"Why, Leo! This is a surprise—"

"I thought we might talk. There's something I want to talk to you about."

I don't know why my blood still ran hot in my veins, but a quiet calm pervaded me. I wasn't afraid.

"Yes?"

"Oh, let's not talk here." He gestured vaguely at the room. "I don't know. It's . . . Let's get out. We'll go to Standard's," he said flatly. He looked at me directly for a moment. "It's about Maria."

I looked back into his eyes.

"But let's not talk here," he continued. "I'd like to go out."

We spoke of trivialities on the way to Standard's. It was a restaurant we had frequented often in our poorer days. We took a table in the squalid little chophouse, ordered our usual meal, as of old, and waited for our lagers. We talked disjointedly to each other, a few words about business, parties, politics. When the beer came, Leo cupped his hands around the glass.

"Do you remember when we were in South Africa?" he asked. We had been in South Africa so many times that it was an absurd question. I nodded. I already seemed to know what he meant.

"That time in South Africa when I had that trouble." The waiter brought our chops. The sight of the peas on the plate repulsed me, I didn't know how I would manage them, Lily, and my mind, my mind was intensely focused on this problem. It needn't have been. Leo never lifted his fork. It was the only time I had seen a plate grow cold in front of him. "That trouble," he was saying. "Because I had too much to drink, and nothing she did helped. It—it came back, uh, just once," he added hastily. "And this time, I hadn't even had a drink. But of course, under the circumstances it isn't surprising. And of course I'm quite over it now." He pushed his own peas around on his plate, and he seemed to have finished with his story.

"Circumstances?" I urged.

"Well, yes. You see, it's about Maria. The night of our wedding, when I tried to . . . She just said, 'Hold me, Leo. Hold me, I'm not ready.' Women, they, you know . . . Anyway, you know what her breeding is. She was in a convent for a time, of course—and after that, those finishing schools. I understood that she didn't know anything about it. She'd never been aroused, she could hardly be expected, I suppose . . ."

He coughed. "I didn't make much of it. It had been quite a day, the wedding was a spectacle, wasn't it? My God. And so the next night—it was the same. And every night after that, for two months. She would say, 'Hold me, Leo. I'll tell you when I'm ready. I just need time. I'll be ready when I've had time.' Two nights ago, I took her in my arms for, for the sixtieth time! I didn't know who to tell during all this, and all those jokes that people make! I wanted to tell you, old man, but I didn't know how. And you've seemed, I don't know, busy. The Dublin pearl is a little bitch, isn't she?" he said stupidly. I could not look up at him.

"And last night she was ready for me. And I—I had that trouble again. Like in South Africa."

I was silent, looking at the fat gathering in little pools on my plate.

He was aggressive in his grief. "Well, well what do you think of that?"

"I think, I think it's very understandable. With her putting you off so long, anyone could—certainly."

"I suppose," he replied morosely. "I didn't sleep last night.

I've never gone a night without sleeping! Not since Father found out what I'd done with the little Thompson girl. Well, you were there too, but you never got caught, you rascal! I was eleven, eh? Do you remember? This morning I had her, Mordecai," he added abruptly. "Everything was all right again. Suddenly, after all that—it seemed immensely important to her that I be all right. She did things that I just—Really, I don't know how she knew them." He shook his head. "I swear I don't know. Some books, I imagine, that must be it. And we're, we're fine now. You don't know what a relief it is. I've been . . . Well, I haven't been myself because of it. I suppose when I told her I had to go away it made her get over this—whatever it was. I've got to go away, you know, to Italy and then to Holland. I'd like to take Maria, but she insists she wants to organize the house. Women are that way, of course. I wish I had a little more time with her, to know if I'm really all right."

"Of course you're all right. It was just nerves. Bride's nerves, groom's nerves."

"Yes, I suppose so. It's just that I hate to leave now. I'll be gone for six weeks, I imagine. I want you to look after things for me. Here, I've brought these papers."

We pored over contracts and account sheets, and spoke no more of Leo's connubial life. I was in such a state as I can't describe, even now. Torn between shame over my rage at my love, when she'd been mine all along, and rage that she had finally given herself to her husband. Eventually my brother motioned for the bill, and we left Standard's Chop House. We shook hands and embraced, and I didn't see Leo again for six weeks.

I gave up everything in my life then, to be with Maria at every possible moment. There were times we snuck away to country inns, or simply lolled in my flat. I became more reckless and more hungry. Her elegant clothes, which she took such care to manage so they wouldn't betray her, were always a little rumpled and unkempt, for no sooner was she in them than my hot hands tore at her skirts, and pulled the pins from her carefully piled hair. In public places, especially, I liked to trace the muscles of her beautiful flanks, beneath starched white tablecloths. I would not allow her to wear drawers when she was out with me. I wanted to touch her and smell her, and see the hot blush spread on her lovely throat. She would pull my hand away and bring it to her lips, licking her liquor from my fingers. Then it was her recklessness that alarmed me.

She seemed happier now, more gentle and more eager. She betrayed no air of shame or sorrow, anymore. I never spoke to her about my conversation with my brother, and I never struck her again. It was an exquisite idyll; we didn't taint it with discussion of our future.

I had received several letters from Leo in this period. His trip was largely preparatory for a voyage to the Orient, and he requested that I join him. It was to be a long journey, as of old, but neither of us could find an excuse not to take it, when the stakes were so high. With the help of Petófi money, Leo hoped to acquire certain gems that would complete his ascent into the first rank of dealers. There were pearls involved as well. If we succeeded, I would have all the work I needed to keep me in London with my beloved. It would take us several months. Finally I got a letter from Leo telling me to meet him in Amsterdam in two weeks, and to bring Maria with me. At least, he wrote, they would have a week together before we set off.

When I met Maria that night, she had a letter in her hand. "Give this to Leo, it will get there sooner," she said. "It will explain why I can't join him. I'm pregnant. I've told him the doctors won't allow me to travel. Darling, of course I made sure — I made sure it was yours before . . . I think I'm three months gone, now." She pressed her small hands to her belly.

I met Leo in Amsterdam at the appointed time, bearing the letter. I sat with him as he opened it, I watched his dismay at her absence give way to ecstasy. It was more than joy at the thought of his progeny — it was the affirmation of his virility. I pretended surprise and pleasure. Leo clapped me loudly on the back. "Ha! Uncle Mordecai! Well, old man. We'll hurry back. We'll hurry back as quickly as we possibly can." We boarded the boat for China as planned.

Leo was full of reverie about his son. Well, if it was a girl, the first one, she would take after her mother. But he was certain it would be a boy. He thought it might be lucky to name him after me. Leo was so preoccupied with his excitement that he seemed not to notice my morbidity, and in any case, I took care to disguise it well. It was our first trip together since his marriage, and while he was not entirely faithful to Maria, he confined himself to the occasional use of a whore. He directed the rest of his energies to drinking, gambling, and eating, and to the pleasure of the adventure.

We had been gone for two months when we received the cable. Our plan had been to return in May, when Maria would be in her eighth month of pregnancy. To this day, I can hardly — Here it is.

> I can hardly take pen to paper, but it is my duty to you. Maria began an early labor yesterday afternoon, and died this morning at 3:00 A.M. of a fever. She gave birth to a girl, who, though small, will live. Everything that was possible was done. I cannot bear to write any more of the details now.
>
> János Petőfi

The most frightening thing about Leo's grief was its quiet. Of my own, I cannot speak. We made our way back to London, but of course the funeral had already taken place. The baby girl was in the care of a wet nurse. She had been christened Dolores, after Maria's mother, and she was a tiny red thing still — she only weighed four pounds. There were so many affairs to attend to, it was the business of grief, and it occupied all my time. Leo could not manage any of it.

After Maria's death, Leo went entirely, and completely, to pieces. We all knew, of course, that he would mourn terribly, but we weren't prepared for what *did* happen. It was horrible. The first time I found him at it was in May. Maria had been dead for two months. I heard noises in the attic, and though Leo had been under more or less constant supervision, he was left alone occasionally. It seemed only dignified that he should be alone sometimes . . .

As I was saying — I found him at it. It was . . . distasteful. No, much more than that. Ugly. Repulsive. Leo, who was so like a child, a brave little child, fearless and guileless and healthy, was mortifying his flesh. In a peculiar way. He had unbuttoned his shirt to the waist, and was meticulously plucking each hair from his chest. When he finished, he burned a hot red hole over the offending pore with a cigarette. Consequently, since hundreds of pores occupy the space of the tip of one burning cigarette, he was burning weal upon weal, his chest was a vicious mass of burns. He seemed to feel nothing, nothing at all. When I tried to pry the fire from his hand, he looked at me, his eyes wet and ringed from crying, his handsome cheeks sunken, and he moaned, "I want to be white and hairless, like a woman! I am a woman! I am not a man, a man would have saved her . . . I am a woman." We struggled heavily for a few moments, and when the cigarette fell to me in our battle, he collapsed, weeping, into my arms. That evening he was delivered to the Maudsley Hospital.

I thought of suicide, of course. It was what I thought of generally. But Leo still recognized me, and his doctors — if you can call them that — they seemed more like jailers — told me that he lived for my visits and spoke of me constantly as his blood and his redemption. That kept me alive.

And of course, I had the little girl to raise. Leo begged me, pathetically, to look after his daughter. I cannot describe to you the shame he felt at being unable to take care of her, and how pitifully grateful he was to me. I asked Maria's sisters to care for the girl; the constant sight of her was too painful for me. It got worse as she grew older and came more and more to resemble her mother. The same beauty, but with dreamy eyes—those were mine. I sent her away to the best Swiss boarding schools, I gave her everything money could buy. She suffered from not having real parents, a real father. She was spoiled, stunningly beautiful and spoiled. I lied to Leo, of course, and told him she was always perfectly happy.

I had Leo moved, as soon as possible, to the best asylum in England. He needed constant supervision. He developed an obsession with fire, with flame and heat of all kinds, and he had to be watched. But somehow he was left alone. He found some matches . . . He set fire to the hospital, and he died. Twenty-three people died with him.

Leo left me his entire fortune, including the Moon of the Celebes, with a note that said, "She was always fond of you, she would have wanted you to have it."

I fell into the habit of living again. Oh, not a real life, but it was a habit, nonetheless. You might say I missed my moment to die. It was an opportunity, if you will, that I did not seize. But I began to collapse under the strain. A soul can only take so much torment, you know, Lily. The body, after all, can only endure so much—until one passes out. If one was being tortured, one would collapse after a certain point. And so it is with the spirit. One wants to die, but it is the art of living to stay just this side of that death, no matter how great the pain is. For once we've crossed over . . . well, we cannot love anymore, can we? A dead soul, a stifled soul, has not even got the gift of suffering and pain to offer the beloved. That's the saddest thing that can happen to a man. I was close to that death, and I longed for it—how I longed for it! To remember her face and not care, to hear the sound of her voice in my memory and recall that I'd once loved her . . . But it never came. My heart would not go mute.

I began to dream of her. I even willed it, at first. These

dreams, in which I found myself back in her arms, exhausted me. Often I awoke at dawn, dreary and empty, spent of all but the longing that flamed in me still. I was like a fire that burnt on air: all flame, no substance, a terrible pain. I was satiate in those dreams of her, and waking, she was lost. If I had thought —oh, really believed!—that dying would be one long dream of her, I'd have gladly rowed across the Lethe . . . But there was no guarantee of that—it might have been one long emptiness, a not knowing, making a criminal of me—the crime was forgetting her. Better to live, then, for my soul-sweating nights than risk an end to the dreams. It was a religious life, and a mad one. Do you understand that? I think you do. One takes a vow, to a harsh order—the beloved is the sacred religion.

Life took its small revenges. Sometimes great ones. I'd wake, racked and bleary eyed, shaken with the exertions of dreaming. I never daydreamed. That belonged to the night. I was anxious for sleep, but when the moment came, I often lay rigid, wide awake, her image before my eyes. Why didn't my body run to sleep, rush to sleep, when she waited there? Why? You'd think I'd sleep like a baby, like an idiot. But no . . .

I began to medicate myself. I tried different balms—chloral, bromides, powders. They all worked for a time. Yet in the end, there was a great sacrifice in taking them—if the dosage was ever a drop too high, I no longer dreamed. It was the normal effect of the drugs, the doctors said—they killed the dreaming centers. It was a price I hated to pay, to wake up, and not have known her again, known her that much more. To wake up, with no interval of brightness that was Maria. Now I moved from darkness to darkness—the darkness that was my life to the oblivion that was sleep. On nights when I went without the drugs, and finally fell asleep, wretched, at dawn, I was barraged by dreams—dreams of her, and other visions. All that had gone unseen for weeks or months erupted behind my drooping eyes —she was everywhere, then, a demon enwrapped in nightmares. Now and then, from sheer loneliness, I suffered this ordeal. The mornings that followed these nights were terrible ones.

The drug Chen Li gave me provided an interval, an interval of peace. Then opium began to exact a terrible price. Fevers came on, and later chills. I welcomed the fevers, in the beginning. In the heat of a long burn, longing is extinguished, and that, in itself, was a relief. But the malaise that followed . . . and then opium, more opium. We were in Shanghai the first time Chen Li gave me the pipe. He said it was better than the pills, and it's true, it *is* a gentler poison.

My dreams had begun to change. Maria spoke to me, she begged for me to join her. She told me I only had to cut the pearl, her pearl, and then we'd be together again. And so I began to write her letters, explaining how much I loved her and why I wasn't ready. I spent opiated days—for now I smoked all day long—writing at my desk, writing her love letters. They're in the book, our book. She called me then and she calls me still, I'm free to go to her, you know. The veil between is just like tissue now, I'm hardly afraid of it anymore, but I haven't any strength in my hands. I would cut the pearl if I had that old strength, but it's sapped by dreams, it's gone to dreams . . . There was no freedom in wanting her, though I thought my desire was a life. Well, let her die! I loved her so, I love her still, but let her old bones rest. I've lived too long, and long enough to kill my curse. I have no more shame. To think I could ever outlive shame, which was like a mistress to me! Lily, be my hands, dearest girl, you'll cut the Moon of the Celebes, won't you? I want to go to her, I'm too terribly old to go on dreaming . . .

But I'm ready to go to my love, my wife. You'll help me won't you? Lily, let me tell you something. That baby girl, my little baby girl . . . Leo died, he left me the fortune that's become Van Velsen's . . . It all went to me. The pearl came to me. And my girl. I raised her; she always thought I was her uncle. I spoiled her so. Fancy clothes, and schools, and parties—I never let her see the world, I was wrong to do it, I know, but she was all I had left. I made mistakes. I hardly knew her as she grew, I traveled constantly. She was my shame, too, you see, I loved her, but—she looked just like Maria.

Lily, when she was a young woman she married a rich businessman, a mediocre sort, I don't know. I should have given her more attention, I—Those were her letters you read, she was your *mother*, not my half-sister, not your mad Great-aunt Dorothy, your mother. Dolores—Dorothy. She died like Leo, in one of those places. I gave you the book when you were going to marry because it's in our blood, darling, it's in your marrow . . . I have some pearls here. They were your mother's gray pearls, I want you to take them . . . And I want you to cut the old moon.

You see, all these years, I couldn't admit anything beautiful had come from my life, when all I wanted was to punish myself. But something beautiful did come—you did. And if I thought I could cut away to the heart of the thing myself, I'd do it. The curse might end with that pearl. It's what she tells me in the dreams. Do you know how old I am? I'm terribly old, and I'm ready to die. Lily? Don't look sad. It wouldn't be a sadness, to go. I'd be with her. It would be a sweetness, all sweetness.

The exertion of the telling was wearing on the old man, and he drank from his bottle of laudanum. He spoke in hazy slurs, now, his pupils tiny and dark in an old man's burning eyes. His head drooped a little, like a dew-soaked stalk, and finally came to rest on his arm.

Lily reached out and shook his shoulder. He started, and stared at her.

"She's my mother? That woman is my mother?"

"Don't call her 'that woman.' You loved her. You visited her, you . . ." Mordecai gave her a dazed look.

"Well, what does that mean, Uncle Mordecai?" She spat the question at him. "What does that mean to me?"

) 163 (

He regarded her sadly. "I'm not your Uncle Mordecai. I'm not your Great-uncle Mordecai, not anymore. You're *my* blood, a line straight and true."

"A line of loonies, you mean. That's right, I said it. But let me tell you something. It's not catching. Madness is not a congenital disease. Anyone can tell you that." She picked weakly at her argument, experimenting with it, unsure. She only felt anger, which crouched over the fear; and the fear that lay on top of sorrow, like a simple veil; and that, finally and truly, lay on top of love.

Love, which couldn't be broken, or tamed, or ended by pain. Love for her mother, mad and possessed, and her mother before her, bewitched by desire and love. Love for her grandfather, and his stubborn belief in his tainted blood. Love for herself, so tired and broken, who grew up in a thicket of lies, lies that spread like a spider's web over childhood. She remembered the scent of that long-ago air, how she had smelt it—how it had stung of untruth, the way you can smell winter in the wind. And now that they were released, secrets only seemed small and quiet, innocent and simple.

"Uncle . . ." she said, then stopped, smiling. "Grandfather." She saw his eyes clear for a moment, she saw him listening.

"Why not have told me? After all . . . why not have told me?" There was an urgency in her, the anger receding. She leaned toward him.

"Because, Lily, because—secrets have a life, they beat with their own hearts. Blood courses in them. It's like a murder to kill them. I was afraid. I didn't want the blood on my hands." He touched his palms together, softly. "And even now—perhaps it was wrong, perhaps this was wrong."

"No, no. The truth isn't wrong. It's not wrong that Maria is my grandmother, or that you're mine by blood."

"No."

"Or Dorothy my mother, or that hoaxster my father. Maybe that was the wild card, the joker in the deck."

"Lily. Dying takes a long time. I don't know if we come back.

If you live long, you'll make secrets too. It has to happen. Secrets stun us, and they tire us. But they make us look, like clairvoyants, inside of every smile, inside of every leaf and into the air itself. Do you understand? They give us a gift: the gift of watching, the gift of seeing inside."

Lily leaned to kiss him, to kiss away the pain of stories, to kiss away what the telling had cost him.

"My dear," he said as they embraced quietly.

There was something in the color of the room's light, an ache perhaps, or a reaching melancholy, that let her watch the scene as if from far away. How truly she felt the old man's silver hair, soft against her embracing palm; his arm that cradled her waist; and at the same time she saw them, as if from outside, two people standing still in a quiet light, holding each other as if they were two memories, two reminiscences played out for the very last time. They seemed fragile, to her watching eyes, like ghosts, yet more alive than flowers, than air or water. I understand this, she thought, there's something old in love itself, interior, like the heart of a tree; we don't have to invent it, only to reach back, behind what obscures it.

Her grandfather's head swayed, tired, onto his arms. He surrendered, like a curling plant, to rest.

"Lily, I miss McConnell; often, you see. You remember, my old friend. Like missing Maria, but as an absence in my core, without tragedy. He was my best friend." He smiled simply, wistfully. "Like missing my other half. We rarely find such people, then God takes them away. How little we are left with, when we're old . . . And then, like turning over the palm of my hand"—he made this simple gesture—"everything is precious. What's left is gold, and you most of all."

They smiled at each other, their smile of complicity. Lily placed the Moon of the Celebes in its little box, laid it beside her grandfather's hands, and left the house.

That night, Alan arrived at her door. He looked tired and depleted.

"Lily," he began, "why are you avoiding me like this? You make appointments with me, as if I were a customer in the store. You don't want to make love. Don't put me off anymore. Tell me what's wrong."

It was the first time she could remember having seen a crack in him, in his ease and his control. It made her falter, the sight of pain on that face, and she took his hand between her hands. He pulled away.

"Alan. I'm so sorry about the way I've been. I'm going to take a month off from work. I haven't known what to do. I don't know how to talk with you."

"Don't think I don't know about him," he said, his eyes narrowing. "That's right. The *Bijou* girls told me. Do you think you're anything special to him? I was waiting for you to get over it. Are you over it?"

"Yes."

"Good. Then we'll forget it. It never happened. It's part of what's wrong with you, whatever that is." He waved his hand, as if to brush away his thoughts. "Which is now over."

"Alan—" She reached out for him again, sickened at the sight of this much pain, this foreign form of suffering. "Alan, it's not him."

"We'll put this behind us, that's all." He spoke as if he hadn't heard her. "This sort of thing occurs. Under strain," he said sarcastically.

"But Alan, it's not him. That's not it."

He looked at her, waiting.

"We're not right," she said finally. "I want us to be. But we can't be."

"Right? What's right? Some horny artist you think—Look, Lily, I *love* you."

She gazed at his bewildered face, and felt a wave of terror. He does love me, she thought, and even so I'm going to be alone. "Oh, Alan, I'm sorry."

"I know you're tired, I know you are . . . Please."

"Alan, don't." She took a breath. "I want to buy you out of the business."

His face went hard. "That would cost a lot."

"I know." She handed him her engagement ring. "Here."

He looked at it in his hand. "That's it? Just like that?"

"Oh." She rubbed her forehead, as if the last words were inside. "Yes. Just like that."

"Let me tell you something—you won't find anyone better for you than me. That's right. All this mooning around—just like that great-uncle of yours. What is it you want? Something heroic, something brave? You'll never find a man to live up to this fantasy of yours, whatever the hell it is. You don't need a man, you need a myth."

"Oh, Alan," she said quietly, "maybe you're right. But I can't change. I wish, I really wish, it could have been you."

Lily threw away the last bottles of laudanum, and went into a cold cave inside herself. It was sickening, there. It wasn't the vomiting, or the icy sweat, or the sick fevers that hurt the most. It was the poignant, absolute experience of exclusion. A tormenting exclusion from comfort, from safety, from peace. She went deep inside, seeking comfort, but instead she met her humiliations, the feeling of being a walking mistake, while she stood outside of life seeking entrance.

She was so violently sick for the next five days that she stayed in her bed. The night demons came with all the angry hunger she feared. As her senses woke from their long death, waves of painful sensation rocked through her, grueling orgasms that shook her, that weren't pleasure but pure sensation, the vivid life of the reborn. Everything was too bright, now. She remembered the first letters she had read in her grandfather's book; she remembered the story of her ancestor locked in her convent room. She thought of what she'd read about the devil, who had an icy penis, huge and terrifying, which lunged at the poor possessed.

Her demons had Johnny's face and hands, hands that moved over her body and pressed against her, white-light rushes in her sickness. She didn't sleep, not really, not for five days; she felt the demons coming at her, pulling at her, offering balm and ice. She had nightmares so horrible she thought she would remember them always. It hardly seemed worth being alive if it meant remembering such things. In the end, she knew she could be haunted and still live, live all the more because she'd punched through the thin veil between her night and day.

In the end she healed. The salty stench of the bed sheets, the faint odor of vomit that lingered in the bathroom, the toxic drone of the air around her—all this gave way to a fragile freshness, a painful, tender, newborn feeling. She washed herself for the first time in five days, threw away the sheets, opened a window, still shrinking from the touch of the air, but alive at least and bright and sharp-eyed and trembling and returning.

When she slept that night, her dreams were mild: a field of snow with the padded imprint of a paw. Waking up, she petted the slothful Curse. He had fallen asleep on the book she was reading, and it was hard to remove him; but once dislodged, he slept peacefully in the crook of her arm, rumbling from time to time with his feline dreams.

She was very quiet for a month.

Chen Li came often; he was the only visitor she permitted. He brought her meals, soups and herbs, and massaged the aches in her limbs.

One day he said, "Your grandfather would like to see you."

"I'm almost ready. I'll come soon. Tell him—"

"He's here."

"Here? But he never goes out. I don't understand."

Chen Li shrugged. Mordecai entered cautiously, carrying a bouquet of lilacs.

"Well, dear girl," he said. "You haven't been well. I thought you might like something to read. I have P. G. Wodehouse, some Oscar Wilde, and *The Tale of Genji*—that takes a while, it might be just the thing."

He paused, avoiding her gaze, looking embarrassedly at the wall behind her.

"And I brought you these. It would be a good thing if you kept them." He handed her a small packet of letters. "They're some letters I wrote to Maria. I don't know what to do with them."

"But they're part of the book."

"Even so . . ."

Lily shrugged and took the letters. They were both nervous. Mordecai looked her closely in the eye.

"You'll get better. You're over the worst, I promise you. I can see it."

"How long has it been since you've been out?"

"Oh . . ." He waved his hand. "A long time."

"Years?"

Mordecai smiled. "I suppose so. You'll be fine now. I can see that."

"It's over with Alan. And the other one . . . that's finished, too."

"Ah, that's very good. In that case, you can begin." He brushed some dust from his suit. "I can't stay long. I'm not used to it. My dear, you know, I love you very much."

"Oh!" She was startled, it wasn't among the things they said to each other. Lily smiled. "I do too, you know."

"Oh yes." He kissed her cheek, and pressed her hand in his. "You sleep well."

"I'll see you soon."

"Good-bye, my dear."

Gently, very gently, he let his hand rest on the top of her head. She closed her eyes and smiled. She was so sweetly warm inside. It's silly, she thought, but I feel as if I've swallowed the sun.

* * *

The next morning she went to open up the shop. She was bent over her desk when the first customer came in.

"So this is where you work."

She looked up at the sound of his voice, and felt a sudden melting when she saw his mouth.

"You haven't answered the phone, or returned my calls . . . I thought I'd just come."

"Well. What is it?"

"Look—Lily. About that night. Hey, I'm sorry. How could I have known you'd come over? Forget it. She's not important. You're important."

"You miss me?" Her fingers curled around the diamond she was holding.

"Maybe. Maybe I miss you. Maybe a lot." He eyed her carefully. "You look different."

"I might be."

"Well, I'm the same. I still want you."

Johnny leaned over and took the diamond out of her hand. "I'm doing some new work now." He set it down. "Everything plain. No jewels."

He reached for her, his fingers listening for the quiet shudder in her blood. "Why do you feel so different, baby? Your eyes aren't the same."

Slowly he began to caress her, familiar routes traced and stroked, feeling for an epiphany, a melting.

"I've wanted you, Lily," he said into her ear. "At night, you know? Sometimes I can't sleep. It's like you visit. I dream things. Isn't that crazy?"

"No."

"It makes me feel crazy."

He eased his hands beneath her clothes, stroking her belly and her nipples, and tracing her spine with the flat of his hand. Curling her skirt up over her hips, he pressed her back against the desk. He stretched his body on top of hers, and the little diamond tumbled to the floor. "You still want it, Lily. Nothing's changed. Go on, tell me nothing's changed. Say something."

She thought she smelt the dragon shop in his hair, as if he were somehow kindred to the Chinese smoke. She pressed her face against his chest and inhaled the narcotic scent of his skin. I'm through with this, she thought. I don't want this anymore. She looked at him, as if watching the receding shore of a beloved home.

Slipping down to her knees, she touched him, her hair falling over her face, sliding over his belly and legs. She reached for his belt.

"Lily, not like that. I don't want that. Later. Stop it . . . I said stop it."

She held his hips, and his fingers curled in her hair, tightly, then touched her hollowing cheeks. She felt his shoulders arch against surrender. He made a last move to stop her, to reach between her thighs and seize her, but she grabbed his wrist and held it.

"Lily, I wish . . ." he said, and then he stopped, a last shuddering moment, a race of blood, a soaring effusion that broke against her lips. Droplets sparkled against her throat, small essential jewels.

He reached for her again, futilely, but this time she pulled far away. He glared at her in loss and confusion.

She found the diamond on the floor, and pressed it into his hand. "Good-bye, Johnny. Don't come back here."

He arranged himself without speaking, but at the door he turned to her.

"You'll be back, Lily, because of what you want." There was a thin, flat tone to his voice, a steady control, but she saw the blood beat in his temple as he spoke. "I know the place where you lose control, and you need that. That's why you'll be back. I just make you hungry, and that's all you really want. Did you think I was romantic? Well, I'm not. So what? It's nothing so refined that makes your blood boil. I know about women." He glared at her. Then he held up the diamond. "Light shines through that—not through people. Hey, I hope you find your luminous hero, but I'm not worried. People are dirty, Lily, and they want to be. The sculptures I make are just dreams. People buy them, because they dream, too. But in here"—he tapped his heart—"there's no gold, not in anyone. That's a dream for fools."

"I never thought you were romantic," she said.

She closed the shop early, and went directly on to Pacific Street. Chen Li opened the door. He saw her in, and showed her to the study. It was empty, but the pearl lay where she had left it more than a month before.

"Your grandfather, he slept last night, and in the morning he had his coffee. He went back to sleep, very contented. Then he died, in his second sleep." There was no crack in Chen Li's voice. "When you wait a long time for something, sometimes it's very quiet when it comes. He said to give you these things." He handed her a string of gray pearls, some blades and a few files, a scale, and a small ivory bowl.

"I'll set to work on it now," said Lily. Chen Li brought them a pot of tea and a plate of buttered toast.

"The book is gone. He said it was a great horror, and you didn't need to keep a thing like that."

She half listened as he spoke, but she didn't quite hear him word for word. She was watching the pearl, and she thought she saw the place where the first skin would crack.

PART III

Scars

My worst habit is I get so tired of winter
I become a torture to those I'm with.

If you're not here, nothing grows.
I lack clarity. My words
tangle and knot up.

How to cure bad water? Send it back to the river.
How to cure bad habits? Send me back to you.

When water gets caught in habitual whirlpools,
dig a way out through the bottom
to the ocean. There is a secret medicine
given only to those who hurt so hard
they can't hope.

The hopers would feel slighted if they knew.

Look as long as you can at the friend you love,
no matter whether that friend is moving away from you
or coming back toward you.

—JELALUDDIN RUMI

UNCLE . . . Grandfather Mordecai. Do you know where I am? I'm sitting graveside, talking to a stupid lump of sod. No, to you. Do you hear me? I talk to you all the time, but today I wanted to come here. I thought you might hear me better. A friend told me to come. Look, I brought some sweet williams and some peonies. You always liked them. I know you can't see anything where you are, I know there's no smelling there, but you know I'm here. I want to talk to you. If the book wasn't gone, I'd have written all this down, but as it is, it seems better to tell you directly. It's a story, a story like the long stories you used to tell me, with a story inside of it. I'm reading again . . . I'm reading the *Lais of Marie de France*. I remember how you loved them.

I cleaved her, and she was perfect, Uncle—do you mind if I still call you that? It's the habit of so many years. She was so beautiful inside—oh, you already knew, you knew all along. You were never truly afraid, but you left it for me to do, because you knew the task was mine.

I thought I'd seen things shine, before. I thought I'd seen things that were alive. But every layer I went to revealed worlds, precious worlds no eyes but mine had ever seen. Can you see where you are? Or is it all sky?

The skin of the blister was hard and cold. The nacre seemed centuries old; it had a prehistoric obstinacy. I thought my tools were too weak, at first, to crack something so inured to solitude, so deeply set. I worked a long time, that first day, in the soft light of the study, just trying to begin. I talked a little with Chen Li, and we ate quiet meals together.

I lay down to rest in the late afternoon, but I don't think I really slept. My head felt strange. I still felt the touch of your hand, and it was warm there. I know it sounds odd, but I feel it still, a gentle pressure, and when I think of it, you're not far away at all, only listening, watching, in a place where you can't hear or see. And as I lay there, quietly, I saw little worlds exploding behind my eyes, small planets reeling, and felt that faint pressure, like the kind, careless touch of a stranger, in my head.

When I got up I saw her, bright inside, and dreaming of release. I took the file and tapped, not hard, but truly and well, and the imprisoning nacre broke with a lazy crackle, like the shell of a black walnut.

I felt like old Lamer, then, filing, cutting, and prying away. In places the skin stuck fast — it took hard work to peel it away — but you know how it is, an old pearl doctor knows how to do these things.

There were eight layers before I came to her — and the treasures at each point were so dazzling I wanted to stop at each one. But time after time I *knew*, I knew with perfect certainty, that they were only places, glorious sites where beauty dazzled, but not the destination. My hands ached from the hours of labor, I wanted to stop, I was dizzy and tired. And then, at last, I saw the shiny moon, peeking out from beneath an opalescent skin. How do we describe glass? Or the molten core of the earth? Or sea? Or wind when it carries an echo? Or the dense bone of fired metal?

She was the moment between night and morning, the crack in the heavens that leads to the gods, the sky over a Celebes sea, the circle that glows around the moon, and the moment before frost. How had the tropical night sunk into her skin, why did she hold the ocean, and yet contain fire? Why was she dew soaked and fresh, like a mushroom from the sea, yet sure as the earth, and verdant like fields?

Ask me to name water—I'll tell you wet, blue, cold, slippery. Ask me to name sky—I'll tell you empty, light, pale. Ask me to name metal—I'll tell you stoic, hard, impenetrable, black. Ask me to name fire—I'll tell you red, hot, jumping, pointed. Ask me to name earth—I'll tell you dense, compressed, fecund, bursting, thrilling. And naming moon—that's cold, flat, blue, woman, heart, eyes, and tears. And naming sun—it's fire, light, sin, beauty, warmth, and sky. But is the naming ever true?

And when all things join—crazy grass to sinking rain, brazen sky to mountain, mad clouds, warm sun—they make a light so great and still that only the gods can see it. That was the Moon of the Celebes—moon now become sun.

Chen Li helped me with the polishing, and when the pearl was finally ready, we wrapped her in a little piece of red cloth and put her in your desk for safekeeping.

I was sleepy and sick for a time after that. It was like having a bone-deep flu that lasted only a little while. I thought I'd be happy when it was all done. But my heart was breaking, the shards stabbing inside, because I knew you were really gone.

I started to dream in blue, then, the month before it happened. As if the tint of sky was in my sleeping. Often they weren't even dreams, exactly, but a fluorescence, a light that trembled behind my eyes. Sometimes I dreamt of depths, and sometimes I saw reeling blue moons.

He came into Van Velsen's, he was looking for you. He was tall and thin, he wore jeans and a checked cap and carried a tattered briefcase. These simple clothes had a slightly foreign air. So did his faintly awkward gait, like that of a boy whose body is still growing. His nose was slightly bent, where perhaps it had once been broken, and his eyebrows were black lines over his eyes. These eyes were bright blue, that blue you only see in certain Irish faces. They were the blue of sapphires from India, of ink, of the sky when it shines with morning, of wells, of shadows. I was so busy with these eyes that I forgot to greet him. I stared at them, thinking about the blue things I'd seen in my dreams. And then I saw his heart glowing, the way I saw pearls. I thought I was imagining things, and I turned away.

"My name is Dermot McConnell," he said. "I've come to speak to Mr. van Velsen. He was an old friend of my grandfather's." He spoke in a light brogue, and the sound of it glided and swirled in the room. There was nothing unusual about his manner, but he seemed oddly displaced, as if he were separated from his proper element. I looked up into his eyes.

"Mr. van Velsen—my grandfather—is dead," I told him. "I miss him," I added suddenly.

He looked at me intently. "Are you feeling bad, then?"

"Yes, I am. Sad."

"Ah," he said, "I understand. I'm a bit of a wreck myself." He smiled, and I saw a broken front tooth. He touched his hand quickly to his head, and then to his heart. I stared at him, at this sudden gesture, and I started to cry.

"Oh, girl," he said, his voice lilting and swaying. "Poor girl." He put his arm around my shoulders. "It's hard to lose someone you love like that. It's hard on the heart." He wiped the tears from under my eyes. "Crybaby," he added genially.

I sat there crying and crying, Uncle, like a little idiot, because I missed you, crying right in front of this stranger. He didn't seem much surprised.

"I'm sorry," I said. "I miss him. I haven't cried like this since he died. I don't know why, now . . . I thought it didn't matter so much anymore."

"You've got to have a proper cry after a thing like that. I know. Do you speak to him?"

"What do you mean, do I speak to him? He's dead."

"Well, I know, silly. You said so. But you ought to have a good chat with him. It's the right thing to do for both of you."

"You're crazy."

"Oh, that I know. But do as I say. When's his birthday?"

"As a matter of fact, it's very soon."

"Well, there you are. Go to where he's buried, bring a few flowers, whatever he liked when he was alive. Don't look at me as if I were mad, I know a few things. And have a proper chat with him. You'll see."

He wiped my cheeks with his fingers, which smelt like salt air.

"God, I'm so embarrassed. Crying in front of you. I don't even know you. What do you want, anyway?"

"Sssh. Let's just sit a bit."

And so we sat. Quietly. He still had his arm around me, and I think he rocked me, almost imperceptibly, back and forth, I don't remember. It was like waves rocking a boat. I might have imagined it. But it was as if I let you go then, with those tears that felt like blue ink running down my cheeks. Suddenly I stiffened, I felt awkward, and I pulled away from his grip. He sat, waiting. Finally I asked again, "Mr. McConnell, what do you want?"

"I've something to sell. But if your grandfather is dead . . ."

"Perhaps I can look at it. What is it?"

He reached into the pocket of his jeans and took out a small, dirty envelope, which he laid on the counter. We both stared at it for a moment. Dermot unwrapped it, and withdrew a strand of pearls.

I'm empty of superlatives — who wouldn't be, who'd seen the Moon of the Celebes? But my first thought, as he unveiled them, was that *you* be alive, that you be here to see. Nothing in these last years so wanted your eyes, so wanted to be seen by you. They were new, new to jaded eyes. Uncle, they were *blue* pearls, nearly a whole strand of them! They were something else, something I'd never seen. No, not like Tahitian blacks, or the Sulu blues. They were cousins to the pearl you owned, in the days of Maria and Leo, the one that gave you so much trouble, that you sat quietly with, the one who never shed its mysteries. I know what you're thinking—I thought it too—no pearls are really that color blue, that bright and lilting azure. They must be dyed, a brilliant fake, they just looked too blue for a crazy moment.

"Nearly enough to make a necklace," Dermot said, a little wistfully, "but not quite." He reached into his pocket again, and withdrew an even smaller envelope. Inside were five more pearls, but these were different shades, varying from gray to greenish white.

"I'm thinkin' these are the same blue inside, and they'll be matchin' the others, but of course I don't know." He paused, and looked at me carefully. "I heard a rumor about the old man, you know, your grandfather—that he had the second sight."

I was still staring at the pearls, but the words started me out of my reverie.

"That's right, but of course he's dead."

"Well," he said, "that's a shame then."

"It is."

"In any case"—and now Dermot spoke a little sadly, a little distantly—"even if these five were a match, even if they were, it still wouldn't be enough. It wants six more, at least, to make a necklace, the way I see it."

"The way you see it? There are ways . . . We could put some other pearls in between, here, like this—It could be lovely."

He looked at me disdainfully. "And spoil her? She's pure. My eyes don't want to see anything else when they look at that blue." His voice was dark and emphatic. "Unless"—and now he smiled again—"it's a pretty girl's throat." He picked up one azure bead, and held it against my neck, to the place where my breath beat fast, like a little heart. "That's all I want to see," he added. His finger brushed the pulse in my throat.

"Yes, of course. You're right. It is a shame."

"Well," he added, a little cryptically, "it mightn't be too late to hope for completion." He seemed suddenly tired. "I've been all around the seven seas, girl, but this is my first trip to the

States. I've no money at all, anymore, and I've been sick." He smiled down at me. "But I'm not a crybaby, am I?"

His hands were strong, and gawky, like his body. He wiped away the last of my tears, brushing his fingers over my cheekbones. "Well, sometimes I am."

I laughed. "Aren't the Irish chronic liars?"

He flashed his amiable grin, but I could see that he was tiring.

"Look, I'm so embarrassed, Mr. McConnell. Crying with a stranger. By the way, my name is Lily."

"Oh, don't be, Lily. You mustn't be. Please don't call me Mr. McConnell. Dermot."

"Well. Have you seen San Francisco at all?"

"No, I came here straightaway." He blushed a little and looked down. "It was important."

"Will you be staying long?"

He shrugged. "That depends. If I sell the pearls for the right price, I'm back home to Dublin. I tried to sell them in London, you know, but buyers think they're fake. If not . . . I'll get a bit of work here. I don't mind."

There was something terrifying in his creeping tiredness, the light dimming in his eyes, an indifference and a settling. I saw it had cost him something to show the pearls at all. I felt a sudden, nervous reluctance to let him walk out the door, as if I might never see him again.

"Well," I said, awkward now, "is there anything special you want to see here? I'll show you around."

"Thank you, that's very kind."

"I have a favorite place. Do you like aquariums?"

"I've never been to one."

"What, really? There's a wonderful one, it's in Golden Gate Park."

We spoke little on the way there. When we arrived we paused a moment to watch the tourists go in — sweating, giddy with sun, bright and gay. The ones emerging were different — glutted with water and the imaginary deep, like so many Persephones returning from Hades. I have always loved the aquarium; as a child I speculated endlessly about the inner lives of fish, about blood that ran cold, about lives lived without the tug of inner warmth.

Inside, Dermot and I stood over the crocodile pit, watching the animals' gums in their snapping mouths. "I've been to Mexico," he said. "I've wrestled a crocodile." He smiled. "I see you don't believe me, Lily. I've got a picture, you know. They do it for a bit of sport down there." I felt a forced gaiety in him now, in this bit of bravado, an effort to please that I hadn't noticed before. We didn't mention the pearls.

We walked past the tanks of fish and snakes, pausing here and there, saying little. A small frog caught our eyes — it seemed to float, on one florid toe, its arms reaching out and up, as if it saw beyond its confines to some imagined sky. He stopped in front of the stingrays, watching them flap and glide in their tiny tank, and beat their slick, velvet wings against the water. They watched us with empty, menacing eyes.

"Imagine running into one of those," I said. I tried to speak lightly, but it was somehow impossible. "Wouldn't it be scary?" I added.

He looked at me then, a long, inner look, and I made myself hold his gaze. The bright blue eyes had something of the sea in them now, a touch of green, the emanation of all the water around us. A murky sea.

"Very scary," he said emptily. He was dark in a new way, and ominous. I sensed danger now in his eyes, which changed every moment, like water.

"Do you think they know they're in cages?" I asked, repeating the oft-asked question of my childhood. I pointed to the eels, the fat serpents that moved moodily, in slow coils, around one another's bodies. "As long as they're in their natural element, they might not notice," I added.

"Only if they were out . . ." He kicked lightly at the bottom of the tank.

"How could they be out? If they were out they'd be dead."

"Do you fancy a cup of tea?" he asked. He said it with a forced ease. I saw he badly wanted to leave. "I'm wrecked. I haven't been too well."

We strolled to the tea garden in silence. Finally he said, "I'm sorry. I don't mean to be depressing. It's just that place reminds me of things."

"Dermot, how did you come by those pearls?"

"Ah, watch out, you'll have me crying. We Irish are very emotional, you know." The irony was back in his gaze, like a tide of life returning as the sea receded.

We strolled through the mock Japan, over tiny bridges, past Buddhas and koi, exchanging small confidences. I felt secrets looming behind his charming stories, and I felt my own truths hovering like birds behind my lips. We came to a bridge over a small pond whose clear water showed a bed of pennies beneath. I touched Dermot's arm and reached into my pocket, withdrawing two coins.

"Here, make a wish."

He was solemn for a moment, and then I watched the penny fall through the air, a spark of sharp light hitting its surface.

At first I chose my favorite wish, my habitual desire—I wanted an infinity of wishes. But then I asked for another—I asked to look a long time into those blue eyes, with their clear, high spirit and their curious sorrow. In the way of the most serious wishes, neither of us told. We stood silently a moment, watching orange fish glide by the shining copper.

"I've cheated," I began.

"Sssh. Don't tell. You might spoil it."

"No, it's not that. I've made more than one. Do you think that's okay?"

"I don't know. It's meant to lessen them." He looked at me speculatively. "But you're a brave girl. You might have the strength to live through more than one wish." He paused a little thoughtfully. "I've only got one, that's the truth. I'll take a chance with it. If you fancy a story, that is."

"Okay—I could use a story—my grandfather used to tell them to me. I haven't heard one in a long time."

Dermot was quiet a moment, then he said, "It's a long story. I'll want to hear one of yours in return. All right then. It's to do with the sea. I love the sea. Do you? I can't imagine living far away from the sea.

"I grew up in Dublin, in Ringsend, by the bay. There were big trees outside our house—huge, they were. My brothers and I used to climb up them and look at the water. It had a gray color to it, slate gray. My brothers got bored with it, but I never did. I watched those waves, and I thought about going deep into the heart of them. I wanted to be a hard man, so I did, and I was always readin' about pirates and sailing ships. I snuck off all the bleedin' time, and stood by that water—it was a ravin' sea—and you could feel the wind in your mouth.

"My mum fussed over me when I came home, she'd rub my hands. She'd make me a cup of tea and say, 'Dermot, I don't like you going in that cold, you'll catch your death.' My mother was a religious woman, you know, and she had a lot of fears. She'd be seein' death all over, and I never fuckin' saw things that way, you know what I mean? I saw life in everything— the world's meant to have life, isn't it? It was in the air and in the rain, and in the garden. But most of all, I saw it in the sea.

"As I grew up, I became a strong swimmer, and I swam in that freezin' water. I didn't mind jumpin' into those waves. I liked it. I used to dive the forty foot, in Blackrock. Bein' a bit of a hard man, as I said.

"Me and me brothers, we used to get into scraps all the time. I remember one time, myself and Goodie—Goodie Thomas, that's what we called him, he was a Brit—we had a row with some guys we met up with. Goodie was fond of a jar, you know; he'd have a few pints, and he'd be throwin' shapes. He was so bleedin' stupid, he was. Calls this guy a handbag, you know?

I had to pull him off the guy, he was huge. Man, we used to get into stupid scraps.

"I remember one night like that, I left my mates and ran off to the sea. I tore off my dirty clothes, and went into that deep water, I could feel the salt bitin' against my bruises.

"Days I couldn't go out, I snuck up into the attic of our house. All my grandfather's gear was stored up there. We knew he'd suffered from a queerness in the head — melancholia, it was. I remember him raving and ranting. My parents never talked about it. Never. I just remember my father sayin', 'If I find you boys muckin' about up there, I'll give yez a clatter across the head, make no mistake about it!' Sure I wanted to get up there! There was meant to be somethin' magic in that room.

"It was a big attic, with a lot of nooks and cubbyholes, all stuffed with boxes and bits of things. We went through every bleedin' trunk and stack of moldy papers. Everything was covered in layers of dust *this* thick. I didn't mind that, but the *spiders*, now that was somethin' else. I remember once one got up my brother's trouser leg. Jaysus, we just fell about — 'cause he was tryin' to scream *quietly*, you know? Hoppin' about like Saint Vitus . . . Ah, that was a sight to see. Anyway, sure we went over that room — tapped the rafters and banged the floorboards, lookin' for a secret compartment.

"After a while my brothers lost interest. But I didn't, Lily. I had this *feelin*' — that my destiny — I know it sounds mad — that my destiny was in that attic. If I didn't keep on, I'd end up like every other git in Dublin, you know? Fightin' and boozin' and workin' and wishin', and giving up wishin' in the end.

"One day, when I was eleven, I rolled my eyes and clutched my stomach and said I was too sick to go to Mass. As soon as I had the house to myself, I was right up those stairs. I was goin' through some boxes in the corner when I heard this weird creak under my foot. The floorboard was wantin' to give, so I took a stick and pried it up. Nothing. I kept on, takin' up five or six more. Then I went fuckin' mad — must've been the spirit of my old granddad got into me—I started pulling up those boards left and right. Sure I was going to tear my parents' house apart piece by piece, just to get to whatever it was. And then, all of a sudden, I saw it, Lily, I saw it for certain—the corner of an old chest, covered with muck and grime. Jaysus, the sight of that trunk! I was *dead* happy, Lily, dead happy. Man, I was sure there was gold in there, piles of it, and maybe a few diamonds as well.

"It took me an hour to pry open that bleedin' lock. And when I finally did, I says to myself, 'Dermot, you're a free man at last. You're a bleedin' rich fucker now.'

"All there was inside was papers. I nearly started cryin'. I looked at 'em anyway, after all my goddamn trouble I thought I might as well. They were diaries, logs of my old grandfather's days at sea. I read a few entries—it was good stuff, you know —but it wasn't fuckin' gold, was it? I kicked that bleedin' chest, and it fell over on its side. And that's when I saw it, under all the papers.

"It was a large burlap sack, tied up with twine. I touched it, and it almost crumbled in my hands. Inside were bundles of rotten silk, and a lock of black hair tied with a ribbon and wrapped in a pouch. There was a thin gold coin as well, and a handful of black pearls. Fuckin' beautiful. But there was better yet to come. Inside another little bag, there was somethin' *amazing*. It was a long, spiny-lookin' skeleton, wound up into a ball. I opened it out, and it was four fuckin' feet long, from head to tail. It was an eel, or a snake. Jaysus, it was weird. I didn't want to put it away, but it was getting late, and I knew my parents would be comin' back from Mass. I wrapped the snake back up and put it in the bag. I replaced the boards, raced downstairs, and got back into bed.

"Well, Lily, you can imagine. Sure I snuck back upstairs, every chance I got. I managed to sort the diaries into chronological order. I read them hundreds of times; that's right, hundreds. I can still recite whole bits of them from memory.

The first journals told my grandfather's adventures in Bahrain. Fuckin' barbaric, it was! Jaysus. Murder and maimin' and all —Ah, don't get me started. I'd never read nothin' like it. But the real adventure didn't start until 1922. It was in the fourth log book, and it had a funny drawing on the inside page, in the same green ink that the ol' fella used to keep all the logs, so I imagine he drew it himself. It was a picture of a serpent biting its tail, a serpent with scales and fins that looked like flappin' wings, and a mad fuckin' look on its face. On top of the page was written 'The Serpent Diaries.' There was a note stuck in the book, which said, 'In the event of my death, these are to go to Mordecai van Velsen, Paris, Rue de Rivoli, c/o Père Lemaître.' Well, I wondered if I was meant to get these books back to where they belonged, you know? But it was my bleedin' secret, wasn't it? I didn't tell anyone, not even my brothers."

Dermot paused, and fingered his briefcase. "I've got the diary here. It was meant to be your grandfather's . . . but you should have it, since he's dead. I can tell you about it, or—"

"No, read it to me. Please."

And so Dermot read, Uncle, what was meant for you. Mostly he recited it in his lilting brogue, because he knew it by heart. I'll read it to you now.

Ceylon
February 16, 1922—
  It's mad, me being here. I should have stayed with the old man. Drinking coffees in Paris, and sitting on the boulevards with Mordecai, and enjoying *les petites putains*. It's bloody hot, and I can't get things working. I've got a lot of responsibility here, and good money for it, too. The native men are subject to more superstitions than I've ever seen before. We've got the shark-talker now—that wasn't half easy, agreeing on a price with the man—that's the fellow who sees that the sharks stay away from the pearling grounds, does ceremonies and such. He's a mangy old bastard, used to be a diver himself, but then, most of the men here were at one time or another.

What else is there to do, to earn enough money for rice? I feel punk about it though, today, really I do, as if I'd made a wrong choice, taken a wrong turn somewhere.

February 18 —

Progress. At last. We're setting out tomorrow. Some of the boats are still docked at Puttalam, preparing to move around the beds at Karativu. The fleet is well equipped. We've got some modern diving gear—rubberized suits, and even sets of helmets and etc. Some of the men are eager to try them, but others say they don't want anything to do with it.

February 19 —

The first haul came in this morning. I was thrilled to bits, so I was, when I saw the oysters up on the deck. Foster opened the first dozen, for good luck, but found nothing. Then he turned the job over to a native. The work went fast, but I think he must have opened five hundred shells, at least, before he found the first pearl. She was nothing special, she had that opal-yellow tint we expected to see, and she was of average size, but we all had a drink to celebrate it anyway. After that we hit a little more often, and even then, it's usually nothing more than a poor baroque. There's no question that the work is slow going. A really fine pearl can be one in a thousand. The divers get a part of the take, as well as their wages, so they do have incentive. Our best diver is a man named Lalit. He can stay down nearly two minutes, so I'm told, but no one has timed him yet. It takes forever when you're waiting. On Foster's insistence he's begun to use the suit, though he doesn't like it.

It was a shock at night to go out and walk by the pens, where the oysters are kept. The longer they rot in the "ko-toos," the easier it is to examine them and pick through them, that is, if you can stand the flies and the maggots. And the sight of them moving. Rotting and moving. A mass of shifting, dying flesh, and the black crows flying overhead. Foster says they look like big, squirming potatoes, like yams covered in algae and mud. Sometimes their mouths open and close, as if they were trying to get a bit of air. But that's not the half of it. It's the stink, really, that will have an effect. It's been years since I'd smelt the stench of the fishery, since Bahrain. It reeks like nothing else. No man who's ever smelt the putrefying flesh of thousands of oysters knows what it is to be really sickened. I can't describe it, but it makes me think of saliva gone bad, and old blood, and a rotten, fleshy marine stink that you smell into your bones. You don't know how you'll ever wash it off yourself, just from being in the air around it. The natives who guarded the pens laughed when they saw my face. I suppose I looked as if I was going to spew.

"Mister McConnell, you don't like, sir?" They laughed. "You first time?"

February 25 —
Haven't had much time to keep the log. We've settled in here. It's a shame the way Foster drinks on the job — he nearly didn't bring Lalit up in time this morning, and I don't know what we'd do without him. Two of the men are sick, and we think it's the beriberi, caused by the rice diet. Drink is a terrible problem with the divers, too; and the pox is the rest of it. They come back from their whoring itching and dripping with the pox, and then they aren't fit to get in a diving suit.

As far as the beds go, we've got a good one and that's sure. But there are plenty of starfish in these waters, and they're the worst enemies of the oysters. Many's the oyster we see with a starfish wrapped around it, cutting off its life's blood.

February 27 —
Lalit had a serious accident. He came in plastered drunk and had a row with Foster. Foster was careless with the hose after that, and Lalit was very sick. He was white in the face on coming up, and said he couldn't breathe properly. He's very sick in the bay, and truly I don't know if he'll be diving anymore. Everyone's in a state about it — Foster said it wasn't

his fault, of course. Now the men want nothing to do with the modern bathing gear, and they're resorting to their old ways of diving bollock-naked. Some of them did this all along, and I will say they didn't do much worse than the other fellows. Brought up as many as 2,000 oysters in a day, sometimes even more.

We found something odd in the net this afternoon. It was a little creature, half earthworm, half centipede. We tried to examine it, but it went to pieces in our hands, and we had to throw the whole business back in the sea.

February 28—

You've got to plan for yourself in this world. It's the only way. I told van Velsen that. There's no god up there who's going to do the planning for you. When I see the way the money—and the pearls—slip through greasy palms, I get a few ideas of my own.

Lalit too sick to dive, and everyone is worried about it. The men are a little happier now that they're diving naked, but we do need another man. I was a strong swimmer when I was a boy, so I had a go myself this morning. It wasn't so difficult, after all. And it's a beautiful sight down there, something you only see in dreams, normally. I'm going to do it again tomorrow—I didn't bring up any pearls yet, just dove for a lark.

March 2—

I fancy myself a real native, now. The men tied a rock to my foot with a piece of twine, just the way they do it themselves, and I jumped in holding it. The bloody thing weighs 30 pounds, so you're down in a second when you do that— and then I slipped the twine off my foot and they began to haul the boulder up for the next man. I had a net with me, and I grabbed what I could. I managed about 60 oysters, not bad for a first haul. I can last over a minute, and the men are impressed with that as I'm not a native. But as I say, I was always a strong swimmer.

March 3 —

Foster very drunk today. He said to me, "McConnell, I don't trust them blue eyes of yours. You've got madness in them, like a native." I asked him what he meant, and he said, "You don't control yourself." He's the one that's mad, if you ask me.

I'm diving like a real Ceylonese now, I will say that. The men are very pleased with me, and I can go down for well over a minute. When I come up I can hear the super calling, "*Ettana chippei?*" That's Ceylon talk for "How many shells?" After the dive I lay back in the sun on the deck, just like a native, and I felt a little wind on my chest. Ceylon isn't so bad when you get used to it.

There was a fine pearl in my haul today, an especially fine pearl. John McSweeney opened her — and when we saw how beautiful she was we decided to name her after the fate of McSweeney's wife, he's such a faithless bastard — we called her the Widow's Tears. I told McSweeney today that sure he'd be happier back in Limerick with his bloody horses, keeping that wife of his a bit happier. A man's got to be where he belongs. He looked at me queerly — he's been talking to Foster, I imagine — and he says to me, "Where do you belong, mate? In the bleedin' sea?"

March 9 —

Something incredible today. Haven't told anybody about it. I was diving around the little reef that juts off the south side, very comfortable, only 30 seconds gone, when I saw a fish like I'd never seen. It was big, I can't say how big exactly, and long. But this fish, it wasn't a normal fish at all, I could see that right away. It was half hiding behind a rock, and I darted behind to look at it. Jesus. It was enormous — it must have been six and a half feet coiled. I'm only guessing, of course, but this is what I saw. More a snake than a fish, really, but not an eel, I'm sure of that. It had a small rounded head, and a curious face that seemed to have a mute expression on it — an expression of dumb alarm. What am I saying? Makes no sense. I wanted to go right back down and have another look, but the men said I needed a rest, and they were right. Tomorrow.

March 10—

I wish I had the gift of words just now, I wish I could express myself the way Mordecai does. I wish he were here to talk to. What I saw—what I saw is beyond anything I ever dreamt of. I went back down to the little reef, where the fish was. It took me twelve dives, and a good part of the morning, but I saw it again. I frightened it, this time, and it uncoiled and began to spread away through the water. The sheer size of it! I ought to have been frightened myself, I've never seen anything like that in the depths. But I was too excited for fear, and I swam after it, hugging the air in my lungs. I followed the thing behind a looming bit of rock, and there I came upon it: there must have been 500 of them, or perhaps there were a thousand. They were crammed together, thickly, as if they formed a great wall, a mass of writhing serpents, pressed in upon each other, coiled and wrapped, amidst the algae and coral. It was a vast, unearthly school of sea snakes. My breath was giving out, and the shock made me lose my wits. I made a quick dart for the surface, and in doing so I unsettled the mass of creatures. They started in a fearsome wave, like some prehistoric wall that shook and shimmered, and they made a frightening, weaving retreat to deeper waters. I broke the surface with not much to spare, and I lay gasping on the deck, confused and stunned. McSweeney thought I ought to have a little whiskey, and he fed it to me with a spoon while I lay there. I wanted to go right back in, though I don't remember this part—I must have begged to do so, for I remember being put into my bed and wrapped in blankets, even in the heat. I fell asleep, and when I woke up there was a cold sweat on me, and I thought I'd dreamt it all.

A little later I found McSweeney standing by the oyster vats, staring at them and drinking. We slugged out of a bottle of whiskey and finally he said, "McConnell, if I didn't know you better, man—if you weren't one of my *countrymen*," and he let the *o*'s roll out—he has that Limerick accent—"I'd say you weren't the full shillin'!" It obviously had taken all his aplomb to make this speech, and he stopped short, staring at me.

"Well," says I, "what do you mean by that?"

"It's what you were talking about when we brought you up. Ravin' you were. About sea serpents. That's right, man, don't look at me like that. You were ravin' about sea serpents. I don't think it's right," he concluded.

I didn't want to talk about it with McSweeney just then, though I like the man well enough. I needed to think, and I still do.

March 14—

I've been down to see them again. It's the draw of the serpents, I can't stop myself going down. They're still there, the mass of them, writhing, their hideous faces leering at me. I didn't tell anyone about it at first—I pretended I was going down to scout some beds, said I'd seen some spat. But they caught on in time, when I kept going down and coming back with nothing. I felt I had to take someone into my confidence. It wasn't my intention to tell Foster at all, but he manages the pump, and if he understood how important it was, we could make an arrangement to keep sending me down, fool the other men. I need more time to examine them. Well. I fancy Foster doesn't like the sound of it. Thinks I'm mad, so I'll have to show him, that's all. I'll bring one up.

March 21—

We've found some beautiful pearls, I really do think so. I wish the old man back in Paris could see them. Mordecai would be dead impressed. Perhaps I'll send a few on if I can manage it. I want them to know I'm getting on all right, and I do think of the old fella. It's a funny thing, but I can't help it. Well, it's only a matter of time before I've made a bit of money and I can go back to him, bring him a fine lot of pearls, too.

We ate "sea pig" for dinner tonight. You wouldn't know it was a fish.

April 8 —

I went back down on Saturday, as early in the morning as I could. Foster was at the pump, as usual. When I got down I saw them there: like a writhing, floating brown wall, a wall of serpents. I thought I heard them hissing, but I suppose that's impossible. I'd thought about them all the time — I'd dreamt of them. I was afraid they'd gone — migrated or some-thing — but fortunately the school seems to want to stay there. They have these little teeth, awful to look at, and small, rounded heads. Their bodies are long, long and coiled and flapping, with fins on the side that look ancient, prehistoric. There's no God made these things: they came from Hell.

It wasn't hard work to net one at the periphery of the group — but for a moment I had a queer fear about them, that they had some sort of hive-mind, that they'd all know what was happening. But it was nothing. I had to spear it, quickly. It struggled viciously — it was a small one, but even so it must be four feet long — and then it stopped flapping and I man-aged to get it up.

It bothered Foster. Well, I suppose I can understand it, when you see a thing like that. But he didn't even want to look at it. McSweeney saw it too, and his eyes got like saucers. He looked up at me and said, "It isn't right, man." And he walked away. The other men were very interested, and we discussed it at length, what it might all mean, and what sort of fish it might be related to. The natives pulled out all sorts of charms and as I expected, they were superstitious about it.

I put it by my bed that night, I didn't want anyone taking it. I bunk with Ryan, and he was mortified, but I wouldn't be affected. He went off and dossed down in McSweeney's room.

April 11 —

Perhaps it was on account of Foster that things went so wrong. I don't know. I think it was. I've been sick in bed for a few days, too sick even to write, but I think I'm on the mend now.

What happened was this: I told the men I'd only brought up a small one, and there were ones three times as big to be had. McSweeney said he dared me to prove it. I said I'd take some of the lads down with me (none of the other white men dive as I do) and they'd tell what was what. But none of them would have anything to do with it. Bloody superstitious lot. So I did the natural thing, what any man would do on a dare — I went down to have another go, and get a big one. I decided to wear the gear again, though I often go down without it.

I got down and there they were, as usual. I thought I felt them shiver — I know that's perfectly ridiculous; but as a whole, as a great mass, they *moved*. I was bolder this time, having got one already, and I swam about carefully, looking for a good-sized specimen. They're bloody frightening, if you stop to think about it. Best not to think about it too much, not if you're down there, at any rate.

Well, I did it, I speared a really large one. It was going off from the group when I struck. It fanned its fins as I hit, and they were like great, watery wings, transparent, so you could see the sea behind them. I was dead scared for a minute, but it was beautiful too, and I went on with it. They've almost got faces — mute, dumb faces — that show pain when they die. It was much too big for my net. I managed to pull it, to drag it up through the water, very slowly. And then I started to get this frightening feeling — the feeling every diver dreads — It makes me sick to write about it. I felt a pressure in my ears, and behind my eyes. I was losing oxygen, and my head was spinning. Ryan knew a man whose eyes popped out under water — when they found him, blood was pouring out the cavities. There was a pressure in my lungs, and a density in my chest that pushed up behind my eyes. I blacked out then, but even as I was going, I knew I was still holding on tight to the serpent.

I woke up in my bunk. A native man was sitting by me, putting blankets around me. There were some bloody towels on the floor, and I could feel the blood caking in my nose and my ears. I had two thoughts, when I woke up—Jesus, please don't let me spew blood—I remember thinking that, don't know why I cared so much. And the other was that I'd lost the serpent.

Ryan came in and looked at me. "You're up. Thanks be to God, man." He was quiet a minute. Then he leaned over and whispered to me, conspiratorially, "Foster was at the pump. Do you know what I'm sayin'?" I shook my head, I didn't understand it yet.

He shrugged and turned to leave, and then he added, "You lost oxygen. Must have been an accident with the hose."

We're going to be leaving in a few days. I can't dive for a while, that's what the doctor tells me. I don't understand why not. I feel well enough.

December 17 —

I've decided to take up the journal again. I think it's important. I'm back in Glasgow at the moment, and I've had a few adventures in between, since we left Ceylon. We set sail from the islands at the end of April. I never went back down again, and some of the men were cool to me after what happened. As if I had something to do with it. Foster and I barely spoke another word. I thought a lot about getting my revenge on him—revenge is important in a man's life; if you've been betrayed, there are scores to be settled, anyone would agree with that. But sure wasn't I a sick man, and I couldn't think as clearly as I like to.

I can feel the call of the serpents. I've felt it ever since we left Ceylon. I've got a plan now, and I think it's a good one. There's a lot of money at the end of it, and that's certain. I've got a little put by from my share of the pearls, and I took a job as soon as I was well enough, on another pearling ship. We went to Tahiti and dove for the black pearls there. This time I had a better cut, and I knew what was what going in. So now I've saved quite a bit, and I've managed to get Williams, the fur man, to agree to put something in. Williams is an unscrupulous bastard, but he's got money and that's what counts.

Here is the plan: I'll buy a ship, and have the hold outfitted to my design. I can store the serpents in the hold, and bring them back here, hundreds of them. It will make a sensation. I can sell them for big money, I know that, and after that I can do what I please, I can go back to the old man. I won't have to scrub any more floors or stand by any filthy oyster vats. And when I'm done studying, maybe van Velsen will want to go into business with me. We've talked about it before. I feel much better having a plan.

February 28 —

Finances are a problem. Fished the rivers around Inverness-shire, particularly the Spey. Then back to Ireland to work the Kerry and the Donegal. Not a bad take for freshwater, I've been able to make a little bit quickly. I'm putting a boat together Monday to have a go at the bay and see if we can't come up with a bed or two. People say there's never anything but edibles in that bay, but it can't hurt to have a look. I once heard of a man finding something.

March 5 —

I found a bed today, but nothing interesting inside. We only had time to take up about 70. Tomorrow better luck.

March 10 —

Sweet Jesus, I've found something down there. We took up another 40 oysters, and when we got about halfway through, I opened one up and found a blue pearl inside her. A great big one, of the finest quality. Worth a bloody fortune, and entirely unknown around these parts. Well, I've never seen that color anywhere, to be truthful. It's a kind of milky blue, that's how it struck me at first, and then later, it seemed darker, and later still almost transparent, like the color of the sky. Old Lemaître would have something to say about this. I didn't think any pearl could surprise me anymore, but I've seen something new, this time. I've a good mind to send it to Mordecai. It's worth a damn fortune, I'd imagine, but I might give it up anyway. We're all anxious to get back to the bed tomorrow, and see what can be seen.

March 15 —

Haven't had much time for writing. I've been diving again myself, I'm well enough now to do it. Lord, it felt good to get back into the sea again, even with the suit on. Made me miss those naked dives into that warm Ceylonese water. Soon.

I've big news. We've brought up seven more over the last month. It takes many more oysters than it ordinarily does to turn up one of the pearls, it's a lot of work, but the *hue* — I've sent the first one off to van Velsen. I couldn't resist. Even though I can't *see* properly, yet, I have a *sense* of that pearl. It's to do with how it changes all the time, I can't explain it. I think there are other blues inside her, finer and richer and rarer than what we can see, fine as it is. Perhaps by now Mordecai will know. I mean to write him and the old man, it's just I'm so bloody busy. And besides, I want to surprise them.

March 17 —

I could get damn rich off these pearls, there's no doubt about it. If I had half a brain in my head I'd stay and mine that bed, but I feel I must get on with it in Ceylon. Those fish are calling to me. I'm not mad, I feel it. The Dublin Bay can wait — it's not going anywhere. It's home, after all. I'll find the real riches in Ceylon. The ship is nearly ready.

May 12, Ceylon —

We've begun. It's an important day, thought I should record it for posterity. I did the first dive myself. I've been dying to get down there. I love the feel of throwing off my clothes and cutting through the warm water. It might do to come back to Ceylon for the pleasure of it, one of these days. Anyway, I knew right where to go, I had no hesitation. And there they were. They hadn't migrated, or moved at all. They just seemed bigger, as if they'd multiplied. Well, I suppose they would, it's been a year. They seemed agitated when they saw me, and I heard that hissing sound again. I'll never get used to the sight of their dull, nervous faces. It shocked me all over again. Sure I'll get used to it. We begin tomorrow. I've had special nets made up. The storage tanks in the hold are all ready.

May 15 —

What a time we've had with the first ones! The native divers have been very nervous — they've gone down and then been unwilling to go after the prey. I had to get the first three myself. Believe me, it isn't as easy to take them alive as it is to spear them! We've had a lot of false starts, and it's taken a lot of dives each day, maybe 50 or 60. It will take forever at this rate. When I've trained the natives, things will go more quickly. It's a lot of strain on me, doing all the work.

I netted the first one at the edge of the group, just as I had before. It wasn't large, but it squirmed and undulated like a big worm, and it snapped its jaw. It has a prehensile jaw, or whatever you call it. The sight of its jaw snapping at me made me reach for my gun, but that won't do — I just had to contain it in the net and get back up. When I broke surface, it really began to thrash. I thought the natives were all going to bolt at the sight of it. I got one of the Brits to help me pull it up on deck, and there it set up a terrible writhing in the net, snapping its jaws, and jumping about. Fortunately, Ellis is a man who can keep his wits, and the two of us lugged it into the holding vat as planned. The vat is on deck, and of course we'll be transferring the creatures into the hold as soon as possible. Once it was back in the water, it calmed a little, though its mouth was still snapping, and I didn't like to look into its eyes. Ellis kept picking at his ear, which is what he does when he's very nervous, but I was pleased with him. The other two catches went similarly, though the third made a tear in the net. Too tired to go on. More tomorrow.

May 24 —

Happy bleedin' birthday to me. Ellis and Walters saved a bottle of Crested Ten, and that must have been tough. Sweet Jesus, what a relief to drink it instead of that local booze, for a change. There's nothin' like a smooth drop of the hard stuff to say to your soul you love it, even though you can't save it. Let's see you do that, Jesus.

Well, we've got the hold filling up nicely with them, now. I just want to dive for them, all the time. Everyone else gets more and more awkward about it. I don't understand it. I've paid several of the natives enough to where they can't refuse, but for every time they go down, there's a big ritual mucky-muck so it takes three times as long. I've tried sacking them and getting new men, but it's all the same. They say the ocean is haunted and I'm interfering with the spirits of the sea, just the kind of rubbish you'd expect. And they think the fish are eating the pearls from the beds! It's an old island superstition, wouldn't you know it. Pearl-sucking serpents. People get mad ideas, don't they? Brown and white alike. It's because they haven't the proper marrow in them; I understand that. So I do the better part of the work myself. It's all right — I feel part of the sea now myself. I hardly ever sleep, there's no time for it.

Half the problem I have is managing the tanks. The men do the minimum. It's a complicated system I've arranged in the hold, very expensive. Some of the men won't go down there at all. I go down every evening, feed them small fish, when all the crew is asleep, and look at them. They look like bloody diamonds to me. They're my fortune. They move around one another like so many big worms, and they hiss, and they flap their fins. Sometimes I fancy I hear them moaning — I know they hate being captive. Well, don't we all.

June 17 —

We've got 73 now — I'm shooting for 100. It's crowded in the tanks, but I know we can manage. It's a lot of work feeding them all, and sometimes the hissing gets damn loud. A few have died, but that was to be expected — I've made allowances for that.

What's odd about them is that the school never moves, though I keep taking them away, every day. It's not half strange. I wonder, just my mad imagination — I wonder sometimes if there isn't a *complicity* among them — they want to see their fellows taken away, always thinking to themselves — it won't be me, it'll be the other fellow — Mordecai would get a good laugh over it. I wish he were here to talk to. I've got no one to talk to, at the moment. If I've learned one thing it's that there doesn't live a man who isn't superstitious. Except yours truly. I've no bleedin' time for it.

June 22 —

Another one died today. We saw it going, and we thought it was done, so we took it out of the tank to toss it overboard. I was busy with the feeding, so I told one of the natives to do it. Well, the bloody thing bit him — tore off half of his hand. And we thought it was dead. The lad cried bloody murder, I thought he was going to faint. But I don't have much sympathy for him — if you get into a thing like this, you have to be prepared to take the consequences. This is what happens if you're not careful.

June 24 —

We're nearly done. I wouldn't mind netting a few more, but the tanks are getting crowded. Ellis is tiring, I can see that, so I've been relying heavily on Dawson. The problem with that bastard is he has to have a poke every damn night. You can't count on him to be there in the morning. He'll come back with the bloody clap any time now. I know, I've seen it before. Time to go down for the evening feed.

June 25 —

Dawson is a randy sod, but he's a good mate. Says he knows a native girl will go with me for a few shillings, but I haven't got the time to give her a length. I told him watch out where he puts that tool of his, some little native snatch will bite it off. Sweet mother of Jesus, I'm so tired, I can barely write.

July 2 —

You've got to be optimistic. It's important. I've docked four of the men for complaining. They said they wouldn't do the feeds anymore, and they said the tanks were over-crowded. Well, didn't I design them? Don't I know if the bastards can hold more fish? When you're an innovator, the world kicks your teeth in, I've seen it before, but now I know it first hand. These men are weak. It's the church, as I always say — makes women of good men. I guess they thought St. Patrick got rid of the snakes — well, I'm fuckin' bringing them back. And as for the natives, well, it's hoodoo from day one till you're dead.

July 19 —

Well, we've set sail. Without half the crew, mind. Walters came to me last night and announced that a lot of the men were uncomfortable, natives and Irishmen alike, and pre-ferred to stay on. Said they didn't quite feel safe with "those things in the hold." I said, "They're not things, they're *ple-siosaurs*, I've been reading up. Don't be a fool. What about your take? You won't see any." He didn't even fight. It's pathetic. He said, "We've discussed it. We don't care, we'll go without. We don't feel right about the thing. It's against God. They belong in the sea." So I said, "Right then. Bugger off. I don't want to look at you again." And that was it. Bloody mutineers. It's a load of Catholic rubbish, what God does and doesn't want. I say you do for yourself.

Johnson just came in. He's a quiet lot, he's never spoken up to me before. But he had a little speech for me. Amazing. He said, "Captain McConnell, on behalf of the men, I want to say we think you're a brave man, sir. But we do want to be sayin' — we think you've gone a bit off. I don't *meself*, sir, you understand, but some of the men do. That you're a bit hard, sir." He turned tail and ran and that was it. The sea gets to men. I've never felt it myself, but I've seen it a lot. Good riddance, they were a sodding lazy lot, anyway.

July 20 —

Ran into Johnson again last night. I said, "How's the form, then?"

He said, "The form's grand, sir."

I said, "People will lie to you, you know that, don't you, Billy?" (That's his name, Billy Johnson.)

"Yes, sir," he said.

"Well, that's it, then. You have to understand that. When you have a grasp of it, it's all right." I had to speak to the boy in a way that he would understand. He's still very young, and doesn't know about the world. I don't mind sharing a bit of what I know. We've got to pass it on, as we learn things.

August 10 —

McConnell's Truth.

Only I know McConnell's Truth. My inevitability. My sea destiny. Those others got undone by the sea, but I have no such problems. I need more sleep, I know that. But with half a crew now there's that much more for me to do: the feeding, the chores, managing them. It's altogether a big job. A vast job. Sometimes the hissing keeps me up at night. Well, it would bother anyone, but I'm more *attuned* to them, if you will. I know their ways. I know if they're crowded or not. They're fine. Some are looking sluggish but I'm not worried about it. That's how it is. I get that way sometimes myself, and who doesn't when he feels penned in.

August 13 —

McConnell On His Own.

That's how it will end. We begin alone, we finish alone. Mordecai has always understood this, that's what makes him my friend. The old man knows something else, I almost understand it, but not quite. About the sanctity of being alone. What am I going on about here? I've written some poetry. Ceylon will have that effect. I call it: McConnell On His Own.

McCONNELL ON HIS OWN

Beware the Siam cannibals
Beware the watery death

Beware the drowning waters
Beware the serpent's breath

Be careful of the nighttime
Be watchful of the dark
Grim reaper strikes at morning
Be careful of the lark

But watch out for the one grim thing:
The devil wants a wife
O guard your soul against this sin:
Beware the half-lived life
Beware the half-lived life

O it's too hot in Ceylon
And it's too cold in the sea
At last I saw the devil's teeth
Leering up at me
He said:

Be careful 'cross the seven seas
The seven skies
And earth
Heaven wants you
Hades taunts you
They're waiting after birth

Watch out for fire
Watch out for water
Be careful where you tread
Bad burns will haunt you
Death will taunt you
You're empty when you're dead

Well once you seized my snapping heart
I saw the sea and sky
I surrendered, but just in part
My heart saw like an eye
And for that crime
I'll always be

A greying man
Drowned in the sea

O it's too hot in Ceylon
And it's too cold in the sea
At last I saw the devil's teeth
Leering up at me

August 14 —
Two of the crew have come from morning watch over the tanks. The weather is bad. They said the serpents are looking fairly seedy, and hadn't we better let a few out to give them more breathing room?

I got angry when I heard this. What do these sodding fools think? I told them what was on my mind, I said, "We've been at sea for months. We're far from Ceylon. If we let them out here, if that was *even necessary*, they'd breed, wouldn't they? They'd let their filthy spawn out all over the bloody Indian Ocean, and then what would we have? Nothing special. They'd be a dime a dozen and then where are we, eh?"

They didn't say much more, so I expect I got through to them, but I can't be sure. We put in for supplies tomorrow at Port Said.

August 15 —
Betrayed. Most of the men have got off here and won't be coming back. I'm not going to try and replace them, I can manage with the few I've got left. It's their funeral.

August 20 —
The fish don't look right. The water is a little too muddy, as if they were letting off filth, and they look weak. Some of the serpents are lying heaped at the bottom of the vats. Little time to write, only time to tend them.

August 27 —
Dead tired. I'm in rags and tatters. The serpents aren't well, and it's got me worried. The men spend all their time

managing ship's affairs, I do everything in the hold. It takes every minute. I've got the answer, though, I really do. I've begun to feed them pearls. I think it's what they eat in the sea, it's their natural diet. I drop them in slowly, carefully, and watch to see they go down. It makes good sense that it will restore them.

September 1 —

Hansen threw a moody. He walked in during a feeding and just lost his head, began striking me. Tried to stop me feeding them the pearls. He landed a few blows. I had to take out my knife, and that stopped it. I don't like to do that, but what else was I to do? He doesn't understand what real money is, he's a poor fool. I told him, "Just hold on, mate. Get a grip. You'll be in your local soon enough having a pint. Settle down."

September 5 —

The pearls all gone. It will bring them up to snuff soon enough. Hansen says they're half dead, but he's got it all wrong. They're in hibernation.

September 19 —

The smell from the vats isn't so bad. I'm used to the fisheries, but it's not even like that. Makes those oysters smell like perfume.

September 27 —

Hansen can't speak too much anymore. He says, "They're rotting in the hold, McConnell," and that's all. He's drinking too much. You have to watch out for the Irish, sometimes. They're my own countrymen, and I hate to say it, but they do drink.

Dermot set the papers into a pile, and reached for his cup. "Tea's cold," he said, and ran his forefinger around the rim. Then, "The diary broke off here. McConnell made his way back, with only two native men and Hansen left on board. Hansen was useless by then, the pearls were all gone, and as for what was found in the hold . . . This is all family lore, mind you. The ship was burned by some vandals after it got into port, and everyone said it was just as well.

"My grandfather, he was safe on land at the time. His trunk, with the diaries and the skeleton and a few pearls, that was safe too. No one believed what had happened. He'd get pissed at the pub and you couldn't stop him talkin'. He was mad for a bit, fit for the asylum, he was, but eventually he calmed down enough to work, mopping floors and such. He married my grandmother, a quiet girl from the town, and they had five children. People said he went to Mass to please his wife, but that may have been rumor. He died when I was seven. I remember hearing him ravin' at times, and telling stories of the sea, and of an old Frenchman in Paris, and a friend he used to love. Sometimes he talked about the blue pearls, which came from his home sea, and how he found them once, then lost them. "I rambled everywhere, boy," he used to say. "I rambled all the seas and skies. You'll wander too, I know it." Sometimes he was so quiet nothing could induce the man to speak. I was a bit frightened of him, but I admired him immensely, and I always asked to see his tattoos. Sure I got a tiger myself when I was old enough. Jaysus, my mum was furious. Here, see?"

Dermot curled back the sleeve of his shirt, and showed me the bright orange cat that glowed on his pale skin. He laughed. "I got an eclipse on the other arm. Just here, the sun and moon together . . . I fancy gettin' a dragon as well. What do you think? Anyway, as a boy, everyone said I took after my grandfather, more than my own parents. That happens. I remember what he used to say to me — 'You've got to do for your bleedin' self, boy. Don't let anyone tell you different.' When he was dying, he told me that again, for the hundredth time. But he added one thing more. 'My boy,' he said, 'where your heart is, there will your treasure be,' and he touched my chest just here.

I hadn't a breeze what he meant. It gave me a funny feeling . . . to think of that old sod quoting from the Lord's book! Well, I expect a lot of people were glad to see him go. He was just a burden to them. It hurt me, though. It hurt me a lot. I hadn't ever lost anything before, do you know what I mean? And . . . and everyone around me seemed different than he had been, and madder, though they said *he* was the mad one. I pined for him, I did, after he died. I was only a boy. Didn't eat, and went a bit dreamy, until my father got fed up with it. I closed up the place inside that missed him, what else could I do? And no one else gave a damn for him. As for the skeleton, no one gave a damn for that either. Until the day I found the trunk.

"This discovery changed my whole life. I only wanted, with all of my heart, to go to sea. But it wasn't even the serpents I was cravin', romantic as the business was. It was the blue pearls, Lily, from the Dublin Bay.

"That Irish Sea is cold. But in the summer, we made a game of it, jumping bollock-naked into those icy waves, and trying to stay down. I forced myself, and I did have a knack for it. I could ignore a bit of pain.

"I was fired up by the dream of the blue pearls. I knew that bed was there, waiting, but I hadn't a breeze how to find it. I didn't have the money for proper scuba gear, and I had to find a way to make some. I began to work the rivers, just as my old grandfather had done—the rivers Tyrone, Donegal, and Antrim, collecting the 'silver-clouded moons'—that's what they call the Irish sweet waters, in the trade. I fished the riverbeds in Scotland as well, and soon I was operating a small trade in freshwater pearls. Well, as you know, they don't make anything like the kind of money to be found in the sea, but I had the knack for it, and soon I bought some gear and some tanks, and I rented a boat. It wasn't long before I was making my first explorations into the bay.

"At first I did what the other divers do, I wore the oxygen tanks. But when I dove like that, I felt weighed down, no edge to it. There's pleasure in that sort of diving, sure, but it's for tourists. Without the heavy tanks I felt like part of the ocean, the animals never shied away, and I could move about among the reeds and starfish.

"And Jaysus, couldn't I hold my breath! The normal limit, even among the best of 'em, is about a minute and a half, or maybe two—I swam for nearly four. Fuckin' unnatural, it was. And painful. But I kept on bit by bit, goin' deeper into that sea. And Mother of God, the things I saw! Colors that don't exist in the air, and swayin' plants, fifty feet tall—when I brushed up against them, fish *this* big—I'm not havin' you on, they were—fish would burst out and swarm around me. Ah, when you're down there, it's so beautiful you don't worry anymore about who made it or why.

"By the time I was twenty, I was longin' for other oceans, for warm oceans, where I could dive deep without the suit. I made a living at it—I dove for the black pearls of Tahiti. I worked the Gulf of Mannar in India. I made quite a name for myself. But summers I always came back to Ireland, back to my home and back to the bay that I knew held my treasure.

"I dove that sea every bloody chance I got, but I didn't find McConnell's bed. Perhaps, says I to myself, it's been washed away, perhaps he just dreamed it—He was mad, everyone knew that. As the years went by, that dream was a holy grail to me. I got a bit queer in the head, and bitter as well. I sat up nights, thinkin' about the oyster that would be holdin' such a prize. My craving made a fool of me. And I started having weird dreams—I dreamt of the color blue. Blue seas, with little white diamonds shining on the waves, blue skies, blue evenings, blue dawns. And I kept taking risks, damned stupid risks.

"One summer night, there was no more blue. I saw blood in my dreams, thin streams of blood that flowed from my body into the ocean. Outside, the trees were blowing against the houses, beating against the sky. I got up and looked out at the night—Jaysus, the stars in that sky!—millions of 'em. I had to go out into it. I put my clothes on and I walked the streets for hours. I thought I saw the lampposts swaying in the dark. And then the stars just went out, and left this queer smoke in the sky. I made my way down to the water, and I sat by the shore until dawn, thinkin' crazy thoughts. When the light began to rise, my thoughts went out in my head, just like the stars that were melting away in the sky, and a quiet came on me as I looked out at the waves. The ocean was so still, I thought it had stopped moving. It lay there flat, like a plate of glass. Fuckin' weird, it was. I noticed the wind had stopped blowing, and the air was completely still.

"I took my boat out on the water, and when I was far enough out, I dove in. There was no movement at all, no resistance. I just sliced right through the deep. I swear, it wanted nothing more than to welcome me, to give up her treasures to me. I loved her, that sea, and I felt my heart beating, and that water, it was sleek and fine. I swam out a long ways from the boat, until I reached a small inlet that I'd seen before, but never explored. The water was deceptive, teasin' like; there were riptides and shards of rock jutting out. I swam over to an odd bit of coral, and under a branching anemone, I saw a small bed of oysters.

"The oysters weren't too big—I wondered if they were too young to bother taking up. But I put some in my bag for the hell of it, and tied it around my waist. Back on the deck I opened them. There was nothing inside. Nothing at all. But I had an instinct. I wanted to plunder the bed, and pry open every oyster. I spent hours bringing 'em up, up and down I went. Then I sat in the boat, prying them open, feeling a bit stupid. I must've done a hundred of 'em, one after the other, all empty. The one that had her didn't look any different. It was right inside, asleep in the heart of the oyster, a bright blue pearl, the pearl of my ol' fella's dreams. It was glowin', Lily, and you can't put a price to a thing like that. I lay back in the dinghy, dead happy, but Jaysus, I was shattered and shakin' from the cold.

"After that, diving those beds became my whole life. I wouldn't tell anyone about it—I had to do it all on my own. I kept going down deeper, to find more oysters. My lungs nearly burst on me. I says to myself, 'Dermot, you'll fuckin' die down here, won't you, blue pearls and all. Do you fancy rottin' down here?' But I couldn't stop. It took me months to get a dozen pearls, all fit for a queen's throat—You've seen, you know. But I wasn't satisfied—I wanted enough for a necklace. The pearls got scarcer, so I went deeper. I didn't use my head, I didn't build up to it. If I'd gone more slowly, more careful like, given myself the proper time, built my muscles and my strength . . .

"One day I went too deep for my own damn good. It was a nightmare—the thing that divers don't even like to talk about. I went down too fast, and coming back I started to cramp up. The light went out behind my eyes, I pushed up but I felt the sea flooding my lungs. My mouth filled with blood, and something went bad in my ears. It wasn't that I was hurtin', dyin' didn't scare me, I don't fuckin' care about that. It was something else, Lily—that water turned against me. It betrayed me, understand? But all that was later. Then it was just fighting against the waves, thrashing under there.

"I didn't feel any big thing about dying, no exaltation, no bleedin' angels like you read about, no grand forgiveness, either. I was just pissed off. And then I scraped against something. Jaysus. It was a huge stingray—the bleedin' size of it! It wrapped around me, it touched me here, on my face, and my chest. I barely got away from those flapping brown wings. My face was burning up, I was on fuckin' fire in the water, and my guts were bursting.

"I woke up in hospital. Someone found me, and saved me, if you want to call it that. I wasn't grateful. I lay in bed, half dead. I was aching all over. That accident opened up something in me. A poison inside me. I tried to sleep, to get away from it, but it was useless. The croakers told me I'd never work again, that my lungs were ruined for diving. If I went down even once more, I'd be a dead man.

"I wanted to leave Dublin. When I was well enough, I took the cattle boat over to England. I was broke—the pearls were all I had. I got onto the dole; I found a squat for a time in North London, and then a bedsit in Crouch End.

"I lay in bed most of the time. All those months of seeing blue, and now everything was gray. I could barely lift my arm out of bed, I was so weak. I dreamt in gray, I woke up and I saw gray, and I couldn't remember blue.

"I lay in that bed for months, so sick I thought I'd die, and so wrecked I wasn't sure I cared. I slept for hours at a stretch: ten, eleven, twelve hours or more. My lungs still ached, my head ached, my heart felt dead inside my chest. As if I was hollow inside. Jaysus, I was weak! My feelings were all gone. Sorrow, especially—sorrow felt like something I once knew, and had forgotten.

"Slowly, I recovered. It took a hell of a long time—it was months before I could get out of my bed. Finally I could walk in parks, and drink a bit. Meself and Goodie got a job tendin' bar. One night, after a party, it was real late, I was sittin' up in my room, doin' nothin'. I didn't feel much of anything in those days, as I say—except when I touched water, or when it rained, or once in a while when I made my way to the sea and swam . . . I drank till everything was dark, till I almost wept. Do you know what I wanted, Lily? I wanted to shut off the fuckin' light—just shut it off. After going to bed with a girl, it was the same thing. A coldness came over me, but I didn't know why. I left girls crying, I went so cold. I never understood it. The coldness got right into me, I couldn't bust out of it until I got in a scrap, or went boozin', or until I felt the cool sea against my skin.

"This coldness reached into me, just here, into my heart. Late one night I cut my arms with a razor. Not on my wrists—I didn't want to die, you know. I just wanted to have the feelin' —that clean connection with my blood, what I felt in the sea. Hah. Sure I was a hard man.

"I wanted to make myself weep, I wanted to make myself feel, but all I saw was blood spilling down my arm. In the end, I did cry—I cried for not cryin', I cried for not feeling. I thought the tears and blood together would make amends, but don't you know my eyes dried, just like eyes will, and my blood caked, just like blood, and left these ugly lines for a memory. Goodie comes by just after I done it, and he says, 'Ah, you're a sick bastard, Dermot. You've gone off your bleedin' shillin', lad.' I says, 'Well you can set that to music. Now fuck off, man, leave me the fuck alone.' He tries to wrap it up in some socks, but I told him to piss off. 'You're a cold fucker, Dermot,' he says, 'but I'm your mate and I worry about ye.' That was Goodie, you know.

"That night I had a vision—it sounds absurd—I've never told anyone about it before. He came to me, the old man himself—he'd been drinking and there were hollows under his eyes—but they still shone blue, though the rest of him was light and flat, like a shadow, or an X ray, or a child's cartoon of a ghost. Another sickly dream, I was thinkin', but it was so *vivid*, I believed it was something more, as if the old man had gathered himself one last time to speak to me.

" 'Dermot,' he says to me, 'as sure as I'm standing here, as sure as you ever knew me—and you, boy, *you* knew me, it's you are my only blood—don't they say you've got my eyes? —don't leave this earth without your treasure. I promise you, if you do, then *you're* the ghost, the walking death, you'll have wasted the spark, your own precious fire.' I was too sick to be scared, Lily, and I already half lived in a world of dreams . . . I watched my grandfather move, a translucent shade, about the room. I had a mind to laugh, even in my pain—I thought for certain I was finally going mad, and that was a relief, and the relief itself seemed funny.

" 'Dermot,' he says, 'it's here'—and his ghostly hand tapped my chest. I could feel my heart beating, but sure it was cold inside, like it had been ever since the accident. I felt him try to pass something on to me, a dying warmth, but he had nothing, he wasn't real, what could he give? And then he said the words again — I hadn't heard them since I was a young fella — 'Where your heart is, there will your treasure be.' The words made me sick, my stomach came up on me, my guts ached and felt thick. I turned away, and when I closed my eyes I saw the bleedin' sea, as if it were on fire. I remember falling into a long sleep, and thinking, When you wake up, you'll be mad. But when I woke, I was no madder than before, just tired and more empty, and more cold."

Dermot paused here, and looked around the garden, as if for a way out. "You see, I've never told that. Makes me sound mad, that's one thing, but that's not the worst, it's the remembering . . .

"Slowly, I recovered. Day by day and bit by bit, but that counsel of my grandfather's did me no good. It might have done me harm. I've got no method for a treasure hunt like that, and I don't know that I see the point. I'll tell you this, Lily" — he stared at me intensely — "I *am* my grandfather's blood, I'll swear to that. And the way I see it, some treasures — pearls and diamonds and such — those are for anyone, they're common. Others are a luxury, and who on the bloody earth can truly afford them?

"That was two years ago. After a time, my strength came back to me, and so did my hope of diving again. I stopped drinking and fighting, and I kept away from women. I rested and I took care. I tried to sell a few of the pearls in London, enough to finance my dream: to buy a boat and the gear I needed, and return to the bay where my treasure was. No one wanted them, you know — the pearls looked dead fake, even to them old masters. I might have sold my grandfather's Tahitian blacks, the ones I found in the trunk, but I couldn't bear to part with them. Your grandfather Mordecai was my last hope." He paused. "That's it. That's my story. The end."

"What will you do if you don't sell the pearls?"

"I'll stay here, I expect. Do a bit of diving on the Mexican coast; there's good pearling in Baja, you know. Make enough money to go back and do what I have to do. It will take a long time. But—" He shrugged. "It's the one thing. It doesn't matter how long it takes."

"I'll buy them."

His eyes were solemn and quiet. I read the surprise in the flicker of light that passed through them, but his face remained steady.

"Do you know what I'll charge?"

"I have an idea. I know what they're worth."

"No one else believes in them. Aren't you going to X-ray them? Aren't you going to test them to be certain?"

"I don't have to. I know what real things are. It doesn't matter what other people see or what they say." I looked down at the tea leaves floating in my cup. "I have a lot of flaws, but that's my one gift."

We went to my home to eat dinner, and we talked. He told me stories of the sea, and I told him about the hearts of pearls. I told him about you, all about you, and what I learned from you. It began to rain, and Dermot made a fire, poking it and coddling it until the first logs gave off a faint smoke. I watched him leaning busily over the grate, his tired eyes and his boy's spirit, deft hands teasing out the recalcitrant flame.

"In Ireland they burn peat," he told me. "They take it from the bogs and dry it. It smells like the earth burning. Do you know anything about the alchemists, Lily? We have all the elements of the alchemical furnace right here." He tapped the grate. "This bit of metal, the wet sap in the wood, the logs, and the air all around. Sometimes the alchemists only wound up with fool's gold, though." He prodded the pile of hissing wood. "Do you think it will catch?"

The tang of the smoke hit the back of my throat. Watching his face by the heat of the flames, watching the shadows that moved like sylphs around the high cheekbones and the blue eyes, the play of light on the white skin and black hair, I felt danger wash through me like a wave of fever, the first flush that comes when an illness is going to strike, and you say to yourself, "I'm not really going to be sick—it's a change in the weather, or this flower that affects me so; it's an allergy, it's a shift in the wind." But, like the destined sufferer, illness falls over you and you can't shake it off.

"Dermot," I said, touching his hand, "stay."

"I shouldn't," he replied. "I have things to do—This will only get in the way of them." He smiled. "I told you—I'm a bit of a wreck." He touched his heart.

The fire began to spit and crackle, and we watched the smoke as it curled between the logs. He looked at me a long time.

"I'm leaving. You bought the pearls."

"I don't care if you're leaving. What does it matter?"

"But it does. Lily, I don't know why the coldness comes over me, and when it does, I can't stop it. It would hurt me if I felt it with you, but I could. I probably would."

I sensed, then, that the blue eyes were dangerous. I saw the other side of the sea—distance, emptiness, coldness, trial. A sea for drowning.

"It's going to catch," he said, pointing at the logs. I turned away, and I felt him in the air between us. I waited, still, like a deer, feeling his gaze on my shoulders. "All right then," he said, his voice tight and angry. He grabbed me roughly, and circled me in his arms. The rage turned tender, mercurial as water.

"You've got lovely, milky skin," he said, pressing his lips against my neck. "It's the color of the moon." I slipped gently into his smell and his touch, into the scent of the sea and the ancient eyes. After a time he stopped his kisses, and looked down at me, weaving his fingers through my hair.

"What if it was just this once, Lily? What if I never came back?"

"I don't care." I felt the lie burn my heart.

He smiled, and kissed me softly, and seriously, and with a vast languor, as if we had years and years, and no enemies, and no obstacles. As the fire blazed behind us, it made a little light, which glowed softly on the scars on his arms. I stared at them, until he placed my fingertips against the angry braille.

"You see," he said, "I told you. It was bleedin' stupid of me. I'm not what you think."

"No, don't say that. It only matters that there was an urge, it only matters that you know what that urge was. You have to ask yourself. Every impulse matters."

"I was stupid. Do you understand?" His eyes were hard.

"Let me kiss them." I touched my lips to the scars, but he flinched away. His eyes were mocking, now, and angry. As revenge, he made love to me with a dangerous, masculine touch, a menacing control entwined with gentleness and tenderness; and struggle as I would, the net only grew tighter around me. His touch made pleasure arc inside of me, made old secrets tremble in my body, but when I looked in his eyes I saw that he had slipped far away, safe from squalls, safe from drowning. He was dead inside; something had died in the sea and I couldn't reclaim it for him. I wanted to see a fire burn inside him, because I loved something in that mad heart, but the sea had taken it away, and it wasn't mine to heal or give back. His hands and body never stopped their skillful work, he coaxed surrender from me, and when I most belonged to him, his gaze was gone, lost in brooding waters.

We fell asleep in each other's arms, and all the layers of coldness left with the night. We slept entwined, and every time I woke, his warm arms held me, he wrapped me in his waving dreams and pressed me tight against his heart. I woke again, at dawn, covered in a soft, warm sweat, and watched his face in sleep, empty of ambition. Perhaps he dreamt of the sea, of his pearls, of his own blue stars. But his face was gentle, and the hard, violent life was gone, leaving the soft, reaching beauty of a boy becoming a man, of a sleeping angel.

He woke beneath my gaze and drew me to him, gently at first, then forcefully, intense and sure, as if the night had changed him. I struggled, it almost hurt me, and I wanted to cry out — At last he'd reached a secret place, all women know it, that place of flowerlike surrender. With his body's clairvoyance he found this center, and held my hips, not moving. I saw his eyes catch fire, the coldness gone, and in one bright moment I yielded, accepting this touch, this shattering fusion. It was the place where life is made, and worlds are born, where reason crumbles and stars open.

Light blossomed behind my eyes, strange soaring bursts of sky, and in a moment of sun I knew that I had changed, and that with him or without him, I was different. Life is made from these fires and these forces, every day, but I bore something else — a vast and tremulous inner life, a new clairvoyance. Where once I saw into the hearts of pearls, now I knew I would see into the souls of living things. By this sweet alchemy I had flowered, and I saw the true, bursting world. For a soaring moment, all things streamed with light and magic, my own glow replaced my pain, my eyes rested, at last, open and unafraid.

I had known, the moment I saw the pearls, that I wanted them — I hadn't felt such greed in a long time. I was scared of the feeling — I had unlearned attachment, after so much loss — or so I thought. That you aren't alive to see them — that's a kind of crime.

My buying them meant he was free to leave. Free to sink to an ocean bottom, free to inhale the sea, free to choke on ancient water, free for the reaper, free for the scythe. I've never been so scared to lose anything. But a love for this man drove me, a gritty, human wish for his survival — that, and a greedy, crazy love for the sea blue pearls. They cost me a fortune — they are incomparable, and I knew I would never sell them; but I had to own them — the price seemed small. Most of them were whole, but a few needed working. You know as well as I do the limitations of the sight. The more we care, the more difficult the task. Perhaps it was a gamble to buy them, not knowing, but it was a risk you would have taken.

Dermot left the next day, on a Sunday. There was a radiant sun in the San Francisco sky, and a blazing light shone on his fair skin.

"Crybaby," he said, but my eyes were dry. In his I saw a faint luminescence, the ghost of soft tears. I looked away, to keep from falling into the sea.

He looked at me long and seriously. "The sea doesn't scare me, Lily. Not at all. Not really. There's only one sea can drown a man." He smiled, and tapped his head, and then his heart. I stared at his broken-toothed grin.

He leaned to kiss me, and then he whispered, "You understand. I can't have anything to hold me here. I can't have anything that stands between me and my risk. If I lost my nerve because I needed you . . ." He shook his head. "I can't write to you. Please understand. It will tie me here."

"Dermot," I said, "take this. It's a charm for luck. I'll feel better if you have it." I reached into a drawer, and I took out the Moon of the Celebes. No one but Chen Li had ever seen it.

"Sweet Jesus," he said, and smiled. "I'll keep it close to me."

I know you don't mind my giving up the moon, Uncle. I fastened it to a chain, so he could wear it around his neck. And that's how I thought of him, in all the months that followed: his long limbs diving into the sea, and slicing through the water, with the Moon of the Celebes around his neck.

I dreamed so often of death, then, that when I woke I was always thinking of it. I dreamed of loss, and abandonment, and I imagined the Moon of the Celebes returning to the ocean, lost forever, and back home again. I drifted into reveries about going to find the lost pearl, searching all the oceans of the world. I wondered how long I could live without a letter, and still think that he was alive.

But in this time, which could have been a hell, I grew less

afraid of death, of its gentle acquaintance. I strung the blue pearls into a necklace, drilling them with great precision. Other pearls I worked on, now, opened up before me, unfolding as they never had before; and other jewels, too, revealed elegant, simple inner lives. I worked slowly, and steadily, turning out very little, but each new piece found its home next to a dreamer's throat, or wrist, beside a breast or on a hand, where it shone in a radiant symbiosis of skin and light. In this patient time, when waiting informed my days like the beat of a steady heart, I stopped seeing blue. I saw green sometimes, in my dreams, or red or yellow, but never azure, never sapphire, never his blue eyes. I decided, after a time, that this meant he must be dead. Dead, or succeeded, and loving somewhere else, dreaming somewhere else.

Inside I was living at a different pace, like the speeded-up films of plant life. Some incomprehensible devotion to him lay over all my moods, making me a mystery to myself. I had said good-bye to Alan, and to Johnny, and I thought, in some childish way, that the heavens would open and deliver a sweet and simple, an easy love. But they brought me a Chinese puzzle instead, a gift beyond my reach and in the marrow of my dreams, someone elementally like me, my mysterious twin, but who lived, unfinished like all of us, in a world of urgent dreams and driving scars. Making love to him was like letting a wild animal loose in my house. It ran amok and broke precious things, it created an exciting disorder. I didn't have you to talk to, Uncle, so I often had angry words with God, the punitive, white-bearded God of my childhood. I addressed him, complaining, a petty Job, demanding to know why I should be sent another trial.

Uncle, I went beyond waiting. His quest might take a lifetime, or two or three. I had reached the point where my heart would not close against him. I had no choice but to love. To love full well knowing he lay in his bed at night, nursing old scars and dreaming of oceans, while I lay in mine, alone. I had to find my own peace, alone. It would have been easy to dissolve into torment, and I often, very often, felt tides of old agony inside me. But I had to go beyond hoping to waiting, beyond waiting to endurance, beyond endurance to stillness, where with him or without him, I was the same. Love is transformative; that is its true power. And in my quiet longing I started to change. I fell over more often than ever before, crying for him, and crying for you—but now I knew how to right myself, with a bone-deep patience born of grief, and of the sunlight I learned from your touch.

The biggest adventure of all was stillness. You almost learned it, from your Père Lemaître, but a restlessness tore you from within and ate you. He taught waiting, didn't he? His teaching was wrapped in it. The seeing was just one part of it, only a small atom of the oldest truth.

I thought I was waiting for Dermot, but he was the disguise, too. He was the irritant that climbed inside the oyster, the last hurdle. We do the job of waiting every day, waiting for sleep, and waiting for wakefulness. Waiting for age, and waiting for death. Waiting for love was just a part of it, like waiting for the moon to spin around the earth—as inevitable as water, as certain as tides. Why don't we let our hearts ripen? I thought I was waiting for him, to be ready, to become a man in his last quest, but while I watched him I nearly missed the very secret I was meant to see: I was ripening, in the mysterious way of fruit and sap; not ripening to be eaten, but simply to fall, and die, and spill the seeds from my heart. And in this swelling, and growing, and changing, uncurling like a frond inside me, were the mysteries I'd always been looking for.

It took me so long to see that our quest was the same: yours in the earth, in death; Dermot's in the sea, among riptides and squalls; mine in the simple sun that cut through the window, in the sap that rose in the spring trees, in the pace of days that are always secrets.

Why are we sent lessons, and who sends them? Why are we

sent lessons that look absurd and meaningless as we live them, and in retrospect shine, our inevitable truths? And when do lessons end, when does rest begin in earnest? Only in death, where you are? Or is there a gentle peace, grown like a pearl inside an oyster, like an oyster hiding in the sea, that lies waiting all the time inside us, waiting to be discovered? I don't try anymore to defend love. That is mystery. I only watch it, sparking inside me. That's mystery, too.

On one hot Sunday, a year from when he'd gone, Chen Li arrived at my door with a small package. It had been delivered, by hand, to your house. It had traveled from overseas, and it was wrapped simply, but carefully. I couldn't make out the return address, it was smudged. I clipped the twine, and unwrapped the brown, crinkled paper, and inside was a little box. It contained six blue pearls, and a note.

Lily,
Enough for a necklace that will reach to your heart. I lost the moon. The chain broke while I was diving. I looked and looked for it, it took me all this time, but it was gone. I woke up remembering McConnell's words.
It's too wet and cold here in Ireland. Wear the necklace to the tea garden at twilight on the next new moon. I want to see the sun.

Dermot

I waited, underneath the mock pagodas. I threw a penny into the pond, and my wishes spun through the air as it fell. I heard him then; the water warmed at the sound of his step. His reflection shone below me, brilliant in the trembling water, bright beside the new moon. As I turned to him he smiled; I saw a flash of blue eyes, a small eclipse, the fading sun on his cheek. The fish that arced in their cages, and ached for the sea. Happy and bright. The new moon hummed in the sky, satiate at last.

Good-bye, Uncle. So deep inside the earth, so high in the airy heavens. Don't fear for me. I lived through longing to its end, as simple as death, as lonely as love, as close as your gift to me.

CHEN LI'S LAST LETTER

Little ghost, I lived to be very old. Old enough to watch your sorrow spin by, the same sorrow that ran down a long line of hearts. We used to believe in the curse, and it ground us down, held us to earth, kept us from sky.

Little ghost, I lived to be very old, and so did you. Old enough for jewels to slip through your fingertips, for children and gardens to grow under your touch. Old enough for me to see you wear your happiness, to see you breathe a crazy joy into the old house.

Little ghost, I too talk to your grandfather. I tell him about what goes on each day, about the stories you tell me of Irish seas and skies, of skiffs that sail under Tahitian moons, of a man who dives naked into the deep. We Chinese dislike the ocean — it's an old tradition. We shun it, and we trust the earth. But I love to hear you tell the stories, little ghost, because then your voice sparkles like sun on water, and a thousand happy dreams live in your words.